Stolen Nights

	DATE DUE	

Also by Rebecca Maizel

Infinite Days

A Vampire Queen Novel

Stolen Nights

Rebecca Maizel

 St. Martin's Griffin 🦁 New York

7-13
10⁰⁰

STOLEN NIGHTS. Copyright © 2013 by Rebecca Maizel. All rights reserved.
Printed in the United States of America. For information, address St. Martin's Press,
175 Fifth Avenue, New York, N.Y. 10010.

Library of Congress Cataloging-in-Publication Data

Maizel, Rebecca.
    Stolen nights : a Vampire queen novel / Rebecca Maizel.
        p. cm.
    ISBN 978-0-312-64992-0 (trade paperback)
    ISBN 978-1-4299-6590-3 (e-book)
    1. Supernatural–Fiction.   2. Vampires–Fiction.   3. Love–Fiction.   4. Boarding
schools–Fiction.   5. Schools–Fiction.]   I. Title.
    PZ7.M279515St 2013
[Fic]—dc23

                                                                        2012038339

First Edition: February 2013

10   9   8   7   6   5   4   3   2   1

For Ryan Quirk, who is brave

Acknowledgments

First, thank you endlessly to: Ruth Alltimes, Emma Young, and Jennifer Weis. How can I thank you enough? What words can I choose that could possibly do justice to your support, patience, and guidance of this novel? I've enjoyed all of it. The Macmillan family has made me a better writer.

Mollie Traver: Thank you for your guidance and your time. I can't wait to work with you again on book three. (If I ever need an elevator buddy, I'm calling you.)

Rebecca McNally: A keen eye, a wonderful editor, and now at a new home. Thank you so much for your editorial guidance. I feel lucky to have worked with you and hope to do so again soon! Book three won't be the same without you!

AM Jenkins: Thank you for that afternoon at the VCFA picnic tables. Your passion and dedication are unparalleled. Working with you made me a better writer. Working with you showed me what it means to be a great teacher. I miss you!

Margaret Riley, my awesome agent: I can't wait to work on book three and dig our heels into this final book.

Matt Hudson: Your guidance from the get-go was always brilliant and always appreciated. I miss our editorial talks and hope we can work together again soon. Next time, the milkshake is on you.

Acknowledgments

All of the VFCA community, especially the Keepers of the Dancing Stars. Keepers are for keeps!

The CCW's: Laura Backman, Rebecca DeMetrick, Gwen Gardner, Maggie Hayes, Mariellen Langworthy, Claire Nicogossian, and Sarah Ziegelmayer. I love our monthly meetings. You add so much joy to my writing life.

Also big thanks to: Franny Billingsley, Josh Corin (a wonderful reader), Amanda Leathers, Monika Bustamante, Heidi Bennett (Vampirequeennovels.com), and Cathryn Summerhayes, my wonderful UK agent.

Also, thank you to: David Fox, Michael Sugar, Anna Deroy, and all of the WME West crew.

And of course, my sister, Jennie. You always know what's best; for my writing and for me. I love you.

Mom and Dad: I don't know how else to say thank you for your endless support. "If you don't try . . . you don't get!"

And last but not least, Kristin Sandoval: Everything I write in this spot seems incomplete. So, simply, thank you. Thank you for reading my novel endless times, for being honest, for having a hawklike editing eye, and for showing me the way when I just couldn't see it. For our Skype calls and for your patience. You are unbelievably talented and giving. This book would not exist without you. I'm so grateful we met. Thank you. Thank you. Thank you.

An ancient parchment lies
in a darkened, sacred place.
Its location, unknown;
its maker, anonymous.
It is legend.
On it is a ritual,
its words inscribed in blood.
This ritual requires the deepest love
and ultimate sacrifice—death.
It will transform a vampire to human again.
My love, Rhode, had performed
this ritual for me, and died.
I performed it only days ago.
And I survived.

Stolen Nights

Chapter One

You're home," Justin Enos said, leading me through the great stone towers of Wickham Boarding School. I hesitated once I crossed the threshold, stopping at the main path that led past Seeker dorm and to the many halls and lanes of campus. In the distance, tall streetlamps lit up brick buildings like tiny beacons.

Only four days ago, I was so sure that this world was no longer my own. I had performed the ritual for Vicken, my friend, my confidant, also a vampire. I performed this ritual to turn him human. That also meant it had been four days since my best friend, Tony, was killed in the art tower, and since I believed I too would die.

"I can walk, you know," I said, though I stumbled and Justin had to grab on to my arm. He gave me a knowing glance. My thighs trembled, the result of lying unconscious in a hospital bed.

"It's a beautiful night," I said, leaning into Justin's arm as we walked. He matched my baby steps, holding a bag of my possessions on his other arm.

Lovers Bay, Massachusetts, was blooming in June, hydrangeas and roses all around us. Coupled with the aromas of the café and the restaurants behind us on Main Street, scents distinct to me in my newly regained humanity filled the air: sauces, perfumes, and fragrant flowers.

After everything that had happened, Wickham Boarding

School campus seemed like an imaginary place. It lived somewhere locked in both dream and nightmare.

The night was quiet. The trees swayed lazily in the June air and I watched students meander across the campus, talking quietly to one another. The moon broke through the clouds, and when I looked back down to the earth, far down the path toward Wickham Beach, a figure leapt over the path and into the woods. Blond tendrils of hair flew behind her in the wind.

I grinned at first, imagining a student sneaking off campus to find something decadent to eat or to meet a boyfriend. Then something about the figure's movements caught my eye. She jumped with the ease of a dancer but with the charge of pursuit as well. She was lean and swift. Too lean . . . too swift.

Alarmed, I scanned the school grounds.

"What's wrong?" Justin asked.

"Want to go down to the beach?" I asked, stalling for time.

Justin left my bag with the guard at the dorm and I waited alone, staring down the pathway. If she came back out of the woods, then I would know whether she was an ordinary human. Students passed by me, calling out:

"Hey, Lenah!"

"How are you! Feeling better?"

I kept my gaze forward. "Word got around fast when you went to the hospital," said Justin, nuzzling my neck.

We walked past the Union and Justin's dorm. I couldn't explain it, the knowing that she was strange, that the blonde might not be human. Perhaps I was just being paranoid. Of course I was being paranoid. I was an ex-592-year-old vampire. Oddities and strange creatures had once been an everyday part of my life.

We walked down to Wickham Beach. I took off my shoes, leaving them by the steps, and sat down on the cool sand. Sitting there, leaning against Justin's warm chest and marveling at the ocean stretching beyond us, I tried to forget about the wisp of blond hair and the unnaturally agile jump.

Justin's hand wrapped around mine. We watched the bay, and I replayed the memory of the first time I met him. During my first week reborn as a human, he had walked out of the water, glimmering and golden.

I leaned my head on his shoulder, breathed, and listened to the water lap lazily on the beach.

Except . . .

A horrific knowing sent a shiver through me. I shuddered and Justin looked down at me.

"Hey . . . are you okay?"

Look left . . . , my mind said.

But Justin felt it too. He looked away from me and his fingers dug into the sand and he rose up onto his knees.

Death is coming, the voice inside my mind said. The voice of the Vampire Queen. The hunter of hundreds.

You know this trouble, the voice slithered.

I looked slowly down the beach.

"Do you see that?" Justin asked.

I did. My heart was a cello string, vibrating as though drawn across with a bow—wavering. Someone was running toward us from very far down the beach. A girl—not a child, but not a grown woman either. A student? Her slight frame swayed as she ran, zigzagging across the sand and then hitting the ground. She pushed herself up from the sand but her arm gave out and she fell again.

"I think it's . . ." Justin's voice trailed away.

She finally got to her feet and started running again. The next time she collapsed to the sand, a few moments later, she cried out. It was a scream that traveled in a long wail down the beach, vibrating her terror into our ears. Goose bumps erupted over my arms.

I knew this kind of cry well.

"She needs help," Justin said, taking a step toward her.

"Wait," I demanded in a whisper, grabbing his arm. I narrowed my focus into the darkness.

"Are you crazy? She's hurt," Justin said. "What are we waiting for?"

My terror was a heartbeat quickened. A dry mouth. Words stuck to my throat, trapped by fear. I couldn't remove my eyes.

For there was someone behind her.

This someone threw her hips confidently side to side. A model's walk. A saunter of death. The woman grabbed the girl by her ponytail. There was a quick yank, animalistic, and brutal.

The wind came through the trees, shivering unnaturally in the summer breeze.

"Justin," I said. "We have to go. Now."

"But, Lenah!", I pulled him to me so we spoke very closely.

"Silence," I said. "Or we'll both be dead."

Justin didn't reply, but an understanding passed over his eyes.

I had to be calculated, purposeful. I could not let the human inside overwhelm me. I scrambled up the steps and turned into the woods that ran parallel to the beach. My legs ached from the days in the hospital and I grabbed on to the trees every few paces for balance.

"Lenah! We have to call for help!" Justin whispered loudly from behind me. I spun around to face him.

"Didn't I tell you? You must be silent," I commanded. "And don't say my name again."

I fell to my knees and crept to the edge of the woods where the dirt and beach storm wall met, and stared at the scene unfolding below. I gasped as I recognized the girl.

Kate Pierson, my friend. A member of the Three Piece—the group of girls at Wickham whom I'd unexpectedly grown to love over the last year. Kate was the youngest of all of us, barely sixteen. Innocent, beautiful, and now in grave danger.

This changed the circumstances.

We would have to do something. I immediately ran through our options.

We didn't have a dagger or sword to pierce the vampire through the heart, so we would have to frighten her with strength, which Justin had.

"Please stop," Kate cried to her attacker.

We lay stomach down and I clawed my fingers into the sandy grass.

The woman sauntered behind Kate, stepping over the darkened sand as though she were simply out for a night stroll. She wore all black. Thick, blond beautiful hair flowed and waved behind her in the wind.

She smiled, her mouth stained red with blood.

I drew in a long breath. "I know her," I whispered to Justin.

My home in Hathersage, England, swept into my mind along with a memory of the staircase that led to the attic.

The maid.

The friendly maid with rosy cheeks.

Now she was whiter than stone and very angry.

Below us, Kate tried to wriggle away from the vampire, but now I could see the extent of her wounds. Justin and I were too late, much too late.

I gulped as the blonde grabbed Kate by the front of her shirt and bit into the nape of her shoulder. Kate cried out a familiar, hollow scream. This was one of finality. Her small mouth opened and she hollered into the night.

"How?" Justin whispered. "How do you know her?"

"I—" A shiver rolled over me. "—I made her."

Slowly, ever so slowly, Justin turned his eyes back to the beach without speaking.

Congealed blood caked the sand together as Kate kicked away. She bled from her arms and her neck. This was a killing of strength. A vampire death can be one bite and virtually painless, but this was a death like Tony's: a ruthless killing, done not out of hunger or need but out of power. Out of joy.

Kate brought her fingers to her throat to try to stop the bleeding.

Useless. I had seen this too many times.

"I don't want to die," begged Kate. "Please."

My heart ached but the once powerful Vampire Queen inside me told me that this blond vampire was strong. She was unyielding in her desire for blood.

Justin and I could not run. We could not help. We would die at her hands if we made a sound.

We could do nothing until the horror was over.

There was one last scream from the beach.

And Kate Pierson was no more.

Chapter Two

We have to tell someone," Justin said as we stepped out of the woods and onto campus.

"No. We can't," I replied. We stood under the lamplight on the pathway and I held a hand over my stomach. "What we have to do is get inside. I have to think this through."

I needed help. I needed someone who understood vampires.

I wanted Rhode, who was dead.

"We can't just leave her on that beach!" Justin said as a girl from the sophomore class and a security officer passed by us on the pathway. Ms. Tate, the science teacher, followed closely behind them.

"You said you heard screaming?" the security guard asked the sophomore.

"A couple times, sir. Down here."

Ms. Tate hesitated next to us.

"Lenah, good to see you, dear." She touched my shoulder lightly. "Did you two hear anything near the beach?" she asked as we stopped next to the greenhouse. "Someone said they heard a fight or argument."

"No," I said, shaking my head and taking advantage of the opportunity. "We were just in here." I gestured to the greenhouse.

She nodded and followed behind the security guard and the student toward the beach. It would be only moments before the sirens began.

My thoughts were at war with one another. What was a vampire doing here in Lovers Bay? A vampire I made. The name Vicken pulsed through my mind.

Vicken. My faithful Vicken. I created him in such darkness and pain. He was my compatriot. But a vampire no longer. I had performed the ritual, releasing him from the endless bloodlust and setting free the human inside.

What if the ritual had failed? What if Vicken had remained a vampire and was working with this blonde?

"Lenah? What are you thinking about?" Justin asked.

"Vicken," I said, focusing on Justin's face. "What happened to Vicken after I performed the ritual?"

A muscle twitched in Justin's jaw and he crossed his arms over his chest.

"I left him in your apartment when I took you to the hospital. I have no idea if he's alive or dead. I haven't been back."

The thought of a decaying Vicken on my Wickham apartment bed wasn't an encouraging thought, but I'd have to see for myself. We walked toward Seeker, pretending we weren't shaking as we walked. Just as I was about to go up to my room, a police car screamed onto campus.

It had begun.

As the car wailed by, it left in its wake an unnerving feeling that wrapped around me from my head to my toes. A knowing within my bones, for the second time that night.

Someone was watching me.

The blonde? Had she been looking for me? Was that why she had killed Kate?

Dozens of students were making their way to the beach

to investigate the chaos. I looked past the Union and up the long slope of an enormous hill that led to the archery plateau.

A familiar figure stood on top, and hope immediately rushed through me. Suleen. The oldest vampire. He would be able to explain everything.

He stood dressed all in white with a turban fitted tightly to his head. He lifted his arm and motioned for me to follow him, then turned and walked onto the archery plateau, disappearing into the shadows.

I ran for it, trying to ignore the weakness in my legs as I sped up the hill. Justin followed behind me.

"Lenah, wait! What's going on?" he called.

I tallied the horrors of the last day as I ran. Kate's murder, the blonde vampire, and now Suleen's arrival? All of this was undeniably connected.

"Something is very wrong. He wouldn't be here otherwise," I said.

"What's wrong? Who is that?" he asked.

We crested the archery plateau. The line of targets sat in the distance highlighted by the moonlight. Suleen was not alone. A figure stood beside him in the middle of the field, clad in black pants, black boots, and black spiky hair.

My god.

The young man turned. His eyes bore into mine—blue. Blue. Blue.

My hand flew to my chest and I stumbled back.

Rhode. My Rhode. His whole body was surrounded by a halo of silver. The light that emanated from around his black hair, his blue eyes, and the curve of his face were nothing compared to the beauty that radiated from within him.

How could it be? I had run my fingers through his gritty vampire remains that first day at Wickham. I'd been so sure he was dead.

Of course . . . the realization rippled through me. If I had survived the ritual with Vicken . . . why wouldn't he survive the ritual as well?

I ran to him. He watched me, completely still. The shock of seeing Rhode coursed through me, over and over again, making my mortal heart race. I was a step from him, close enough to reach out and touch his skin.

I would touch him! Feel his skin with fingertips that were alive with nerves and pulsing with blood. Suddenly, Suleen stood between us. I stepped to the left to avoid him but Suleen blocked my way. I moved to the right—blocked again. Rhode kept his eyes locked on mine, but didn't take so much as a step toward me.

My fingers shook as my hand stretched out to him. "Rhode . . . ," I whispered. "You're not dead. You're not dead."

He stared, marveling at me as if I were an unknown creature or some rare bird.

"Rhode?" I said, panic rising from my stomach to my chest.

"Lenah . . ." Suleen's slow voice broke my gaze. "We haven't much time."

"Damn it, Rhode, speak to me," I commanded.

Rhode closed his eyes for a moment, seemingly gathering strength to speak to me. Instead he took a deep breath. When he opened his eyes to look at me, I nearly fell back from their coldness.

"Rhode?" I said. "Do you know how long I've dreamt of this?" He didn't respond. "I love you!"

A pressure on my arm fell away. Justin. I had almost forgotten he was there. His cheeks were streaked with dirt and when I moved my gaze to his hands, those too were caked in mud and sand. It reminded me of our terror that night, of what we had been through in the last few hours. And Kate Pierson had died.

"This is Rhode?" he said faintly. The wonder and hurt in his tone made me want to clamp my hands over my ears.

Rhode stared at Justin with the same curiosity he had for me, as if we were some strange animals. Justin reached for me again.

"You don't want to be here," he said.

At this, Suleen stepped between Justin and me.

"What are you—?" I started to say as Suleen opened his palm, face out to Justin. A great gust came over us all at once. My hair flew about my face and tree branches creaked. There was a loud pop as Suleen thrust his arm forward. In a blink, a wide vertical whirlpool of water separated Justin from Suleen and me. This watery shield hovered in the air between us. I reached out, extending my fingers and ran them through the whirlpool suspended in air. They made lines where they broke through the water.

I had never—ever—seen a vampire with that kind of power.

"Lenah!" Suleen said from behind me. *"Rapidement."* Quickly. He turned back to Rhode and left the swirling shield hanging in the air as though it had always been there.

Justin banged a fist onto the watery barrier, then stepped back. He rose onto his tiptoes, trying to see over the water, but the barrier simply stretched upward too. Our eyes met through the water, his face rippling strangely.

"Lenah!" He yelled my name and the sound of his voice breaking made a knot form in the center of my chest. I could not go to him. Not even after everything that had just happened that night.

I turned to Suleen in frustration. "What the hell is going on?"

"When you performed the ritual for Vicken, you alerted the Aeris."

"The Aeris?" I said with surprise. I had heard of them, but only in ancient vampire texts and Celtic mythology.

"What you both have done with the ritual. It must be reckoned," Suleen said.

"A reckoning? Like a trial?" I asked. Rhode wouldn't look at me; his arms were folded across his chest. The muscles in his forearms contracted, drawing my eyes down for a split moment. Then he swallowed. I watched, just to prove to myself he was human, that he was real. His chest rose and fell in an easy rhythm. We had both performed the ritual, we had both intended to die, yet there we were together—both very much alive. Both human.

"You must focus right now. This will affect both of you—" He placed his warm palms on my shoulders. "—indefinitely."

I wanted to tell Suleen and Rhode about the blond vampire. About Kate's death and the horror unfolding down on Wickham campus.

The watery shield still hovered in the air but Justin was gone from the other side. All that lay behind it was the rippled green of the darkened trees speckled with silver glints by the moon. The knot in my chest tightened again when Suleen spoke.

"Rhode must explain to the Aeris why he manipulated the elements to perform a ritual to turn a vampire into a human. He must explain why he passed this information on to you, so you could perform it as well."

"Well, that's easy. I was losing my mind. Going insane. Tell him, Rhode."

Rhode sighed, then spoke for the first time. "Lenah . . ." It didn't even sound like my name; it sounded like a swearword, a rotten word spit out, wishing to be forgotten.

"You never said this ritual was elemental magic," I said to Rhode. Elemental magic would be the only reason the Aeris were involved. For they represented the four elements of the natural world: earth, air, water, and fire. Not human. Not spirit. The Aeris exist as the Earth exists.

"We have to do this," Rhode said. His voice was calm. "We have to clear up our own mess."

"It's time," Suleen said, and finally moved out from between us. Suleen looked to the middle of the green, but I kept my eyes

12

on Rhode. The long trunks of trees behind him were a blur. The flat summer leaves were nothing but a wash of darkened emerald to me now.

"You won't even look at me?" I asked quietly. "Did you know the Aeris were coming?" I didn't dare move closer to him. "Why didn't you come back sooner?"

Again, his silence was his answer.

"I don't understand you," I said.

"I didn't want to come back," he snapped. "I had to." He lifted his eyes to mine. "For this."

His words cut into the center of my chest.

He didn't want to come back?

It was then I glimpsed a white light out of the corner of my eye. I knew that light—it was supernatural light.

Rhode's words hung in the air, stinging me like a burn. There was a large expanse of land before me, and the archery targets sat deep in the distance of the plateau. My heart beat in the base of my throat; I brought my fingertips to my skin to feel it. The white light in the center of the green grew to be as long and wide as the field that stretched before me.

At first it was difficult to see anything discernible in the whiteness, but eventually the fuzzy forms took the shapes of human bodies. Four female bodies. The Aeris stepped forward.

Their dresses were flowing as if they were made from water, and the hue of the gowns changed color every few seconds, one moment blue, then a darker blue, then red. I wondered if it was the trick of the light. One of the women had impossibly white eyes and her hair swayed around her head as if she were submerged underwater. The woman next to her had hair that fluttered around her like crackling flames, a bright red. When she looked at me, her gown flickered a poppy orange. Fire.

Behind the Aeris were hundreds—no, thousands of shapes that looked like regular people.

The four spoke together. "We are the Aeris."

Their light took over the entire sky now.

"Who are the people behind you?" I asked.

Fire gestured across the field of people.

"These are your victims, and the victims of the vampires you made."

My victims? I shook my head quickly. It couldn't be.

Yet there they stood. They were amorphous, their identities shielded in the light. Included in their masses was a bright being no more than three feet high. A horrified chill ran through me.

A child.

She was the child I had killed hundreds of years ago.

Looking from Rhode to me, Fire said, "Your lives are destined to be intertwined. You are held together by a power that cannot be undone by the Aeris."

"Destined?" I asked.

"Yes, Lenah Beaudonte. You and Rhode Lewin were born under the same stars. The course of your lives has brought you here—together, as soul mates."

"You never interfered with us before," Rhode said.

"You, Rhode, were meant to die when you performed the ritual to make Lenah human. Yet your soul mate tied you to this earth. When you went out into that sunlight, you were meant to die. But you could not. Not without Lenah."

"And the same for me?" I asked. "When I was performing the ritual on Vicken?"

She nodded. "So now we have come to undo what you have created with this ritual."

I racked my brain, trying to understand what she was saying. Fire's hair crackled. "You cannot manipulate the elements in order to bring life out of death. Not without consequence."

"So you've come to punish us?" I asked.

"We have come to hold you responsible."

Fire gestured toward the ghostly figure of the child to illustrate her point. There was nothing to say. Nothing I could possibly try to defend.

"It was our nature then," Rhode said plainly. "To kill."

"We are not here to hold you accountable for your endless murders, as heinous as they might have been. The Aeris are not responsible for, nor do we police, the vampire world. Vampires are dead. Supernatural, night wanderers. We cannot hold you responsible for the killings you performed in that world," Fire said as she paced between us. "What interests me is what you have done to become human. It is against the laws of nature to manipulate the elements. You forced yourself back into this natural world with the ritual, and once you did, you became our responsibility. This will not go unreconciled."

Rhode said nothing. I was unable to keep my eyes away from the thousands of figures collecting behind the Aeris. All those people . . .

Fire clasped her hands together at her waist, then let them hang. My legs were so weak, they shook, and I wondered if I would fall to the ground right there.

"The choice is this: Either you can go back to your natural states and Rhode will return to 1348 as a knight under Edward III. You, Lenah, will live your life in 1417 as it should have been."

"When we were human?" I asked incredulously.

"Natural states means when you each had a white soul, a pure soul," Fire explained.

"You'll send us back in *time*?" Rhode asked.

Fire glanced behind her at the crowd of our victims. A question rose in my mind.

"What about all of them?" I asked, gesturing.

"When you go back to the medieval world, these souls will return to the natural course of their lives too."

"I don't understand," I said.

"Every person you murdered will live again, as will those killed by the vampires you created. They will never meet you—because you won't become a vampire. It will be as though you had never met." She looked to both Rhode and me.

In 1348, when he became a vampire, Rhode was nineteen. I wouldn't be born for another sixty-nine years. He would be dead by the time of my birth or, at best, a very old man. That was their purpose. To send us back so that we would remain apart.

"It is a balance, Lenah. All the four elements of the world create balance. You were made a vampire against your will. You are Rhode's original victim, so it is your choice to decide his fate."

"What is the other option?" I asked.

Fire stepped to the edge of the white light. Her pupils were bright red, but the iris around them glowed a pearl white. I held my breath until my cheeks and whole body tingled.

"You and Rhode have unleashed a chain of reactions that cannot be undone unless you separate. You may either go back to the medieval world or you may remain here. If you choose to stay here, you and Rhode may not commit to each other."

"'Commit'?" Rhode asked. "What do you mean?"

"Commitment to love is a choice deep within the soul. If you choose to bring your lives together in this world, we will know."

Could we touch? Talk? Kiss? . . . All these questions popped into my mind.

"You may talk, speak, interact, but you may not commit to be the couple you once were," Fire said, reading my mind.

"But how will we know if we've committed to each other? If we're the couple we once were? I can't just stop loving Rhode."

"You have always, always loved whomever you wanted, whenever you wanted. Rhode, Vicken, Heath, Gavin, Song, and Justin. But who filled up your soul? How many of them have you committed to? You didn't share a life, you didn't grow with them as you did with Rhode. It's over. You must do to Rhode what you've done with the rest of the men you've come across. Keep him at arm's length."

"I don't understand," I barely said, knowing deep in my soul that she was completely right. Had I used everyone except Rhode? I had, hadn't I? Fire took another step to me, and I could feel the heat emanating off her.

"Like the whitest shores on a beach as far as the eye can see. You want that ocean. You see that ocean. But you can never go back in. Ever."

I swallowed hard, unable to formulate the words I so desperately wanted to say. I wanted to convince her. Could I keep Rhode at arm's length? Could I pretend we didn't have the history we had? The silver light around all my victims pulsated behind Fire's head, reminding me of all that I had done to deserve this moment on the archery field.

"And them?" I asked with a nod of my head. "What happens to them if I stay?"

"You see this light around me?" she asked.

I nodded again.

"Your victims. They have white souls. And they will keep them."

I imagined my soul to be black and hardened, like a lump of coal.

"And if I return to the medieval world? If they go back to their lives?"

"Then they will be left to their own choices. The fate of their souls will be their own."

I had already decided their fate. They were safe where they were, safe in that light. How could I release them into a past I knew nothing about? Was I being selfish? Did I want to protect their souls or my own? I knew more than anything else in the world that, if I had a soul, Rhode and I were meant to be together.

"What is your choice?" Fire asked.

I looked at Rhode's profile. He wouldn't meet my eyes. I wanted to kiss his mouth, even now, even with the Aeris's decree that we would never be a couple again. Just seeing him there, knowing I could be near him when I had been so convinced of his death . . . I didn't want to go back. No matter what we had to face, if Rhode was by my side, even at arm's length, I could do anything.

"I choose to stay," I said, looking into Fire's poppy-colored eyes. "Here in Lovers Bay."

In my mind, a perfect apple orchard, painted in thick swirls of color, dissolved as though left out in the rain.

"And they'll be safe?" I asked, meaning the people behind the Aeris. She nodded, then said, "You must fight her, Lenah." She didn't need to tell me whom she meant.

She took a step back into the light, and her distinct form began to fade.

The white light dimmed too and Suleen, who stood beside us, held a hand out toward the Aeris. He turned his palm left, then right, and then made a fist. He was performing some sort of communication that I did not understand. Fire mimicked these gestures. A palm left—right—then a fist. She and her sisters were almost gone, fading into the scenery as if they'd never been there.

Rhode watched Suleen, but I couldn't stop staring at his chest, rising up and down. I had stared at it for hundreds of years, wishing we were both alive, breathing and living together.

You cannot commit, Fire had said. I jumped forward, past Suleen and toward the vanishing Aeris.

"Wait!" I yelled. "Wait!"

I threw my arms out facing the light, but it dimmed, leaving nothing behind but misty cobwebs. The Aeris were gone. Fire was gone.

Rhode stared around the archery plateau, now shrouded in darkness.

"We have to do something!" I cried to Suleen.

"You did," Rhode said. "You chose to stay."

There was sadness in his voice, anger too. I just couldn't part with Rhode, not when it came down to it. I couldn't go back to the medieval world without him.

The grass under my feet was gray; the sky black. I swallowed and a lump in the back of my throat hurt.

"Your hundreds of years of experience on this Earth must be your conscience now. Stay away from each other," said Suleen. His even tone broke the spell of my thoughts.

Rhode met Suleen's eyes. A tremor traveled from my shins to my knees to my thighs. I needed to grasp something hard, clench it in my fist and break it, like a branch.

My mind sped up, as though coming back to the world I existed in before the Aeris came from their white world and lit up the archery plateau.

Justin.

I spun around to look back at the slope of the hill where Suleen had conjured up the water shield. But Justin had long gone. I supposed I could not blame him. I would not have wanted to linger at the scene either.

"There is no other way, Rhode," Suleen said.

Rhode replied in Hindi—a language I had not learned. While I could speak twenty-five languages fluently, Rhode had chosen one I could not understand.

He walked past me and descended the hill without looking back.

Was he leaving? Right when I had found him again!

"What did he say? Rhode!" I yelled, and followed. Suleen caught my arm. "No!" I screamed. I pushed against his strong grasp but he easily held me back.

Rhode ran across the meadow, then onto the pathway.

"Rhode!" I screamed. This heartache made me sick. "Rhode!" He did not look back.

I could not tell him about the blond vampire. I could not say, *Stay, for I love you. I've always loved you. Stay and we can do this together.*

Because without a second look, without a glance, he was gone.

Chapter Three

When the years of vampirism began to chain my mind to madness, I yearned for my parents' apple orchard. I ached for the succulent red apples dangling from the branches. For almost three hundred years, I begged Rhode to accompany me back to Hampstead. When we finally made the trip, I wore black for the occasion. My hair fell in long tendrils over my shoulders, my ribs constricted by a corset. The 1730s was the era of panniers, wide hoops attached to a woman's hips underneath her dress. Women were meant to take up space, to be a spectacle, to be admired. It was a time of opulence. I loved this era most of all. I could shine when the light of the sun was no longer upon me. As for the men, many wore wigs, powdered white. But not Rhode. He always wore his hair long, black, and tied at the nape of his neck. The leather of his black boots reached almost to his knees.

We were gorgeous Angels of Death.

"Three hundred and sixteen years since I stepped on this land," I said, glancing at Rhode.

"Same for me," Rhode replied. A brilliant sunset descended over the Heath, washing the fields in a tangerine light. Behind him, set off by a field, was the stone monastery where I'd spent so much of my childhood. The Hampstead sunset washed bloodred hues over the grass. As a vampire, I was relieved to know that the daylight would start to dwindle soon.

"Are you sure you want to see this?" Rhode asked.

I nodded, moving my eyes from the monastery to the lane ahead. I had often padded these fields as a child. Images of dirt caking my toes, my hair flowing behind me in the wind, and the rich earth burned in my mind. The wind brushed through the branches again, and a shower of leaves layered the ground. The Earth seemed to shiver as though it knew someone unnatural was walking its lands.

As Rhode took a step, his sword clicked against the side of his leg. I lifted my hand and gently intertwined my fingers through his. Even though almost every finger wore a jewel, he chose to rub his thumb over the onyx—the stone of Death. We stepped down the long, tunneled lane that led toward my family's home. As we passed the monastery, my eye followed the gray stone and well-kept grounds. After three hundred years, it was still a place of holy reverence.

Was it possible Henry VIII had spared it? That it had escaped the dissolution of the monasteries in the sixteenth century?

"It is a church now," Rhode said, and when I looked properly, I could see that the monastery of my childhood was no more, though the core of the building remained the same. I could hear the sounds of a service from inside, soft murmuring and chanting.

When I was nine years old, I used to hide underneath the stone-framed windows, my feet pressed into the scratchy ground. I would listen to hundreds of haunting voices. The hum of the monks' soft tones would echo out into the field, sending a vibration through my chest.

One night, my father told me the light from the monastery was the most beautiful light in the world. "Candlelight," he had said, "is a human's beacon to God. A little piece of God on Earth."

"It's just ahead," Rhode said. There it was. I stared at the house on the orchard.

"It's the same," I whispered. "Just as it is in my memory."

The same slate roof and evenly spaced stones. The same two-story manor overlooking manicured lanes of trees that stretched back in straight vertical lines so far that I couldn't see their end. And the trees were in bloom. Green, green everywhere—lime green, sea green, bottle green, and long grass that tickled your ankles.

I gripped the heavy fabric of my gown, lifting it up so as not to drag it along the muddy ground.

"I don't believe anyone is at home," Rhode said as he took in the smokeless chimney.

It didn't matter to me either way. I pressed my hands against the glass, wondering if it was cool—I could not sense its temperature. As a vampire ages, her sense of touch deadens. I leaned in closer. The wooden beams on the ceiling had been reinforced over time but it all looked the same. The familiarity sent a wave of comfort through me, and that feeling overtook the anger, pain, and misery that so overwhelmed me as a vampire. The comfort was a gift.

"Lenah, look," Rhode said from behind me. "There are—"

"Fifty acres," I finished for him, turning from the window. A sense of calm settled over me as I looked at Rhode. I expected him to be marveling at the acres and acres of land.

"No," he said. "Tombstones."

As though I had been drenched from head to toe in icy water, the calm vanished. It was replaced by the unrelenting familiar constant: grief. The most common feeling of the vampire. Grief. Loss. Pain.

My eyes followed the long point of Rhode's finger. I paused at the doorstep a few moments before walking toward the little graveyard. Rhode squatted down on his heels and ran his index finger along a deep engraving on the front of one of the gravestones.

As I walked past the house, I glanced at my reflection in the windows. So many years before, I had seen myself as a child in the wavy lines of the glass. Now, in the same glass, I saw my long dark hair falling over my shoulders. The black of my dress stood out against the lush green of the rows of trees behind me. I took another step to the side of the house and came upon the cemetery.

Rhode's finger was tracing the *L* in my name.

It was my gravestone.

God, it was a rotten piece of stone, but despite three hundred years out in the elements, my name was still etched clearly. There was no epitaph.

LENAH BEAUDONTE

1400–1417

Long ago, I thought. Long ago, I belonged to the world. I could have made a difference to my family, to my neighbors, to the monks, and to myself.

"Now you know," Rhode said quietly, and stood back up. "You were given a tombstone." That had been one of my many questions about my human death.

I nodded. "I wanted to see it. No matter how painful."

"Your father died not long after you," Rhode said.

The tombstone next to mine plainly read that Aden Beaudonte died in 1419. Next to the rounded curve of his gravestone was a cluster of jasmine flowers, dainty and white. Grow jasmine if you need to live, someone had once told me, not just exist but live. Grow jasmine so you'll never be alone. I took a step, leaned forward, and plucked three sprays of flowers. When I turned back to my father's grave, Rhode had stepped down the lane and was standing at the end, staring down at another tombstone.

I placed one jasmine spray on my mother's grave; she had died alone in 1450.

"Lenah . . . ," Rhode whispered. I looked to the end of the lane. His chin pointed toward his chest, and his eyes were fixed on the stone before him. He squatted to the ground. I walked toward him, and once I was by his side, I saw the name on the tombstone. I gripped his shoulder, stumbling backwards. I had no breath to take. No heart to thud. Just the simple shock of seeing the name:

GENEVIEVE BEAUDONTE

MOTHER AND SISTER

1419–1472

"You had a sister," said Rhode in awe. "She was born two years after your disappearance."

A sister. I had a sister? I stared at the name, unmoving. If I'd known she existed, I could have come to see her, I could have watched her live. I spun from the tombstone, walked past the graves and back to the orchard. The train of my gown trailed behind me over the dirt of my father's land.

"Lenah!" Rhode called.

What had they told her? That her sister had been taken away by demons? That she was there but then gone? My sister lived to be fifty-five, uncommonly old for her time. She outlived my mother. My mother hadn't been alone. I stopped once I reached the orchard.

A sister.

I heard the sound of Rhode's footsteps over the grass and he stopped right behind me.

"You were right. You had to come. To find out about your family," he said gently.

The sunset almost fully settled over the land, I knew that if I scanned the sky, I would see the beginnings of the constellation of Andromeda. I brought my eyes back to the orchard. Whoever lived in my house would return soon. They were most likely at the evening service at the church.

Rhode's hand linked through mine. When two vampires love each other, their touch will produce warmth. Without love, we feel nothing. In that moment, his touch was the brightest sunlight on the warmest day.

"Lenah, every person who has a tombstone in that graveyard carries the name Beaudonte." He motioned with his head toward the house. "Your family lives there . . . even now."

I grasped my hands around Rhode, pulling him to me.

"Promise me. Promise me that no matter what happens, you will always be there for me." I pulled away and looked into Rhode's vampire eyes. So glorious, they were the color of a summer sky. My sky. "We don't know what will come, but if I know you will always be there for me, I can bear it."

"I promise," he said. "No matter what may come."

He took my hand into his. With a glance back at the house and the graveyard beyond, the burn of tears that would never come stung my eyes. So I let the only person left in my heart take me away. As darkness swept over the long lane leading out, I could hear the singing of a few people in the meadow behind the old monastery. They were heading away from us, back toward the orchard. That was my family singing. Although they were many generations later, they were still my blood. I gripped Rhode harder, and let him take me as he had done three hundred years before, into the night.

Chapter Four

Time does not tick on for the dead. After we die, we cannot keep it. It is the master of the living. For the dead, for the vampire, time is a hornet's nest. Dangerous, best to be avoided—always humming in your ear.

When Rhode had run from me after our meeting with Suleen and the Aeris, he was leaving me for the second time in our long history. The first had been in 1740, when my mind was starting to string itself into pieces of lace. He had said, "I will never leave you," hundreds of times, thousands of times. Vampires like to count; they like to tally their sadness.

The last time Rhode left me, I went mad. The last time Rhode left me, I had created a very different kind of family for myself. I had made a coven of vampires. This time, I vowed, standing on the Wickham Boarding School pathway, with the moon filtering through the lattice of branches, I would not relive that misery. I would resolve to be me . . . whoever that was.

But where had he gone this time? Back to where he was hiding during the year I believed him dead? What could possibly have been strong enough to keep him from me?

His words gnawed at my mind.

I didn't want to come back, he had said. *I had to.*

Rhode had said he would never leave me. He said that as we stood in the lanes of my father's orchard hundreds of years ago.

Security vans pulled through the campus. Guards and police officers corralled students and pointed them to their dorms. Trees swayed; the stars above twinkled in a lazy dance.

"Hey, you!"

I turned. A security guard I had never seen before walked toward me in the darkness. His badge shone under the pathway lights, which seemed brighter than usual.

"Curfew is nine P.M. tonight, fifteen minutes. Let me see your ID."

I reached into my pocket, extended my hand with the ID. The guard reached for it, then froze, motionless, struck dumb.

"Sir?" I said, but he stared into the distance. Unmoving.

After a moment, he shook his head quickly and then turned on the spot, heading down the pathway away from me.

I stood on the path, unsure of what had just happened.

Suleen stepped out from the shadow of a building nearby, making me jump. "Walk with me," he said.

"How did you do that?" I asked, breathless.

He did not answer. We walked in silence down the path by the building, past maintenance crews working in the dark. I could not tell what they were doing, but sparks flew into the air like tiny fireworks.

"They are changing the locks," Suleen said. We were quiet again as we crossed campus and approached the beach. Across the steps that led down to the sand was a piece of yellow tape that read, POLICE LINE DO NOT CROSS.

Suleen lifted the tape right beside a police officer who was reading something off a clipboard. We walked under the tape, and the officer gave no indication that he had seen us.

When we reached the beach, they had already moved the body, but Kate's blood was still soaked into the sand.

Suleen and I stood beneath the light of the moon. The summer wind blew gently and I admired my silent protector. I wondered why he had involved himself in my life for so long. And how it was that he had such power. It radiated off him; it positively hummed.

I inhaled the scent of ocean and salt. When I was a vampire, I could not smell anything other than flesh and blood. My sight, on the other hand, was unlimited, needed for hunting and resulting in countless murders. I could see the veins in my victims' skin, the flow of their blood. But touch and feeling? There were none. And taste?

"'All you shall taste is blood and it shall be the fruit of your darkness.' So say the books on vampirism," I said aloud.

"Vampires love to record and pass on their misery. They use anything they can find to do so. Ancient documents, printed and scrawled on the oddest paper, bark of trees, or human skin," Suleen said.

I was quiet.

Then, "I created the vampire who killed Kate Pierson," I confessed.

He nodded. "As you saw tonight," he said, "our past is not an immovable thing. It defines us; it can undo our future."

I exhaled loudly. "How do the Aeris have so much power? Are they actually capable of time travel? . . . Could they have sent me back in time?"

"Yes, I think so. You see, in this particular decree, they are trying to repair the damage you have done." Suleen seemed to think about his words, then said, "The Aeris are not human. They do not have human desires or wish you any ill."

"Yet they're hurting me in the most effective way possible— separating me from Rhode."

Suleen drew in a deep breath, which surprised me. I watched him inhale, though he would never need the breath. He drew it in and when he breathed out, he blew toward the ground, so the grains traveled in infinitesimal movements, making patterns on the sand.

When he was done, the faint outline of a body lay below us. Like a silver ghost, Kate's body lay on its side, mouth gaping open exactly as Justin and I had last seen her.

The wind picked up but Kate's apparition glowed on the sand.

"They said Rhode and I could talk and touch but we couldn't commit to each other." The word "commit" hung in the air for a few seconds.

"Yes, this is the rejoining of soul mates. If you choose to form a life together, if you give in to your love despite their warning, you will return to the fifteenth century and Rhode to the fourteenth."

My vision blurred, the ocean a mess of watery lines—I didn't dare meet Suleen's eyes, and pressed my lips together hard. The images from my first human life swam through my mind: a graveyard peppered with ancient stones, hazy light cast through thick glass, and monks chanting in the night.

Kate's misty body glowed underneath the bright moonlight. If I went back to the fifteenth century as the Aeris threatened, no one I loved from this world would be there. No Vicken. No Justin. Wickham wouldn't even have been built yet—no Lovers Bay Main Street.

Kate would be alive, however. Tony too.

"Be the human you wanted to be. Revel in it," Suleen said.

"How can I be that human when it's so dangerous here?" I met Suleen's eyes and then sighed. "The blond vampire has most likely returned for revenge. She seemed so delighted with herself and her murder."

It came to me then: Suleen should stay. Suleen could help me!

"Stay," I said simply. "With you here, no vampire would dare attack." Suleen's expression was one that I had seen before but not in a very long time. A kind of parental concern. Emotional pain rippled in my chest. I visualized my father and mother in the white light of the Aeris. I could only imagine what my disappearance had done to their lives.

"Your father was no victim," Suleen said, reading my emotions and perhaps my thoughts.

I knelt and Suleen joined me at my side.

"You made a choice on that archery field, Lenah," he said.

"I know."

"Then you know you chose to stay here, in this world. That means you must deal with the repercussions, even if that means fighting this vampire."

I didn't want to fight the vampire. Not alone.

"What about the Aeris?" I asked.

"No supernatural being has ever accomplished what you and Rhode have. Just as the Aeris did not interfere with you and Rhode, they cannot interfere with this vampire."

Guilt spread over me. The only hope I had was that Suleen would stay.

"I cannot," he said, reading my thoughts once again. He hesitated a moment, looking over Kate's body, then said, "May I tell you why elemental magic is so powerful?" Suleen asked. "Why your ritual called the Acris?"

I nodded, saying nothing.

"Elemental magic is life magic," Suleen continued. "We vampires take life. It is our curse. The more powerful the magic, the more we are drawn to it."

"Why?"

"Magic is drawn from the elements. Supernaturals have summoned it, created it with our power. That is why when a spell is performed, vampires can sense it if we are near. We crave it like we crave blood. It reminds us that we have some control in this world that ticks by without us."

"I didn't know the consequences."

"Of course you did," Suleen replied, and even as he said it, I knew that he was right. At the time, I didn't care about the power of the ritual. I put my selfish wishes above all else. "And so does this vampire, who has come to Lovers Bay. She craves that magic."

"If you can't help me, then why are you telling me this?"

"We are much more connected than perhaps you realize."

My lips parted. "How?" I asked.

"That is for another time," he said. "Just know, when you most need me, I'll find you."

Suleen stood above the body and held a palm above Kate. He moved his hand as if he were simply wiping the air, and the sand looked as it had before we arrived. We walked back to the pathway onto the campus, and Suleen stood with me at the entrance to Seeker.

"I suggest you get inside," he said.

"I could die," I said to him.

He examined my face a moment; then the corners of his lips lifted, just barely. Just enough that a smile shone from behind his eyes.

"Not a girl like you . . . ," he said.

I blinked. That was all it took. In that fraction of a second, I stood alone. No one walked along the path. No one called to me from the meadow. All I heard was the pervasive sound of silence.

Chapter Five

stood outside the glass doors of Seeker dorm for the first time since I'd performed the ritual for Vicken and been rushed to the hospital four days ago. So much had happened since I walked back onto campus earlier that night. I looked at my reflection. A sixteen-year-old girl, almost seventeen. How I had longed to make it here. I would age this year.

I took in my appearance in the shadow of night. Same thin nose. Same long hair that reached down to my ribs. Long, lanky legs, ending in black combat boots. The shadowy light illuminated my humanness. My perfect, white skin used to glow in the moonlight. It had healed instantly if anything or anyone dared to sully it, but now, red raised scrapes lined my hands. I turned my cheek to see another, smaller scrape. These were the physical reminders that Justin and I had crawled through the brush of the Wickham woods while Kate was being murdered.

Justin.

I sighed, feeling the weight of the night's ordeals in a slouch of my shoulders. I had to go in alone, and back up to my apartment. I pushed open the door and walked inside.

The foyer was the same as last year, and the familiar guard sat behind her desk, in her blue uniform.

"Lenah Beaudonte has checked in," she said into her walkie-talkie, and checked my name off a list. As I headed for the stairwell through the long hallway on the first floor of rooms, I could hear people speculating about the police cars on campus.

"I heard Kate Pierson died."

"First Tony, now Kate."

"Has anyone seen Tracy?"

I listened to the whispers all the way up to the top floor. When I opened the door to my apartment, I found a glass ashtray blackened by cigarette butts, dirty plates in the sink, and three empty pizza boxes on my coffee table. Next to them was a familiar silver flask given to Vicken by a count in the 1890s. I picked it up and opened the top, expecting to find, as usual, a stash of blood. I sniffed for the metallic rusty scent but instead found . . . whiskey? I shook my head, unable to stop a smile.

Oh yes, Vicken Clough was now definitely a mortal.

I put the flask down and turned to my bedroom; the door was open. I walked slowly across the living room, passing messy piles of books and an empty pack of cigarettes. When I placed a hand on my bedroom door, it creaked, echoing in the silent apartment as I pushed it open. There on the bed, where momentarily I expected to see ashes and blood, were messed sheets and a couple of pairs of jeans in a heap. When I came out of the bedroom, the living room decor was unchanged from when I'd left it four days earlier.

The longsword on the wall.

The red couch.

The thorned, iron candleholders.

And then there was a bang on the door. It had to be Justin, wanting an explanation after everything that had happened on the archery field.

I walked to the door and as I grasped the handle, I noticed something out of the corner of my eye on the balcony.

"One second," I called out. I walked slowly, heel to toe, over the hardwood floor. My toes curled over the metal of the balcony doorway. On the black tiles, thousands of glittering particles shimmered under the moonlight. And there, in the center, was the clear outline of a body—my body. It must have been where I lay after I performed the ritual for Vicken. The golden particles were scattered unevenly near the door, as though I had been lifted from the spot and brought back inside.

There are three ways to kill a vampire: a stake through the heart, beheading, and very powerful sunlight. When a vampire is killed, she leaves behind only the dust of her supernatural form—and there it was before me, like small crystals.

Bang!

"Coming!" I spun around, walked quickly to the front door, and opened it.

It was not Justin.

A young man with hair like a lion's mane and a proud chin leaned an elbow on the doorjamb.

"About bloody time. You'd think I have all night to wait around," Vicken Clough said.

"Vicken!" I cried, and threw my arms around him.

"Yes, that's my name." His muscles contracted as he squeezed his arms around me. It sent goose bumps rippling over my arms to feel him so close to me and to hear him breathe in my ear—in and out. I pulled away.

"Vicken! My god." I placed both hands on his cheeks. His fierce brown eyes warmed as he looked at me. "Look at you," I said with an amazed sigh. My hand pressed onto his back and I waited for it, for his chest to rise and then fall. It was fast but he did—a quick inhale, a quick exhale.

The ritual had worked. He was a living, breathing human. Officially an ex-vampire.

"Hello, love," Vicken said, pulling back. He appraised my face. The side of his mouth lifted, and he winked. Vicken walked into my apartment, plopped down on my couch, and rested his black leather boots on the coffee table. His shaggy hair was purposely unkempt. He leaned back into the pillows and crossed his hands behind his head. It was so him, I wanted to hug him again.

"You look . . . ," he said, ". . . terrible."

I appraised his sleek shoulders and lean frame. It seemed impossible that the Aeris could hold Rhode and me responsible for giving someone this gift. Looking at Vicken, it seemed so justified. I wondered briefly if the Aeris had made an appearance to Vicken too. He too had reentered the natural world as a human without their consent. They might have visited and threatened to send him back to the nineteenth century, before I made him a vampire.

"Vicken, have you seen the Aeris?"

"Seen the Aeris?" he asked, and his features darkened. "You mean they exist?"

Suleen was right, then. The Aeris did not show themselves to vampires just because they were evil. They had come for Rhode and me. They had come to make an example of us.

I explained to Vicken what had happened on the archery field. That Rhode had run off and left me with no answers.

"That explains that, then," Vicken said with a sarcastic chuckle.

"Explains what?" I asked.

"I've been staying here in your room. Rhode walked in, grabbed a bag, and said he had to leave."

"Wait! Rhode was staying here?"

"Yes, well—" Vicken paused guiltily, then cleared his throat and continued. "Anyways, I tried to follow but when I walked on campus, it was bloody chaos. Police cars, sirens, and ambulances. I haven't exactly got a pass to be on campus yet, you know what I mean? What happened out there?"

I stood up straighter and clenched my hands. I did not answer him right away. I couldn't.

Rhode had been staying in my room the four days I was in the hospital, while I assumed he was dead? Last year, he had existed. Somewhere in the world . . . just without me.

I groaned. How strange it was to stand here now, looking at his longsword and our photos without the pit of grief in my stomach. It was the same apartment, but everything was different.

"Oh!" Vicken said, interrupting my thoughts. He stood up and reached deep into the pockets of his jeans. His fingers curled around something I could not see, and he opened his palm. "This is for you."

A ring dropped into my palm. My onyx ring.

"I found it out on the balcony after I . . . after I awoke," Vicken said. "You were gone."

The legend of onyx was that it could hold on to spirits left lingering in a world that no longer wanted them. I immediately thought of Rhode holding my hand on our long walk to my orchard so many years ago. I tried to push away the words he'd said on the archery plateau but they sifted into my mind anyway. . . . *I didn't want to come back. I had to.*

"I'm sorry I wasn't here for you," I said, clearing my throat and pushing the ring onto my finger. "Justin took me to the hospital after the ritual was completed."

"Typical mortal . . . ," Vicken grumbled. "All you would have needed was some simple—"

"—lavender water," we said in unison, and shared a smile. I kept looking down at the onyx ring on my finger. I focused on its smooth black surface. The stone had no end, no beginning, and no glint of light. Just darkness.

"Hey . . . ," Vicken said. "Your hands are shaking."

Were they? I sat down on the couch, placing my head in my hands.

"Is it me?" he continued. "I just got back here, you can't possibly be angry with me yet." I met his eyes. "Seriously—what is it?" he asked.

"The chaos on campus was caused by a murder. A student was murdered tonight. By a vampire."

"Anyone we know?"

"Yes, I recognized her. Remember the maid from Hathersage? In 1910? I can't remember her first name."

"Was she alone?" Vicken asked.

"As far as I could tell. I didn't see anyone else."

I rested my elbows on my knees and looked to Vicken for answers. He would know what to do. He was once one of the leaders of my coven.

When he offered me no answer, I stood up and walked to the balcony door. Outside, I watched the moonlight shine over the sparkles of my vampire remains . . . such a strange remnant of a life so dark, so empty.

I thought of Rhode running from me, and a pulse of pain rippled through me. I hoped, wherever he was, that he was safe.

Vicken stood beside me, joining me at the balcony door. "We didn't tell anyone," he said, referring to my coven and their arrival at Wickham Boarding School only a few weeks before. "No one in the vampire world knew we were coming for you."

"No," I said as Suleen's words echoed in my mind. "It's not your fault. This vampire was drawn here by the ritual."

Vicken turned to me, a thought forming in his mind. I could see the excitement building in his eyes.

"She'll probably wait around. Wait to see who was performing that kind of magic."

"You can count on it," I said.

"Let's go," he said, walking back across the room.

"Go?" I asked. "Do you have any idea the kind of night I've had?"

"Bollocks. Let's go find her. See what we're up against. See if there's more than one."

"So you've gone mad. The ritual destroyed your mind," I said.

"A simple hunt. That's all. Just to size up what we're dealing with."

"Now? Tonight?"

I was exhausted to the core, truthfully, but something in Vicken's idea made adrenaline fire up my muscles.

"Why not now? She killed that girl tonight. Should we sit around until there are more murders?"

I had to admit it was a better idea than sitting around and waiting. But I had to be logical about this.

"We don't have Song or Heath. We've got no coven. We're human, with no backup and no supernatural abilities," I added.

"Not true. I've still got my vampire sight and extrasensory perception. If vampires are nearby, I'll be able to feel it, sense their intentions."

True! Vicken still retained some of his vampire abilities because he had only recently been transformed. He would have sight like a vampire and a sixth sense. He would be able to pick up other people's emotions.

"Come on, then, let's go," I said, walking out of the apartment.

"Oh, please," Vicken said, shutting the door behind us. "Don't act like this was your idea."

We sneaked out a side door and waited in the alleyway running the length of Seeker dorm. Down near the library, a security van was pulling toward the chapel.

Vicken motioned to the trees. "Go," he whispered.

We darted down the path into the shadows, keeping close to

the buildings. We turned at the infirmary and ran down its length toward the woods beyond it. I couldn't make out the stone wall, but I knew it was there. Vicken's footsteps matched mine and when I caught sight of him out of the corner of my eye, I saw that a small smile still played on his lips.

"You're enjoying this too much," I whispered fiercely. We reached the stone wall, which was as high as Vicken stood tall. He placed a motorcycle boot in between the mismatched stones and pushed himself up, then pulled me up behind him. We climbed down to the other side on Main Street, outside the protection of the Wickham Boarding School walls.

Now that I stood there on the street, it did seem a rather stupid idea. Vicken and I hadn't taken any precautions. We could have tied rope around our necks in a knot with a protection spell. We could have tried an array of spells to arm ourselves.

I drew a deep breath, taking in the long view of Main Street.

"I can do this," I said, extending my hand to Vicken. "I'm not bad with a knife."

"There's my girl," Vicken said, and reached into his boot. He handed me a dagger wrapped in a leather sheath. We continued along the wall, down Main Street, away from school, away from the cafés, and in the direction of Lovers Bay Cemetery.

"Besides," he added, "we're here to see what she wants. To observe. We won't have to fight anyone if we stay out of sight."

I couldn't be afraid, even though she was more powerful than we were. We weren't helpless. By nature, vampires did not have super strength or speed. They were just hyperaware: They could smell flesh in an instant, read thoughts and intentions, even track a person from miles away. Vicken and I could outrun a vampire if it was over a short distance, but eventually the need for breath would weaken us. We just had to stay out of sight so she couldn't sense us or see us.

Already, I was feeling better. I had been a Vampire Queen for almost six hundred years, and I knew vampires. I had to know more than she did. Vampires were loners. They usually traveled only with a maximum of four others, a coven. Too many vampires together were too many vampires fighting for power. We walked past the cemetery, down toward the end of Main Street. As we walked, we could see the ocean at the end of the street.

"Do you sense anything?" I asked Vicken.

"Just how scared you are," he said with a devilish smirk. But it vanished immediately. He inhaled deeply. I did too.

For there had been a shift on the air. A light breeze picked up, bringing with it the smell of . . .

"Musk," we said together. Musk was a very specific fragrance, one used in many spells.

"Where's it coming from?" I asked. He pointed toward the end of the street. The wind blew again, and the smell was stronger this time.

I touched Vicken's arm. "What are the odds?" I asked.

"Pretty good, actually. You said it yourself," he whispered, his eyes darting down the street. "The ritual drew her here."

I inhaled the strong scent of musk again and looked to the sky. Right above where we stood was a constellation I knew very well.

"Pegasus," I said. My old friend. The winged horse. Vicken and I shared a knowing gaze. Vampires looked to Pegasus for the time—you could tell how long you had until sunrise based on its position in the sky. The time now was nearing midnight, a powerful hour for vampires performing spells. Even though we were mortal, I hoped Pegasus might give us some strength.

With the musk came a hint of earth and vanilla. The smell deepened—this was not traditional musk; this was different. I had smelled that combination before.

"Of course," I said knowingly. "This musk is being burned over a fire. Don't you smell the wood?"

I had performed this exact spell with Heath, Gavin, Song, and Vicken when they first became my coven. The annunciation spell was used to cement a coven, binding their lives together. Forever.

And it was meant to be performed before midnight at the beach.

"They'll need seawater," I said, and with renewed focus, I ran toward the end of Main Street.

"That's why she killed Kate. She had to be full so that she could share her blood with her coven," I continued breathlessly.

"Yeah, I remember," Vicken said darkly as he followed me toward the beach. "Look, if there's only one or two, we can stab them right in the heart. Get it over with quickly." The smell of musk was nearly unbearable now. "Get out your knife," he commanded.

I slid the knife from my boot, and my fingers gripped around the butt of the dagger. The sidewalk ended with a string of houses gated off from the street by a long driveway. Vicken's fingers wrapped around my wrist and he pulled me into the shadows at the edge of a small parking lot.

His profile was serious as he looked down to the sea. "Come on," he whispered. I followed behind, crouched over as we made our way across the parking lot to a seawall that bordered the sand.

Vicken crouched down and leaned forward.

"Stop," I whispered. "They'll be able to feel our presence."

"Not if they're in the middle of their ceremony," he said. Vicken inched forward so he could see around the side of the wall. His body was still as he looked down the beach.

"Well?" I asked, unable to bear the anticipation.

He sat back on his heels. In the moonlight, his mouth opened and he looked at the ground before quietly saying, "There are five. Four men and the one woman."

Without letting him go on, I positioned myself so I could look. There was room for only one of us to peer down the beach. Without any remaining vampire sight, all I could make out were five figures, just as Vicken had said. The fire burned before the coven, and tiny flickers crackled in the blackness. I inhaled musk and frankincense.

It was done. She had a coven.

As I watched, she turned her head, highlighted faintly by the moonlight so that I could see her profile. She had a small upturned nose and a pronounced collarbone, as if she hadn't eaten enough as a human. In a moment, she spun on her heel to face me, then lifted an arm and pointed up the beach directly at me.

"Run," I said, scrambling backwards. "Vicken, run!"

I pushed my body as hard as I could as we ran down Main Street back toward civilization. My legs, my poor legs, were shaking so badly that if it weren't for the mental image of the vampire's arm, pointing right at me, I would have collapsed onto the ground. That blond hair and the familiar slope of her nose. How could she have known I was here? In Lovers Bay?

Run, Lenah. Stop thinking and run.

If we found a crowd, we would be safe. Vampires don't expose themselves to humans en masse. But she wouldn't give up. She had seen me, her maker.

Oh, what was her name?

"Here, here!" Vicken said, skidding to a halt at what seemed like a particularly random part of the street. He started to climb over the stone wall, and only then did I realize he knew exactly where we were because of his lingering vampire sight.

I checked the street again. Luckily, the long trees curved over it, protecting us from her view, and it remained empty.

He extended a hand to me and we climbed over the wall together. Once my feet hit the grass of Wickham, I felt a bit better. Vicken and I crept back toward campus through the trees, but when we were close to the pathway, he stopped.

"Wait," he said, holding out an arm.

A security car drove by, causing both of us to retreat deeper into the shadows. Once we were safe in the darkness, Vicken asked, "What did you run like hell for? Did they see you?"

"Yes! Of course," I said, still trying to catch my breath.

"Let's keep to the back of the buildings," Vicken said. "We have a better chance of staying hidden."

We walked toward Seeker.

"Her name was Odette," Vicken said. "After you changed her, she did not linger long. She left shortly after you took your hibernation."

I could see the back of Curie building and the greenhouse as we walked.

"Odette?" I said. Her name felt odd and foreign as I said it aloud. "I don't remember that." I remembered her face, though. I never forgot the faces of those I killed. "If the power of the ritual called her to Lovers Bay, then she's here to find that elemental magic," I said. "She'll want it to use herself."

I didn't need to explain to Vicken that she desired power.

"Well, we won't be performing the ritual again anytime soon, so maybe she'll leave when the magic doesn't present itself again."

I hoped that was true, though I didn't know Odette's intentions. But as Vicken and I hesitated at the back of the infirmary, I did know this: A vampire's number one priority is blood. Second on that list would be power. If Odette wanted to find out the source of the magic of the ritual, she would have a plan. Vampires always had a plan.

Vicken and I ran to the media building next to Seeker. We hesitated as two Lovers Bay police officers patrolled the pathway ahead of us. I looked all the way up to the top floor to see my balcony. The balcony where I'd performed the ritual.

I tried to ignore the voice in my head, the one that had haunted me since she lifted her arm and pointed at me up the darkened beach.

Odette would be back.

Chapter Six

rested my chin in my hands and sat on the couch with my legs tucked under me, studying the longsword on the wall. I analyzed the slim reflection of my body in the sword's metal. How many times had I stared into its silver and asked how I could possibly survive without my Rhode? How many times did I have to turn my eyes away, because it was just too much?

And then I had met Justin, who brought me out of the depths of despair and back into the light.

Two days had passed since Vicken and I discovered the vampires on the beach. We did not venture off campus after dark. No matter how hard I studied that longsword, looking into its infinite mirror for answers, I found nothing. Why had Rhode stayed away from me for so long after he survived the ritual to make me human?

All I knew for certain was that our souls had linked us to Earth.

For two days, I had walked back and forth from the archery plateau to my apartment, searching for answers where the Aeris had stood. But nothing came from sitting for hours on the grass. For two days, I wondered: Where was he? Where had he hidden for the year I believed him dead? I found no answers and Rhode did not return.

Two days
  became
  two weeks . . .
  . . . two weeks
  became
  two months.

··─◄⦂··

The summer passed in a blink. I had whiled away the time by taking summer classes, and as we got closer to the start of school, I found myself marking off the days on the calendar. On August 31, I resolved to take a trip. Wickham students were set to return in a couple of days and I had not seen Justin or his brothers on campus all summer.

No letters. No e-mails.

I had tried calling Justin but my phone calls went unanswered.

Three days before school was to begin, at dawn, I took a drive to Justin's parents' house in Rhode Island. I intended to give him an explanation. He deserved it. I practiced my speech during the hour-long drive there. When I finally pulled onto his street, I rolled down the window. A cool breeze floated into the car, brushing against my cheeks. The big houses slept in the early morning. Not even the sprinklers were on yet.

I stood at the foot of Justin's family's driveway, looking up at the house. The last time I had been there was Halloween, and now the trees were lush and heavy with leaves. I associated freshly baked cookies, home-cooked meals, and soft hands touching my skin with this house. At any moment, I expected to see a light click on in the kitchen window. Justin's mother was an early riser. Did she know we hadn't talked all summer? Would she welcome me inside?

How could I explain how sorry I was? Okay, one more rehearsal.

"Justin," I said aloud to myself. "You don't understand. When I saw Rhode, I was . . . surprised."

I heard the sound of a latch; the front door opened. I lifted my chin to see Justin, shirtless and in a pair of sweatpants with WICKHAM down the leg. He squinted.

This was it. I had to tell him.

"Lenah?" he said, and rose onto his toes to try to see me over the top of a hydrangea bush.

I shifted the weight from my left foot to my right foot. My heart was unable to find a comfortable rhythm. I couldn't scream "I'm sorry" across the lawn. I started up the long driveway, but there was no need.

He slammed the door.

❦

Here's what I don't understand," Vicken said the next evening. Still careful not to venture out after dark, we had a couple of hours left before sunset. We had planned our days that way the entire summer. It was just after six and we were at Lovers Bay Herb Shop, at the end of Main Street. "Why do we need to stay in this bloody place? Skulking about in daylight just in case we run into a vampire you might have made a hundred years ago. In case you forgot where that happened, we have a house in Hathersage. In fact, we murdered lots of people there."

"Yes, our house that is likely to be overrun with vampires in our absence," I said.

"We have money," Vicken reasoned. "Let's go to Paris. Drink wine. Relax."

"You know why we can't leave," I replied, and held up a jar of dried jasmine. Might be useful. I scooped some into the paper bag. "I'm not leaving now that Kate's been killed. Especially when I feel so responsible."

"Maybe it's all a coincidence. It's been ages since you performed the ritual. Those vampires probably came to town, ate your unfortunate friend, and left. Let's go. We can find Rhode on our own. He won't be that hard to find," Vicken groaned. "Blue eyes, scowl, self-righteous attitude."

"We're staying," I said, and piled the items on top of the counter. I didn't mention to Vicken that I didn't want to leave Lovers Bay because I had put down roots here. It was my home now.

"You know, just because you were Queen for a few hundred years doesn't mean you still are."

The Herb Shop owner had disappeared behind the curtain to get me some newtfeet. I placed a twenty-dollar bill on the counter and waited for her to return.

Vicken examined some chanting crystals on the bottom shelf of the case but then he slid up slowly and whispered under his breath, "White skin, so delicate. As a human, she's truly so small, easy to break her neck."

A tingling feeling crept over me. I shot a glance at Vicken. He stared behind the counter, his eyes wide. "I'll siphon her blood out, slowly," he said. His intonation was different, female and almost reptilian. He was speaking for someone else; this was what happened while using vampire extrasensory perception. "It'll be easier to get Lenah alone," he hissed.

He took a step back. "Lenah," he said in his familiar raspy voice. "Go. Now."

The woman behind the counter had long, cascading ringlets of blond hair that curled perfectly across her blouse. This was not the shopkeeper. Her skin was abnormally polished and pale. Her eyes were glassy. Their color was an unnatural jade.

Odette.

There was a screech against the glass. A white hand adorned with knifelike fingernails made a claw around the bill. She ran her crimson red nails along the shiny countertop and wiped a drop of blood from the corner of her mouth. "Getting comfortable, were you?"

She licked her lips and grimaced from the taste. "Blech. She was overweight. I'll be full for days," she said, and with a sleek bend of her legs, jumped and landed on top of the counter. "My, my . . . ," she said, looking down at Vicken and me.

With paper bag clutched in my hand, we backed toward the door.

"Lenah Beaudonte. The Queen. Backing away from me?"

Blood dripped down her chin like wine running down the side of a goblet.

Vicken whipped out a dagger and stepped before me. Odette jumped to the floor just inches from Vicken's dagger, and her eyes slid back and forth between us.

"Very good, Ms. Beaudonte. I see your ritual works. He makes a very good human."

My blood pounded in my ears and throat. Vicken held his arm outstretched, gripping the dagger tightly.

From the floor behind the counter, I heard a groan. The shop-keeper was still alive.

"If you want to die, then by all means, come closer," Vicken said to the vampire.

She cocked her head to the side and smiled eerily at him.

"I had always admired the stories of your greatness, Lenah," she said, licking the blood from her chin. "And your evil. They are legend in the vampire world."

A lump in my throat made it hard to swallow.

"Your friend Kate, was that her name? She crawled away from me. Cried and screamed. It was such fun," Odette snarled.

Vicken lunged at Odette, thrusting out his hand to plunge the knife into her heart. She kicked up a leg, and the dagger flew in an arc through the air, clattering onto the floor.

"Damn it!" Vicken spat, and scrambled across the floor for his weapon.

Chin dipped to her chest, the vampire bored her eyes into mine. She opened her mouth—fangs bared.

When my coven came for me all those months ago, when I killed them in the gymnasium, I never understood. It was not until this moment as the blood pumped through my heart that I realized what humanity meant. I was filled with it. She needed blood. I would be next. She wanted to drain me of my life force; I knew that feeling too well. How I had hungered to suck the blood from two small holes, siphon it out in rhythmic swallows as life slowly drained away from my prey.

I dropped the bag of herbs to the floor and raised my hands, ready to defend myself. I turned to my side to avoid giving her a larger target. She ran at me, extending one arm, and thrust outward, slamming me in the chest. I fell backwards to the wall behind me. Small brown and black vials clanked and clattered together. Some fell on me, spilling their contents, and others broke into pieces on the floor. My chest throbbed from the force of her hand.

Instead of coming after me again, she linked an arm around Vicken, pulling him from the floor and hooking him around the neck. Vicken's eyes locked on to mine. He jerked against Odette's strong grasp. His hands were balled into fists. The dagger lay on the floor, useless.

I jumped up to grab on to Odette's fingers and pulled back, jerking, but they were immovable. I was like a child pulling at a metal vise. I tried again. How was she so strong?

Odette smiled and her fangs slid down.

"What is this?" I growled.

"Such questions," Odette said. She squeezed harder and Vicken grimaced from the pain. Then she pushed me away with her right hand, but it felt like an anvil hitting me in my stomach. I fell back into the shelves of bottles, so they popped and exploded around me, and I hit the floor, shaking my head to clear my vision.

The force of her hand had made the muscles tender. When I touched them with my fingertips, they seized, sending an ache through me.

"Lenah. Give me the ritual. Now," Odette ordered. Vicken's face was turning red. My eyes darted to the knife. I pushed up from the floor just as Vicken lifted a knee.

He stamped down hard on Odette's foot, and out of surprise, she let go. Vicken jumped away and scrambled for the knife. Instead of going after Vicken again, Odette clawed through the air at me. I ducked, missing her knifelike nails, but slipped on the slick oil from the aromatherapy bottles, falling back to the floor with a smack.

Odette stepped down on my chest and grinned.

She pressed harder. Surely she would crack a rib. My chest felt so tight. Behind her, Vicken was getting to his feet. She pressed down even harder, right below my neck. I coughed, unable to breathe. I needed to breathe!

Vicken picked up the dagger.

"I'll kill your friends one by one," she said through clenched teeth. "Kate was easy. The rest will be painful and slow."

Vicken plunged the knife through the air, but he was not as fast as the vampire.

She jumped off me and ran out the door. Vicken scrambled after her, dagger in hand, but she was gone. I gasped for air, drawing in heaving hot breaths and clutching my chest, rubbing at the skin where her boot had pushed against me.

Kate was easy. The rest will be painful and slow.

"Vicken!" I coughed, rolling onto my stomach and snatching my bag of herbs from the floor. I pushed up from the mess of bottles and inhaled a mix of scents—fig, patchouli, others. Vicken darted out the door and onto the street, but he was no match for a vampire who needed no breath to run. When I stumbled out of the shop, Vicken stood in the middle of the street. All we could see was her blond hair and lean form disappearing into the twilight over Main Street.

I walked slowly to join Vicken. He scanned the street to see if there were other vampires about. The only movement came from the fast-flying clouds sweeping by above our heads.

He sniffed a couple times and looked over at me. "You stink."

"Gathered that," I replied. My blouse was slick from the essential oils.

"We should go back and check on the shopkeeper," I said. "Though if someone comes in and catches us before she's awoken, we'll be implicated."

"I'll go," Vicken said. "I'm not afraid of human idiocy." He bent down and dropped his knife with a plunk into his boot. "That vampire was quick. I couldn't get a clear shot if I threw the dagger." He sounded like he was trying to justify it to me.

"Mind you, she didn't kill us," I said.

"No, she didn't," he said, and grabbed on to his shoulder. He winced. "But she tried to take me with her."

"She wants the ritual."

"Gathered that too," Vicken said, and sniffed in my direction. "Wait here, where I can see you—" He hesitated. "—and smell you."

So do the movement again," Vicken demanded, sucking on a cigarette. We stood on Wickham Beach and I mimicked the motion Suleen had made earlier that summer. "So he waved his hand, and her body just appeared?" Vicken asked.

"Not really. It was an outline of it. Like a ghost."

That moment seemed a thousand years ago now. The yellow tape and police officers had gone. Someone had combed through the sand. Combed it, cleaned it, taking away all evidence that anyone had been killed there.

"I told you," I continued, "we were indiscernible to the people around us. Invisible."

Vicken stood up, dropping the cigarette onto the sand as a Wickham security vehicle pulled past the entrance to the beach. The car window slid down and a security officer called out to Vicken and me in the darkness.

"Curfew in twenty minutes!" he yelled.

"Thank you!" I called back.

After a moment, I said, "She had that look," recalling Odette's saunter on the beach. "That power-hungry look. The one where the madness has just begun to take over."

I stopped pacing as Vicken lit another cigarette. He stood facing the ocean, his back to campus.

"Hey, kids! Fifteen minutes to curfew!"

On the path, a different security guard pointed down at us, this one portly with a beard. "No one out past nine," he reminded us.

When the students came back to campus in the next few days, they would find it much altered. Vicken and I had walked off campus that morning to see a construction crew erecting a heavy steel gate. It was set to connect between the two Gothic entrance towers. By the time we returned that afternoon, a twenty-four-hour guard manned a booth at the entrance. A booth that had remained empty the entire previous year.

Now, on the beach, a guard was watching.

I joined Vicken at the water's edge.

"How are we going to protect ourselves if there's five of them?" I asked. "I'm not exactly a sunlight-wielding vampire anymore."

Vicken was quiet and then said, "That's just it, isn't it?" He nodded to himself. "We need to rely on sunlight."

"That depends. She was strong enough to hold you, paralyze you. We don't know what kind of strength she has. And she was out before sunset this evening."

"It was almost sunset. And she might just be very strong. We don't know her powers. We'll have to try to let it play out until we know what we're dealing with. I'll nose around for some more information."

"You be careful. Your ESP has not waned at all?" I asked, hoping that some of Vicken's vampire traits had not yet faded after his transformation. He shook his head. Like Vicken, all I'd had left of my vampire powers after the ritual were my sight and my extrasensory perception. There was no telling when they would disappear for Vicken, but both of mine weakened the longer I was human. The more time he had them, the more advantage we had. We walked away from the beach and back toward Seeker.

When I returned to my room and Vicken to his dorm, I lit a white candle on my coffee table and collapsed back onto the couch, watching the candle flame flicker and dance. The light became just a golden blur. I leaned my head back on the couch and as I watched the flame, its dancing rhythm lured me to sleep. I drifted off, visions of Justin slamming doors, and Justin screaming at me in front of an audience of people lingering in my mind. More nightmarish images came: Justin racing his motorboat and driving it head-on into Rhode, lying on the shore and helpless.

Then the images changed.

I walk down a familiar pathway. I am at Wickham. There are brick buildings covered in dirty snow. No students. Windows are blackened; the Union, vacant. I walk the long path toward Wickham Beach.

"What is this place?" I ask the empty campus, and suddenly, I am not alone. Suleen joins me at my side. We walk in the snow toward Wickham Beach. As I look toward the shore, a discarded broken rowboat sits in burned pieces on the sand.

Behind us, quartz dorm windows are blackened, abandoned. No one walks in and out of the dorms; no one hurries with cups of coffee to their classes. Wickham is darkened, deadened. A ghost town.

"Is this the future?" I ask.

"This is Wickham if Odette achieves the ritual," Suleen says. "No one that wicked can pour evil intentions into a ritual that powerful without repercussions. She will destroy . . . everything."

I stop, gasping in the bitter winter air.

I shot upright on the couch, placed my hands on my thighs, and tried to catch my breath. I froze a moment—the tip of my nose was ice cold. It was as if I had been walking around outside on a snowy day.

"Suleen?" I said aloud. "Suleen?"

I twisted about to look around the room, but it was just a dream. And I remained alone.

Chapter Seven

A sea of black cloth. Black T-shirts. Black dresses. Black skirts. Black boots.

It was black for miles. I knew I wore everything in that closet last year, but . . .

"Do I own anything that isn't black?" I asked the closet. Everyone already had reason to stare at me: I had left for six months at the end of last year; my best friend, Tony, had died; and I was now back at school with no explanation. What would Tracy and Claudia say, I wondered, holding a skirt in my hand. There were bound to be questions and talk about Kate, the third girl in the Three Piece, who was now dead. I pulled a black blouse and black jeans from the closet. My breath caught in my chest. Would Tracy and I be friends this year, without Tony around?

I sighed and tried to shake away the dream from the night before. Odette's reign, if she achieved the ritual, would turn Wickham into an abandoned hell. A hell without those I loved, without Justin or Rhode.

Hello, I thought, holding the blouse to me. *I am Lenah Beaudonte. I wear all black, all the time, and at one time was a harbinger of Death.*

I sighed again and made myself a cup of coffee.

When I stepped out onto the campus, I slid on a pair of sunglasses. For the briefest moment, I expected to see Tony waiting for me, as he had done so often the year before. I expected to see the gauge earrings in his ear, the charcoal on his fingertips, and the backward baseball hat. I could have seen my beautiful Japanese friend if I imagined hard enough.

But he was dead.

School, on the other hand, was lively despite the new security presence. The campus was vibrant with students from the upper schools scrambling from building to building. Some exited the Union grasping mugs and cups; the others held to-go boxes filled with a quick breakfast. I walked under the shade of the branches though I no longer feared the sun. I looked down at my palms, at the lifelines I knew so well. I wondered briefly, though I knew it would never be answered, why sunlight once came out of my hands in my second life as a vampire. Who made those decisions in the world, and why had that power been given to me?

As I walked toward assembly, I knew that when I could wield sunlight, I harbored an enormous amount of power. I gulped my coffee and stopped short as a realization came to me. If I had remained a vampire, I would still be one of the most powerful vampires in the world. The desire for power, the high I had once felt as a vampire, throbbed deeply within me for a moment, then ebbed away.

I started walking again. Vicken stood up from a bench about ten paces down the pathway. Seeing him there, with a backpack slung over his shoulders, made me smile. Beyond, in the distance, the harbor sparkled in the morning sun.

"I'm skipping this," Vicken said flatly.

"You can't," I replied. "They take attendance."

"Attendance?"

"Roll call," I clarified.

"I should never have let Rhode convince me to go to this sodding school."

I stopped. A spark of surprise flickered in my chest. Just at the mention of his name, I immediately imagined scenarios about Rhode. Rhode in Hathersage, walking through the empty halls; Rhode watching me from afar, protecting me. Was he wondering if I was all right?

"So," I said. "Rhode convinced you to go to Wickham?"

"Not convinced exactly, but you do realize I haven't been in school since there were horses and buggies?"

"When did you speak with Rhode?"

"Early this summer. Right after you met the Aeris," he replied, though I didn't exactly believe him. I stopped short again and looked straight ahead. Standing together by the entrance to Hopper were Claudia and Tracy, Justin's brother Roy, and some lacrosse players I did not know. And there, standing by his brother, was Justin.

"What is it?" Vicken said, alarm coloring his tone. Perhaps he was a bit more ready to grab for his dagger than usual. "Oh . . . ," he grumbled when he saw whom I was looking at. Justin embraced Claudia with a big hug. When he pulled away, she wiped her eyes and I saw that she was crying. This unit had existed before my arrival at this school, before I darkened their doorstep. Now they stood together, shoulders slumped, looking smaller to me, somehow. Not in numbers, but in their energy.

"I liked her perfume, the pink one with the twisted bottle," Vicken said suddenly. He had closed his eyes in concentration. His wild hair framed his face in manelike waves. "She'll miss that smell," he said, though the words he was saying were not his own.

"What?" I asked quietly.

"Your friend Tracy. She wishes Kate were here. Because—" He hesitated. "—because she listens better than Claudia."

I watched the group a moment. Tracy was looking at Claudia, though she wasn't speaking.

"And your other blond friend, she—" He hesitated again.

"—she wants her friend to go shopping with, to walk with, she misses her presence. But I don't get it. It's been over two months since she died. Why haven't they calmed down by now?"

I understood mortal grieving, even if Vicken couldn't.

I would miss Kate plopping down in a seat next to us, offering us gum first thing. I would even miss her digging endlessly into my love life, asking inappropriate questions. We weren't close, I knew that, but still, her death left a ghost in my mind.

"Two months is nothing," I said, thinking of Tony. His death, unlike Kate's, left a hole in my heart that I was sure would never heal. "The sorrow of death can linger for years."

Death had been so easy to understand when we were vampires. But for a human, the death of a loved one was a point in history always to be referenced. A fixed point.

The pin in the heart.

"Well, let's just go get attended and get to class," Vicken said.

"Attended?" I said, tearing my eyes away from Justin and his friends.

"You know—roll."

Vicken dug a piece of paper out of his pocket while I sneaked another look at the group I'd once considered my friends.

"I have World Literature first," Vicken said, squinting at his schedule.

Justin walked toward us purposefully and I prepared myself with a shake of my hair over my shoulders. *You deserve this. Take it, accept it. You deserve what he is about to say to you.* He picked up speed. In fact, his feet carried him faster and faster in our direction. Vicken looked up from his scrap of paper only at the last moment.

When Justin's body slammed into him, Vicken blasted into the air and hit the ground flat on his back. Justin knelt over Vicken and, with devastating force, punched him in the face. I reacted out of instinct. I kicked Justin directly on his hip, which disarmed him, and he fell away from Vicken. A rather large crowd had formed already and I bent down to pull at Vicken's arm, helping him up. He stumbled on his feet and wiped his right eye. Blood blossomed in the skin below it. It was already swelling.

"Give me a mirror!" Vicken demanded.

"Odd time to be vain," I replied.

"I want to see this!" he said incredulously. He shook his head as though it were preposterous that I wouldn't know this was an important moment.

He turned toward Justin. "Nice shot, mate."

Ms. Tate, our science teacher, ran out of Hopper building. Her eyes were wild and she pointed at Justin. She had obviously seen what happened. "You!" she cried.

Justin shook out his hand; his fingers must have been hurting.

"Come with me," she said.

"And you," she said to Vicken. "Go to the infirmary." She pointed at a junior, Andrea, and ordered her to go with Vicken.

Justin stepped dangerously close to Vicken and me. He could easily have thrown another punch. I'd never seen him so calm . . . or so angry.

"That," Justin said so quietly that only Vicken and I could hear. "That," he repeated, "was for Tony." He turned to follow Ms. Tate but kept his eyes locked on Vicken.

My gut clenched and I waited for Vicken to react. A muscle in his jaw quivered, but that was it. Ms. Tate pointed again, this time toward Hopper. "Justin!" she yelled. "Go!"

Justin's eyes drifted over to me. They were cold and distant now, so angry, so disappointed in me. He broke our gaze when he turned around and followed Ms. Tate. I watched him go with an ache in my heart. This was different from how I ached for Rhode. I wanted my old Justin back. The one smiling at me, teasing me, the one helping me to understand the human world.

Andrea stood at Vicken's side, ready to cross the meadow with him to the infirmary. She glanced back at Tracy and Claudia, as if to ask, *Who is this guy?*

Vicken leaned toward Andrea. "Tell me honestly, is it more purple? Or red?" he asked her. "Actually, do you have a mirror, love?"

Claudia and Tracy walked directly toward me. They wore gorgeous sundresses; Claudia's was a canary yellow. I wished for a split second I could shine like them—like they always did. But when Claudia got closer, I realized how truly sad she was. Her eyes were red and puffy from crying.

"Wow," Claudia said. "A fight over you already." She smiled, and it warmed the grief that had settled on her face.

"That wasn't over me," I said.

"Sure it was," said Tracy seriously. "Who was that?" she asked with a nod in Vicken's direction.

"My . . . cousin," I stuttered. "Vicken."

"Cute," said Claudia, and it was a relief to see a glimpse of her old self.

"We should go in," Tracy said. "It's time for morning assembly."

As I followed them, I glanced around, searching for Rhode on the virtually empty campus. It was pointless, I knew. He wasn't coming. He was taking our promise to the Aeris seriously—and I knew I should be doing the same.

Inside Hopper, a general murmur echoed through the auditorium. Students congregated together, chatting about their summers. I stepped into the doorway, then stopped. So many people. A hundred—maybe more. What I had learned with regard to human behavior came to be tested at that moment. I stepped into the spacious auditorium, and a hush rolled over the crowd. The younger classmen didn't know any better, so they just stared. My classmates who had seen the events of the previous year stopped their conversations and turned toward me.

Tracy and Claudia had made it to the third row, in their regular spot, although now, Kate's seat was empty.

My hands curled nervously into fists. Why did Justin have to pummel my only ally?

Rhode . . . , I said to myself, but it came out as a groan.

I passed by some silent juniors whom I recognized from the year before. My confidence, it seemed, had disappeared along with my fangs.

I hated the human desire to gossip. Once I was past them, they started up again.

"That's Lenah. She dumped Justin Enos. Idiot, right?"

"Those were Kate Pierson's best friends."

"Lenah was Tony Sasaki's best friend."

"Yeah, she is the stupidest person alive, to dump Justin."

"Sit with us," Claudia called, and moved her backpack off the extra chair. I tucked my hair behind my ear and headed gratefully toward the two girls I hoped would still be my friends. These girls who had been on the Earth sixteen piddly years. But they had been kind to me when I needed them and were still being kind. I sat down and listened to Claudia talk about her summer at sailing camp.

"What about you, Lenah?" Tracy asked. "Did you go home to England this summer?"

I was about to explain I had spent my summer at school when Ms. Williams, the overcontrolling headmistress of Wickham, tapped the microphone.

❦

". . . the second you even think about signing out. You must be in twos," Ms. Williams dictated. "Off campus? Twos or lose the privilege."

I have always admired your greatness, Odette had hissed.

And your evil . . .

"Security is more important than ever. We have lost a good

third of our student enrollment because of the accidental deaths of both Tony Sasaki and Kate Pierson," she said with a frown. "So it is our responsibility to reassure Wickham Boarding School community that we remain vigilant and committed to your safety."

Tracy looked down and wiped her eyes but I kept staring forward, pretending not to notice. Claudia reached for Tracy's hand.

"Kate Pierson," Ms. Williams continued, "died off campus. So, while we'll miss her, please do not misconstrue the facts. These incidents are not specifically related, nor are they directed specifically at students. We will, however, maintain our new safety precautions."

Mortals will lie about anything to protect themselves.

I sighed, tuning out her voice. I turned my onyx ring around and around so the silver band rubbed over my skin. Without Rhode, Vicken and I had no chance of fighting more than one vampire or maybe two. We needed Rhode. His years of experience could really help us now. And as much as I thought I knew about him, there was clearly so much I didn't know. So much he could do. So much he kept from me.

No, I thought, and threw my hair back over my shoulders. *Don't go down that road. The pity road, where you dwell on all that Rhode has done. He's gone. He's gone and all you can do is wait for him to return.*

But he was alive. And that rotated throughout my mind. Where was he?

Once assembly broke for the day, chatter immediately started up again. Most people were discussing the new sign-out policy and pointing at the security guards who stood at the auditorium entrance.

"I'm so glad you're back," Claudia cried, grabbing me into an embrace. I inhaled fresh soap and a spicy perfume. I couldn't help looking over Claudia's shoulder at Tracy, who watched us with the remnant of a tear in her eye. Claudia pulled away and her eyes were wet too. "Especially with the whole Kate thing. You know?

Now, promise us. You're not going anywhere? Right? No running off like last year?"

"No," I said to Claudia, who had now taken both my hands into hers. "I'm staying." Her hands were warm and tight around mine. If I were still a vampire, we would have been in perfect proximity for me to snap her forward and bite her neck.

I glanced at her wrists. To investigate her veins. It was so shocking that I would still feel the urge to do this, a silent horror overtook me. Immediately I pulled my hands from hers. *Must get away from her,* I thought.

It seemed that old habits died hard. Wasn't that the expression? The feeling passed and I bent forward to grab my backpack. I was mortal. Not a vampire. Not like Odette. I started after Tracy and Claudia to the front door of the auditorium.

Turn around, a voice in my mind whispered. Perhaps it was intuition or the Vampire Queen deep inside me. *Turn around, Lenah. Look behind you.*

Slowly I turned, and I froze. Standing at the top of the stairwell at the back of the auditorium . . . was Rhode.

A deep gash, scabbed and blackened, ran horizontally across the top of his head. Running down the top of his beautiful lips was another scab so dark in color, I couldn't be entirely sure there wasn't still fresh blood oozing out of it. His right eye and right cheek were puckered and swollen.

My jaw dropped.

"Come on, Lenah," Claudia called from the auditorium door.

But I couldn't look away. A couple of seconds passed; then Rhode did the honors for me, walking down the back stairwell and out of sight.

Rhode!" I called, running toward the back door.

"Lenah!" Claudia called after me, but I ignored her and ran out into the quad.

"Rhode!" This time, I screamed it. He spun around; sunglasses hid his eyes. I could see my horrified expression reflected in the shiny plastic.

That close to him, I was able to really see the damage. A purple bruise ran over the thick ridge of his nose. The black tinge on his skin made him look ill. Beneath the ridge of his forehead was a deep cut that probably needed stitches, but it was much too late for that. The skin had scabbed and would most likely scar. His lips, his beautiful lips, were split down the middle and brown from scabbing.

I lifted a hand to touch his forehead, but he backed away from me. Pain ripped through the center of my chest and I lowered my hand. In the reflection of Rhode's sunglasses, I could see my downturned mouth and the squint of my eyes from the sun.

"What happened to you?" I asked.

"Nothing," he replied. "I told the headmistress I was in a car accident."

His right eye was so purple, I couldn't help but lift my fingers to touch the mutilated skin. He stepped back again.

"What happened isn't really any of your concern," he said. "I have to go to class."

He walked past me toward the science building. If I were lucky, we were headed to the same room.

Chapter Eight

A line of students snaked out of the classroom and down the hall. Geology was a popular course for the senior year— there were three sections full of seniors and a few select juniors. I rose up on my toes to try to see Rhode at the front of the line, but all I could see was the short crop of his black hair. My heart fluttered as I remembered how his hair used to fall past his shoulders like black silk. Oh, how I had loved his top hat and the angle of his fangs. Back then, fangs were a part of our physical being. The thought of the sharp point of Odette's fangs made me press my fingertips to my neck as though to protect it.

"Ah good, Lenah," Ms. Tate said.

I dropped my fingertips. Oh. Apparently, I had made it to the science room doorway.

Rhode sat in the front row, chin pointed down, writing something in a notebook. Ms. Tate looked over her roster, pointed a pen at Rhode, and said, "Rhode Lewin, you stay there. You'll sit with . . . Justin Enos." Ms. Tate was planning the seating charts for the year. "He'll be able to get you up to speed." She was mostly talking to herself.

Very, very bad idea.

Ms. Tate handed Rhode a sheet of paper. "I heard about your car accident. How are you feeling?"

"Better, thanks." He placed his pen down and, with trembling fingers, picked up the sheet. His hands, both of them, were wrapped in thick gauze: one around the wrist and one over the knuckles. I froze when he looked up. Beneath those purple and black bruises were the blue eyes I'd spent half a millennium knowing and loving. My stomach knotted and I took a shallow breath. We did not break our stare, and his gaze lingering on mine was enough to make my head spin. Much to my confusion, he sighed, closed his eyes, and broke the spell.

"Lenah," Ms. Tate said, "you're in your old seat. We have a junior who placed for this class and once she comes, you'll sit together." I nodded and tried to keep my eyes away from Rhode as I walked toward my desk.

I loathed that empty chair next to mine. Tony's. I was about to sit down when Ms. Tate spoke again. "Oh. Hmm."

Justin and two other students had walked into the class. Ms. Tate looked down at her list. "On second thought, Justin, you sit with Lenah. And Margot, actually, we'll put the two newbies together, you sit with Rhode here. Caroline . . . ," Ms. Tate continued to the new girl who'd just walked in, "you sit at the back with . . ."

I stopped listening to the jumble of names. Avoiding my eyes, Justin sat down, and when he placed his books on the table, I noticed his knuckles were wrapped in white gauze. He gripped his textbook, and his knee jerked up and down, trembling from either excitement, rage, or possibly too much caffeine.

I swallowed, unnerved by his silence. I twisted the onyx ring again, around and around, and finally, as I opened my mouth to talk to him, Ms. Tate called the class to order.

"Let's get to today's plan. We'll review some basics."

Justin stared forward purposefully. The aching in my gut surprised me. Why wouldn't he talk to me or even look at me? I anticipated his familiar touch, his warm hand on my knee or my lower back but he did not touch me.

"Okay, today we'll be analyzing the pH levels of local water samples from Lovers Bay. I know, I know—it's very elementary, but I think we need to consider it here as we go forward in our experimentation process."

I looked over at Justin again and he pressed his lips together.

"What?" he said coldly, and kept his gaze forward. It took me a moment to realize he was speaking to me.

"Oh. Nothing," I said, and looked back down at my notebook. "I just . . ."

"What?" he said again, this time with a slow turn of his head. The green of his eyes was hard, cold. "Want to humiliate me some more?"

"Humiliate you?" I whispered, and glanced at Ms. Tate, who was writing something on the board.

"Your boyfriend is up there. You should be sitting with him," Justin growled.

"I just want to—"

"If you talk to me again, about anything other than this assignment, I'm leaving the room."

·-·

Hand me the litmus paper." Justin's tone was icy. Silently, I handed it over.

"Seven," he said. "What's yours say?"

I checked the coloration of the paper and then recorded our results. When we finished, he scooped up the papers, dropped our classwork on Ms. Tate's desk, and swiftly left the room. At the front of the class, Rhode placed his pens and notebook gently into his bag. His jaw was clenched and he winced as he placed his bag on his shoulder. I followed him out of the room.

"Rhode," I called quietly once he was out the door and a few paces down the hall. "Rhode!" I called again, a little louder. He walked quickly down the hallway. I'd had enough of being treated like the Invisible Woman. "If you don't turn around right now, I'll scream bloody murder."

He turned on his heel and looked at me.

"There was a vampire in a herb shop," I began. "Here in Lovers Bay. I recognized her from Hathersage. The maid I killed before my hibernation. And she knows," I added, "about the ritual." I stood a foot or so away from Rhode and watched for his reaction. "Vicken and I wanted to tell you earlier, but you were unreachable."

"Were you hurt?" he asked, keeping his stance the same, arms folded, back straight.

I shook my head. "She's already killed one friend of mine," I said simply. "She said she'd be back for the ritual."

It was as though Rhode were having the conversation with me against his better judgment. He was respecting the Aeris's demand that we stay apart, but surely he was allowed to speak to me?

"She's fashioned her red fingernails to a point." I gulped, imagining my flesh splitting in two from the strike of her fingers. Rhode brought a gauze-wrapped hand to his chin, nodded once, and kept his eyes on my feet. "She created a coven. Vicken and I saw the ceremony ourselves."

"Five?" Rhode asked.

I nodded, but couldn't help myself. I had to know. "What happened to you?" I asked. "You look terrible. What kind of fight did this? Was it because of the ritual?"

"No, and I already told you it was nothing."

"You're lying," I said in disgust.

"I have to go," Rhode said, but before he turned completely away from me, he added, "We should meet tonight. About this coven. I'll have Vicken alert you when and where." He walked a few steps and I listened to the echo of his heels on the floor.

Anger bubbled up inside me. "You know," I called after him, just a little louder than my natural speaking voice. "It was always this way."

He stopped, keeping his back to me. We were alone again, now that the next period had started.

"For hundreds of years, you were in control and I knew nothing."

Rhode turned to me now, our eyes locked in a stare.

"It's true," I said, my voice faint. "I had other distractions, but it was always you who held the power. I loved you, so it didn't matter."

Rhode walked toward me until we were inches apart. This close, I could see the tiny hairs growing on his chin and the faint bruising along his jawline—bruises I hadn't noticed before.

"I don't care about power," he whispered. He seemed to catch himself in a moment of real anger. He took a deep breath. "Always, always my thoughts were with you," he said in an angry hiss.

"You kept me in the dark," I challenged. "Perhaps if I had known about the particulars of the ritual, I could have helped you. We wouldn't be stuck, cursed by the Aeris with no possible way to be together."

At the back of my mind, I wondered why Rhode had said he would never have come back to Wickham, and where he was for the year he'd been gone. It kept nagging at me. What could possibly be a strong enough reason for him to stay away? Another secret, another truth he was keeping from me.

"I told you, I didn't know we would face these kinds of repercussions from the ritual," Rhode said.

"You said a lot of things, Rhode. Made promises, which you have since broken." An image of my sister's grave laced with jasmine flowers flashed into my mind.

"Such as?"

"I do not need to remind you. The point is that if I had helped you with the ritual, if you had told me what you were doing, we might have found another way. Maybe we'd have done things differently. You wouldn't have had to fake your death," I dared to say.

"I really do have to go," Rhode said. He looked at my lips, and my anger dispersed. How quickly it evaporated into the air and away from me. We were so close. Close enough that our lips were just a kiss away. My body wanted it so badly that my muscles ached. His eyes, surrounded by those bloody bruises, gazed at me.

We'd never touched before. Not as mortals.

If he just leaned forward, he'd kiss me—lip to lip, skin to skin—and we'd know what it was like to touch. With human feeling. What we'd craved for hundreds of years. The Aeris wouldn't mind. Would they? Just a simple kiss . . .

"Can't you feel that?" I asked.

I looked up at him, peering into his eyes. I stared at the purple bruising, wondering if it still hurt.

"Can't you?" I repeated.

In the pit of my stomach was a tornado of feeling, churning and spinning, pulling me toward him. I continued to stare at him, drinking him in. My feet were rooted to the ground, but my body swayed just slightly. My body was on fire, the glorious feeling of blood racing through my veins and into my heart. I extended my hand and watched him do the same. His hand, so different from the cool, smooth skin of a vampire, was now the weathered hand of a human. We stood like that almost touching, enjoying the electricity between us. I let every pore, every cell feel the sensation of heat.

"Yes," he answered at last, and dropped his hand.

It can't be like this for everyone, I thought. *Not everyone feels love like this.*

Finally, I took a tiny step toward him, but he stopped me.

"We can't," he said.

I didn't want to come back. I had to. His words echoed inside me. I ripped my eyes away, and the space between us opened up.

I looked at the ground. "You should leave. Permanently."

I took a step back. "If it's such a torment to be near me. If you didn't even want to come back as you said, then go." Even as I said it, I knew I didn't mean it. And Rhode was not so easily fooled.

He blinked slowly. "You know I couldn't leave. Not now."

My anger bubbled again. I swallowed hard. Rhode inched closer. I could breathe him in: soap, deodorant, and his skin too. He smelled sweet, of humanity. He clenched his jaw as though he was fighting tears, and when our gazes met, I saw that Rhode's eyes . . . were glassy.

"Lenah," he said, drawing my eyes to his. "I stay because there is an extraordinary difference between thinking of you and seeing you in the mortal flesh. I stay for the one moment you smile throughout the day. Or to watch you run your hand through your hair. Because I must, must"—his breath was short—"must be near you, in any way I can."

I was speechless. I wanted to say something—anything. Tell him I felt exactly the same way, but I couldn't stop him in time before he turned from me.

And then . . .

I was engulfed by the pungent smell of ripe apples. Apples everywhere. As though I were standing above a wooden crate holding dozens of shiny red apples for the September harvest. I shook my head to shake it away, but the scent was so strong, I was compelled to close my eyes to escape from it for just a moment. Images flooded my mind. A scrapbook of memories from my life ran through my brain, unstoppable.

Rhode and I kiss on the great hill at the foot of our stone manor. I wear a great black gown with a long train. It is moments before sunset. We are vampires. His hands press against my back, drawing me near. My skin

73

has a porcelain sheen. My lips are rose colored and I can see the pointed knives of my fangs. Why can I see myself? A hand holds a cane. I know that cane and its owl head handle made of onyx.

I opened my eyes, shook my head, and focused on my breath. *In and out, Lenah,* I thought. *In and out.* Slowly, the images dissipated along with the scent of apples. The sound of Rhode walking away brought me back to the world of the present.

I must be near you.

My breath couldn't catch up with me fast enough.

Rhode walked down the hallway, his words ringing in my mind, and the smell of apples lingering on the air.

Chapter Nine

I t's September third. We have twenty-seven days before the start of the month of Nuit Rouge," Rhode explained that evening.

As promised, Vicken had summoned me to the library after dinner. I stood at the glass window of a study atrium. From the back of the library we faced the great hill that led to the archery plateau. I tried not to follow the slope of the hill, especially since I intended never to go up there again. I doubted a vampire would watch from there, so exposed. There were no trees to hide behind and no cover of shadow. Vampires liked to watch and examine their victims. By knowing their weaknesses, they could kill them with ease. I pressed my body weight against the glass, letting it cool my skin. I used to do that as a vampire to make sure I still retained some semblance of my sense of touch.

I turned from the window to the two men of my past. Vicken leaned against the wall, arms crossed over his chest. His brow creased and he kept his gaze on Rhode. Rhode sat at the table and rested his bandaged elbow on top of the study desk.

"Why does Nuit Rouge matter?" Vicken asked.

"It's when the connection between the supernatural world and the mortal world is at its weakest," I said. I could feel Rhode's gaze upon me. "It's why our Nuit Rouge party was always particularly bloody. Ever notice if you felt stronger on those nights? More . . . animal-like?"

Vicken considered this with a frown. "Yes. I guess you're right."

"Until October first, it's unlikely Odette will be able to attack on the campus," Rhode said.

"She attacked on the beach," Vicken said.

"Technically, they're not the grounds," Rhode replied. "The ritual was performed on campus more than once. It might have called Odette initially but it may offer us protection as well. The energy may be lingering, as a shield. At least until October first, when Nuit Rouge will endow her with extra powers."

"Brilliant. So in the meantime, we're prisoners in this loony bin," Vicken said.

I ran a hand through my hair, massaging my scalp to relieve some tension. I finally met Rhode's eyes. There was a zing in my chest as though he was touching something within me, very near my heart.

I wanted to tell him about Tony's death and Justin's defense of me. I wanted to explain how it felt when I was able to wield sunlight. But Rhode had not asked about the coven. He had not asked how they died. Again, I reminded myself, I still had no clue to his whereabouts the year before. He had revealed nothing.

"Let's go, shall we?" he said. "I think we've covered everything."

Vicken turned off the lights to the study atrium, bringing our meeting to a close. Rhode glanced at me just as we walked onto the courtyard in front of the library.

As his bruised eyes locked on to mine, I stopped short, inhaling the smell of apples again. But it was different this time. Now the scent was just like when I was a child. I brought my hand to my eyes and rubbed at them and brought with it the smell of cider in winter. In the back of my mind, I saw the geology classroom from that morning.

I am sitting in the geology classroom at Rhode's desk at the front of the room. I look up to the doorway, and my chest clenches. I see myself walk into the classroom. I am wearing all black, my brown hair falling over my shoulders.

How can I walk into the classroom and sit at the desk at the same time? This is someone else's vision. Someone else's mind!

Beautiful, *a voice says. A deep voice, a man's voice. Someone is looking at me. I am aware of the pain in my hands, the cracking sensation whenever I move my lips. I have been in a battle.*

It was all worth it, *the person thinks. His whole body aches. But there is something else too. As I walk by, the person inhales deeply, hoping to smell something familiar. He grips onto his notebook so as not to lift a hand to touch me. He hurts just looking at me. This is painful. This love, he thinks, is so deep, it cannot be undone.*

A realization overwhelms me: I'm in Rhode's mind. These are Rhode's thoughts.

I breathed in the familiar smell of campus: the Union, the fresh-cut lawns, and of course, the ocean. The sweet smell of apples had vanished as if it had never been. I took a moment to replay what I had just seen. I could see myself in Geology exactly as Rhode saw me. I smiled at the green grass at my feet. He thought I was beautiful. *This love is so deep, it cannot be undone.*

With the mechanical click of a lighter, and a plume of cigarette smoke, Vicken tugged at my elbow. Vicken did not fear my touch, but Rhode did. With that realization, another burst of happiness pumped through me. Rhode wanted to touch me but was resisting. I could feel the conflict within him during the vision. Hope rippled through me again as it had in the hallway the day before.

I stay because there is an extraordinary difference between thinking of you and seeing you in the mortal flesh. Because I must, must be near you, in any way I can.

"We will always be in love," I said aloud.

"Oh Lord. Let's go," Vicken growled.

We headed across the courtyard and onto the main pathway.

"Where are we going?" I asked.

"The star tower at the top of Curie." He called the science building by its official name.

Vicken puffed at his cigarette as a collection of junior girls passed by.

"Hey . . . Vicken," one of the girls said with a curl of her lip and a breathy tone to her voice. "You shouldn't smoke," she added with a giggle. He walked backwards to maintain eye contact.

"I heard it could kill me," he said with his Cheshire cat grin.

Another round of giggles and I rolled my eyes as we approached Curie.

"One of them is jealous—she thinks I have a huge crush on you," Vicken said, and I wanted to roll my eyes a second time.

"Are you ever going to finish that cigarette?" I asked.

He drew another puff. "I like to fully experience things that are bad for me."

"You know," I said as he blew out the last breath of smoke, "contrary to your vampire life, those will actually kill you."

Vicken exhaled angrily and stubbed his cigarette out on the brick of the building.

"So will your friend Justin. This actually hurts," he said, and pointed at the yellow and purple bruise beneath his right eye. "I keep touching it with my fingertips. You know, it's easy to forget physical pain when you haven't felt it for more than a hundred years. Glorious." He brought his cheek toward me. "You touch it. I wonder if it feels different if someone else presses on it."

"You're sick," I said, and ran my student ID through the scanner—just one of the many precautions introduced at Wickham Boarding School since Tony's and Kate's deaths.

"I'm sick?" Vicken said, following me into the building. "Need I remind you of the time you killed an entire beach party by yourself?" He paused and we climbed the six flights up. "Don't get me wrong," he said between breaths. "It was brilliant."

❦.

After an hour, the bright moon cast a milky light through the glass ceiling onto the observatory floor. We opened the ceiling windows and instead of using the enormous telescope, Vicken and I admired the passing constellations with our naked eyes, lying on our backs on the floor. Even though the sun had descended only a couple of hours earlier, with every moment, the sky darkened and more stars popped out into the night sky.

"You know, as a point of conversation, Rhode may have gotten into a fight here," Vicken said. "Not in Hathersage like you think."

"All right," I replied. "Then why didn't Odette mention Rhode at the Herb Shop. She clearly doesn't know he survived."

"You're speculating."

"How do you know she has anything to do with Rhode? Wouldn't she have said something? Wouldn't she have mentioned Rhode?"

A shooting star raced across the sky. I pointed straight up and so did Vicken. In unison, we counted in Latin. . . .

"Unus, duo, tres . . ."

Waiting . . . waiting . . . Another shooting star flew across the sky. The exhilaration of seeing that bright light streaking over our heads faded quickly, just as the Aeris's words echoed in my mind.

You are soul mates. Your lives are destined to be intertwined.

"Leave it to me," Vicken said. "I'll figure out what happened. Oh, hell. I was a soldier! Snooping around won't be too hard. Difficult to miss Ol' Bludgeoned Face these days."

I laughed. "Old Bludgeoned Face?"

"Spot on."

"You're funnier as a human," I replied.

Vicken waited a moment and then asked with a wide smile, "Do you want to touch my bruise?"

"Still no."

He turned onto his side and inched forward like a seal out of water. "Come on, Lenah. Touch my bruise."

"No!" I cried. He was so close, I could smell the tobacco on his skin.

"Just do it. Are you afraid of it?"

I smacked him hard.

"A little tiny blood mark!" he exclaimed, and we were hysterical before I heard another kind of laughter echoing up the stairs. I froze. A squeal of girlish giggles followed by a voice I recognized. We sat up and I twisted around to look to the doorway. Justin walked into the observatory with the junior I recognized, Andrea.

"If it isn't my escort," Vicken said with a devil-like grin. Andrea smiled.

Justin's eyes shifted from Vicken to me. "Let's go, Andrea. This room is occupied," he said.

"It's not occupied," I cried, and scrambled up.

Vicken scooted back against the wall and lit another cigarette. "Oh, let them go. He's a twit," he said from behind me, and crossed one ankle over the other. "By the way, he came in here to take her clothes off."

I glared at him.

"ESP," he said with a shrug.

"Put out that cigarette," I hissed.

I clambered down the stairwell after them. As if Justin didn't already hate me enough, now he thought I was with Vicken.

"Wait!" I called, and burst out onto the quad.

Andrea and Justin stood by the door; her expression was murderous.

"This will just take a second," I said to her. "Will you excuse us?"

She looked to Justin, eyes wide, waiting for him to say no. When he didn't, she scoffed. "You're pathetic," she said with a dramatic turn, and stalked off.

"Andrea!" He called after her again, but she was already on the pathway, joining other students. It would be curfew soon.

Justin moved to follow after her.

"Can you please give me a moment?" I asked. He turned back to me with a huge sigh.

"I'm not with Vicken," I said emphatically.

"Did I say that you were?" Justin said, his tone stinging me like a smack against my cheek.

"No," I said quietly. "You didn't."

"On the archery field, you left me for Rhode," he said. "But I guess I wouldn't be surprised if you were with Vicken now. It's tough keeping up."

I didn't have the heart to tell him the actual order: Rhode, Vicken, and then him.

"Vicken and I are really just friends," I said.

"Friends with a murderer. He helped your coven kill Tony!"

"It's more complicated than that," I said.

"Yeah, well, it doesn't seem too complicated to me," said Justin. "I have to go."

That seemed to be a common phrase these days.

But Justin didn't go. He looked down at the ground and then at me. "What do you want from me? What about Rhode?" he asked. "Aren't you guys soul mates? Ritual mates? Whatever?"

"I'm not with Rhode," I said after a pause. "I'm not with Vicken. I'm with no one."

His nostrils flared and his cheeks reddened. He blinked a few times and I struggled to read his expression. "Don't you love him?" he asked. "Rhode?"

"Things just changed," I said with a shake of my head, and it was the truth. As much as Rhode consumed me, as much as I would love him forever, everything was different now. I had to move on.

"Kind of seems like a hard thing to change," Justin said.

We let the sounds of the campus resonate. People were talking and laughing. Cell phones chimed and somewhere close, cars whooshed by on a street.

"Look," I said. "I don't want you to hate me. I know I deserve it. . . ."

"I don't hate you," he said, and shifted his gaze from the ground to my eyes. "I just don't want to know you anymore. I want to live my life without rituals, and covens of murderous vampires killing my friends. I like dating girls who, you know, stay alive."

His words cut through me. It seemed to me then I'd never again feel the joy and comfort of lying in his arms. I remembered how powerful his warmth had felt after being cold for hundreds of years. Warmth, touch, tenderness—that was Justin. He was a reminder that I could truly be alive and feel love. He'd helped me move on last year. I wanted him to help me now. Help me in the way only he could.

But he turned and walked down the pathway after Andrea.

"Wait," I called. "Please."

He stopped next to the pathway light. "What?" He kept his back to me.

"I'm sorry," I said, then hesitated. I chose my words in my head but none of them sounded right. "About all of it," I finished.

He shook his head but faced me again. "Sorry, Lenah, but it's not enough."

"I just want you to know—" I took a step to him and raised

my palms to say *stay*. "No, let me rephrase. I want you to try to imagine someone in your life that you've known forever. Let's say Roy, your younger brother."

Justin frowned but nodded once.

"And then one day, he's gone. How he held a cup of coffee or laughed or touched his face is left only in your memory. Gone forever. I want you to try to imagine that grief."

"Tony died. Kate died. I know what grief is like."

I dared to take another step. "Humans can learn to live again after grieving, but for the vampire, that grief is constant. It's what makes us so dangerous. And when Rhode died, or I thought he did, you were there, at the moment when I was human for the first time. You brought me out of that curse. You healed me."

Justin avoided my eyes by looking across the campus. I waited for him to respond, to say that he was touched, that he understood. But he just exhaled and put his hands in his pockets.

"I know you heard me talking to Rhode that day, on the archery field. I was surprised to see him," I tried to explain.

"I bet," he said, still looking away.

"It's not that I don't love . . ."

Justin's eyes snapped up.

". . . love you," I finished.

He kept my gaze but didn't reply. Didn't say, *I still love you too.* I gave it a few more seconds.

"Fine," I said, and turned on the spot. I hurried down the path.

"Wait!" Justin called from behind me. "Lenah, wait!"

But I did not wait. I kept walking, embarrassment rolling over me in waves. *I can't believe I told him how I feel and got no reaction. No reaction!* It was so unlike him. I walked and walked until I found myself almost back at Seeker.

I'd stopped on the path directly next to the library when a desire to go inside swept over me. There was another hour until curfew. I wanted to go inside the listening room, where I could sit and listen to music at the push of a button. Where I could be alone. Perhaps I would play Mozart. I saw him play in person several times—four, to be exact.

I had walked away from Justin's words. I hoped the listening room would help me forget the look in his eyes. I entered the library and walked down the main aisle toward the rooms in the back. I had worked in that library the year before and knew its contents well. I checked through the small rectangular window into the listening room. It was empty. I opened the door and stepped inside.

There were no CDs anymore. Instead, a computer sat on top of a small desk. I had spent the last year learning to navigate computers. I sat down and clicked on a small icon that said NEW SONGS. Someone had classified them as well: romance, classical, New Age, death metal. Death metal?

I searched through the songs for a few moments, marveling at the thousands of choices. A hand reached over my shoulder. I jumped a little as it then gently grazed the top of my fingers and rested on the mouse. I hadn't even heard the door click. The hand was warm and golden bronze.

"Pick this one," said Justin quietly. He double-clicked, and a ballad, a very soft song with a woman singing, echoed in the small room.

"What are you doing?" I asked quietly as he pulled me up from the chair.

"Dancing with you."

The image of him shoving his hands in his pockets came to mind.

"But I thought you were angry with me," I said.

His strong arms pulled me to him gently and his grasp was firm around my shoulders. His palm rested on the center of my back and I lifted my chin to him. Underneath his shirt collar was a black leather strap. A glint of a silver pendant peeked out from his shirt when he moved, but Justin drew me closer. I wondered what kind of pendant it was and what else could have changed over the summer. The sound of a guitar filled the room, and the melancholy piano swirled through me. Our eyes met and Justin's gaze compelled me to speak.

"I really am sorry. About Rhode, about—" I hesitated. It felt odd to apologize for almost dying when I performed the ritual. "Well, like I said. I'm sorry. About all of it."

He hushed me gently and nuzzled his nose to my shoulder. He grabbed on tighter and we started to revolve.

"About Tony . . ."

"Shhh," he said again, and this time I closed my eyes. I was back at winter prom with Justin, dancing under the sparkling lights. In this modern world, people danced so intimately. Body to body, chest to chest. I could sense Justin's desire in the heat between us. This close, the music made me aware of his wanting. The vampire in me longed to feel Justin's heartbeat. And when I closed my eyes and listened to the song . . . I did.

Imagine if this were Rhode. What would he say about modern dancing? There were no choreographed steps as we'd had in the medieval era. Just two bodies, together, moving. If this were Rhode, his hands would come up my back, landing at the base of my neck. Justin's hands slipped under my arms. Goose bumps swept over me. Justin pulled me even closer so my lips kissed the nape of his neck.

Yes, he's here. Rhode's here. This is not Justin, but Rhode.

Rhode squeezed me closer as the musical serenade echoed in the room. I swallowed nervously as I let myself give in to my fantasy. Rhode and I spun in that room, his graceful hands flowing up and down my body. His warmth, his human warmth, overwhelmed me. Rhode pulled me closer so there was no space between us. He kissed my neck, sending chills through me.

Love. What a strange word. How endless. How it had defined my beliefs for so long. Because we had run through decades of time, hands held, always, always waking with the moon. We reveled in every color of sunsets.

"I love you so much," I whispered.

"I love you too," a strange voice replied.

The American accent startled me from my reverie. I blinked a few times, holding on to the wisps of the fantasy, but knowing as I lifted my chin that I would look into Justin's eyes and not Rhode's.

We kept dancing even though my spell had broken into a thousand pieces.

"I thought when you saw Rhode, it would be over between us," Justin said.

I can't have Rhode. I'll never touch his hand again. It's over.

I refocused on Justin.

"I thought it would be easier to be mad at you," he continued.

"I'm not used to the angry version of you," I said.

"I can't stop loving you, Lenah. I can't," he replied softly. "I keep trying. But I can't."

I looked into his eyes as the song slowed to its last bars.

I can make this happen. Can't I? Justin and me?

This was so much easier than the endless rejection from Rhode. Nothing supernatural telling us we couldn't be together. Nothing stopping us.

Justin held my cheek with his hand and ran his thumb across my cheekbone. I searched his eyes. What was love anyway? Love was warmth and comfort. Love was for the living. Justin could help me feel alive again. I knew he could. I'd felt it last year.

I didn't want to come back. I had to. Rhode's words reverberated in my mind.

Justin leaned forward and kissed the top of my nose. "Want to walk back?" he asked. "Thirty minutes until Williams's stupid curfew."

We shut off the lights in the listening room. Justin stole one more kiss before extending his hand and leading me home.

Chapter Ten

Late-night rain had left the grass glistening the next morning. As I walked the path to Curie, Ms. Tate came flying around the corner, into the courtyard.

"Lenah," she said, stopping in front of me. "I'm glad I found you. We need to discuss your semester project." She rambled on about Justin and me and the importance of teamwork. I took some papers from her load of files and held them for her.

"Oh, thank you," she added, continuing her diatribe. I listened for a few moments, but the wind distracted me. It was stronger than a breeze. It had intention. The air snaked through the trees and lifted my hair from my ears as though acting of its own accord. I smoothed it down as quickly as I could. Ms. Tate's voice floated off and I turned my attention away from her.

The leaves above us shivered again. The water from the fountain fell away in an unnatural hush. I needed no vampire ESP to know. I would always harbor the knowledge. I could feel it in the air.

I was being watched.

I searched the shadows. Any clue would do. The lift of a sly smile or eyes still as death.

"Okay, Lenah?" Ms. Tate said.

"Right. Of course," I said.

Ms. Tate nodded, though I had no idea to what I had just

agreed. I scanned the grounds in front of me, but without my vampire sight, it was impossible to see as far as the other side of campus. When I turned to follow her into Curie, I realized I had forgotten to search the woods behind us that circled the school. They were perfect to hide someone watching an unsuspecting victim.

"I'll need those papers in class today," Ms. Tate said from the darkened entrance to Curie.

My eyes lingered on the trees and on the morning sunlight shining through the breaks in the branches. I did not have time to search for eyes watching me.

I walked into the building with an absolute certainty in my gut.

I was being hunted.

slid into my seat next to Justin, trying to shake off the goose bumps still lingering on my skin. Justin's hand was wrapped in gauze and momentarily I thought of his arms around me in the listening room.

"I can't get last night out of my head," he said.

He reached under the table, placed his hand on my knee, and squeezed. I smiled at him. Perhaps this wouldn't be so hard, being with Justin? He knew how to calm me. Perhaps the girl from last year still existed, the girl who wanted to be human, who needed Justin to help her feel that way. Not like Rhode, who was much better at following the Aeris's decree than I would ever be.

"Guess she's just jumping right into this," Justin said. "Yesterday pH tests, today sediment something or other. I can't even pronounce whatever that other word is."

The experiment was complicated—very complicated. Justin and I stood up to gather our assignment tools from the storage chest. I made sure to avoid looking at Rhode or even in his general direction. That was all I needed, to look at him and have another strange connection that I couldn't control. I wasn't sure yet what had spurred the overwhelming smell of apples, the memories, and the window into his mind.

"Maybe we can have dinner tonight," Justin said quietly.

"Oh," I said, hating that I wished it were Rhode asking me to dinner. In my mind was a dark room lit by candles. Rhode and I sat at a long oak table and raised goblets filled with blood. I'd never eaten a meal with him. I wondered what he liked to eat in the modern world.

"Lenah?" Justin said. "Pizza?"

"Sure," I replied, thinking instead of linoleum tables and plastic cutlery. Greasy food from the Union and paper napkins, just as we had the year before, dozens of times.

I felt the empty space between my seat and Rhode's. I knew very well that the candles, the ones in the darkened dining room in Hathersage, were long burnt out.

I bet Rhode hated modern-day pizza. Too messy.

Justin grabbed a box of slides. When he reached up, I saw the leather necklace again. I rose up on my tiptoes to try to have a better look at the silver pendant.

"Andrea's not speaking to me," he said with the slightest of smiles.

"Sorry about that," I replied, and we moved back to the desk. Justin handed me a dropper and some iodine. With a wink he added, "I'm not."

⚫

I attempted to nap later that afternoon, only to be awoken by sirens screaming onto campus. I threw off my covers and ran to the window, looking down at the campus below. Security guards pointed students to the sides of the pathways. Across the quad, teachers were corralling students into the Union and away from Hopper.

The sound of another police siren traveled in a wave, swelling loudly as the car curved along the pathway and stopped in front of Hopper. I tried not to think about Tony's death in that very building. As I caught sight of Vicken and Rhode standing just to the side of the building, Rhode's blue eyes locked on mine.

With a casual nod of his head, he requested I come down, and in a heartbeat, I followed his orders. As if I could ever say no.

What happened?" I asked. There were hundreds of students on the green. People inside the Union stood against the circular windows, pressing their hands against the glass.

"I need to get into the art studio," a student said to a police officer. She held a portfolio under her arm. "My portrait is due tomorrow."

"Hopper building is going to be off-limits for a couple of hours," the officer said, moving out of the way for a security guard.

"Did someone else die?" a student asked.

"Just go back to your dorm, please," the officer ordered.

"Someone else totally died!" the student cried. People were already taking out their cell phones.

A third police car pulled onto campus. Its siren was off, but the blue lights swirled around and around. Vicken pulled on my shirtsleeve and we walked to the side of Hopper, away from the fray.

"One of the gymnasium windows is open at the back," Vicken said with a nod of his head. The back of the building met the bottom of the large hill that led up to the archery plateau.

"Let's go," Rhode said.

"Casual," Vicken said, always thinking like the soldier he had once been. "Slow."

One by one, we walked to the back of Hopper. Once we

stood together at the gym windows, I said, "Odette. It's got to be. She warned us in the Herb Shop. She said she'd be back. And I sensed her this morning."

"You sensed her?" Rhode asked.

"I felt someone watching me. I can only assume it was Odette."

"Well, there's only one way to tell for sure," Rhode said. "We need evidence. Clues."

"Clues," I parroted. I ran my hand along the edge of the windows. They were horizontal and at least three feet tall, but narrow. I could easily fit through, but Vicken and Rhode would have to wait for me to open a door for them from the inside. If I could reach the handle on the inside, I could open the window wider and slide into the gymnasium.

I did just that and landed on the floor in the darkened room, then took a few steps and looked back through the window.

"Go," Rhode whispered.

"She shouldn't go alone," Vicken said.

I tiptoed toward the double doors. "I'll be fine."

I pushed them ever so slightly, just enough to peer down both ends of the hallway. Once I turned the corner of the first-floor hallway, I would be in the administrative section of Hopper building. The headmaster's office was there, along with admissions. I hurried quietly, finally turning the corner. Voices echoed from the offices.

When you're a vampire, it is of the utmost importance that you remain confident. As the years go on, you gain more and more confidence, but it was hard to find that confidence now, as a mere human. I hunched over, careful to tiptoe in my heavy boots, and crept toward the voices at the end of the hall. My body wasn't so agile as it had once been; now my organs were filled with blood that moved. I kept tiptoeing forward and stopped near the office door.

"She's dead. We're absolutely sure?" Ms. Williams's questioning voice echoed out of the room.

"I'm afraid so. Been dead for at least a half hour," a voice replied.

"What do I tell the students?" Ms. Williams asked weakly.

"Our team is going to have to do a thorough investigation, ma'am. It would be best if you got Ms. Tate's classes covered and temporarily moved these offices to another building."

My hand fell away from the wall; I hadn't realized that I had been clenching my fist.

Ms. Tate. My science teacher?

"I don't understand," Ms. Williams said, and her voice cracked. There was a moment of silence and then the sound of noses being blown. Their footsteps collected near the door, and Ms. Williams spoke again, her voice nasal and closer now. "Why leave that note with the body? What does it mean?"

"It's like a riddle," said a voice I did not recognize.

"It'll be taken with the rest of the evidence," an officer said.

"What evidence? You said there were no fingerprints."

"It looks as if she was murdered just like the other two. Puncture wounds. Depletion of blood. We'll need to photograph the body and have our forensic team investigate."

"You make it sound like a gothic horror movie, Officer."

"We get cases like this occasionally. Some psycho who has watched *Dracula* one too many times."

The footsteps echoed again. *Oh no.* They were going to come out of the office. I looked across the hall. A door. I ran, opened the door, and jumped inside a janitorial closet; then I sank to the floor, pressing my back against the cement wall. I drew my knees to my chest and held my breath, my heart thudding in my ears.

"Ms. Williams, we're going to need you to keep this area off-limits. We'll mark it off with police tape and have it manned overnight."

"And she really drove herself onto campus? Bleeding?" Ms. Williams pressed.

"There's blood all over the car, but we don't know the specifics yet, ma'am."

I had to see the body to be sure. I hoped they wouldn't take it away just yet.

The voices trailed off as the group of people walked down the hall and out of the building. I kept my arm tucked close to me to avoid a precariously positioned broom and bucket and cracked the door just barely, peering back into the hallway. One officer had been left on guard inside the office. I would have to sneak in through the connecting door from a neighboring office.

The officer stood, legs slightly apart, hands held behind his back. I needed him to look away for just a few moments. Be distracted by something, *anything*. I waited. As the moments ticked by, I knew Rhode and Vicken would become impatient and come looking for me. *Oh just look away, you idiot.*

Right then, a girl screamed from outside, and the officer spun to look out the window. Perfect! Her scream trailed away into laughter just as I crawled out of the janitor's closet. I had to leave the door cracked open behind me. I scrambled across the hallway and into the office next door; then I stood up, waited a moment, and pressed my back against the connecting door. I tried to breathe quietly, and waited to see if the officer had heard me. Unlike Odette, I would leave fingerprints so, again, I kept my hands close to my sides. I knew how to be quiet. If I applied pressure to the whole foot instead of the ball of my foot, I would make less noise. I had to go in. I had to see if it was Odette who'd killed Ms. Tate.

I took off my boot and removed my sock. I used it to twist the doorknob as quietly as I could. I placed my boot back on, and on my hands and knees, I crawled into the room. The officer stood in the office, but near the hallway.

94

I would never fear the dead. Never. It was Ms. Tate's heels I saw first. She was on the floor, on her side. She had driven back to campus and died here, in this office.

A vampire's bite mark will ooze for hours, even after a person is dead. As I knelt beside the body, I could sense it was cold without touching it directly. Body heat emanates from a live body. This body was hard. And there they were: two puncture wounds in her neck, still thickly oozing, following the depletion of the vampire's bite. The last of Ms. Tate's blood. It would stop soon. The thicker the blood, the longer it had been oozing out of the victim.

Her eyes were closed; someone must have closed them. There, on the floor next to the body was a small piece of white paper. The note Ms. Williams had mentioned.

In curly, old-fashioned handwriting, it read:

> *Like the lick of a flame, death can be quick.*
> *Or drawn with a knife slowly.*
> *Endlessly.*
> *Over skin.*

I gulped away a scream. At the bottom of the note was one more line.

> *You know what I want.*

It's like a little poem!" Vicken said. "How lovely. You know, if you enjoy threatening poems about murder and death."

"She's doing it on purpose," Rhode said.

"Of course she is. It's exactly what I would have done. It's sick."

"One by one, she'll take out anyone who she knows is close to you, Lenah," Rhode said. "She must have been watching us for days now," he explained.

I paced back and forth at the gymnasium window.

"The second line of the poem is threatening more deaths. Prolonged torture. She'll never quit," Rhode said.

Vicken crossed his arms over his chest. "So what do we do? We can't give her the ritual."

"Of course not," I said. "Think of the consequences." I had seen the consequences in my dream with Suleen.

"We have to join the rest of the school. Ms. Williams has called an assembly in the Union," Rhode said.

Another death would bring the school one step closer to closing. They would surely have to if there were any more deaths. The only place we could go was Hathersage, and that would mean leaving Lovers Bay.

We walked around to the front of the building, passing by Ms. Tate's car, which was being photographed by an officer. Security officers were already leading students toward the Union, to the assembly. Tracy and Claudia walked together at the front of a mass of students.

"Here's something," Vicken said, stopping near the car. "Ms. Tate wasn't killed on campus. You said"—he looked to me—"that she drove back here. She drove herself, bleeding. She got away."

"Or was set loose," Rhode replied.

"Either way, the power of the ritual is still working. Odette can't come onto campus. Not yet," Vicken said.

"This way, please," a security officer said, and we walked into the Union and into pure mayhem.

Chapter Eleven

repeat, this accident occurred off campus. Off campus. There is no connection between Ms. Tate's accident and the safety of your school. Now, let me continue. . . ."

There was uproar again but Ms. Williams roared into the microphone.

"Silence! Now, only seniors are to be allowed off-campus privileges at this time and must sign in and out. If you go off campus, you must go in groups of at least two. Ms. Tate's accident was off campus, so it appears to be unrelated to Wickham or the other unfortunate accidents. Regardless, we must insist on a buddy system, no matter where you go. Wickham continues to be the safest environment for our students."

The Union exploded in voices and questions.

"Why did she drive back onto campus?" someone yelled.

"Please, please, I don't know." Ms. Williams put up her palms, and the room quietened. The cafeteria windows were closed due to the emergency meeting. Metal grates and empty counters surrounded us. "Lovers Bay, Massachusetts, has never before seen this level of violence and I am sure this will be the final incident."

"If it was an accident, why do we have to walk in twos?" someone called from the crowd, and the Union erupted in jeers and questions again.

"I want some answers!" a sophomore girl cried, and broke into tears.

"Quiet!" Ms. Williams yelled into the microphone. Some people put their hands over their ears. "A buddy system is best for student safety on or off any campus, and Wickham is no different."

As I looked around, I finally spotted Justin. He sat with the lacrosse team across the room. "This school remains the safest place for all of you," Ms. Williams exclaimed.

"Guess not!" someone called from the audience.

"I understand some of you would like to go home and we cannot stop you. As we've assured your families. Ms. Tate's car accident off campus was surely that, an accident."

"She's lying," I whispered to Vicken.

"Everyone in this room can sense she is lying," Vicken said. "The disbelief is actually overwhelming."

"What else?" Rhode asked.

"Well, they can tell she's upset. Most of them are angry. They know something connects these incidents. Their trust has been broken."

"Wouldn't you feel the same?" Rhode whispered.

The assembly ended with most of the people staying in the Union to talk about Ms. Tate. Some people were crying; some were asking what they should do about their homework. Some wanted to know who would teach Science.

I couldn't cry.

I didn't want to cry. I had seen the mark of death.

I sat there, waiting to feel something, some sorrow. But all I could muster up was anger. Anger and rage at myself. At Odette. At Rhode and the memories between us that I didn't understand.

"Lenah!" My head shot up. I looked at Rhode. "What?"

He motioned to Claudia and Tracy, who stood above me. Clearly they had been trying to get my attention.

"How are you?" Claudia asked.

I shrugged. "All right, I suppose."

I scooted over as they sat down next to me, but Claudia sat next to Vicken, and I wondered if she did it on purpose. I smelled something sweet from her, like vanilla. "You smell nice," I said. "I know that scent."

"It's Kate's old perfume."

I immediately focused on the Formica of the table. "Oh," was all I could say.

"Weren't you sort of close to Ms. Tate?" asked Tracy. She raised an eyebrow and I realized she was talking to me.

"Not really," I said, and considered last year. I wasn't close with Ms. Tate, though she was the first adult I had spent any time with since my parents. And that was 592 years ago.

"She's the third person to die," Claudia said.

"Keeping count is morbid," Tracy said, taking a sip of soda. She thought a moment, then added, "Or appropriate. I guess that's the kind of school we are now."

"Nice . . . ," Claudia replied.

"These deaths are a coincidence, nothing more, nothing less," Rhode said, and stood up, then walked off. Tracy followed him with her eyes all the way to the Union door until he was out of sight.

"You're not saying much," Claudia said to Vicken.

"I don't worry about much," Vicken replied.

Claudia exhaled heavily. She shook her head. "I don't want to see Ms. Tate when they . . ." Her voice trailed off and she shivered. "When they take her out of the building."

"Me neither," I said, remembering the sight of her lifeless body and the heels of her shoes.

"Want to go off campus with us?" Tracy asked. She got up from the table and smoothed out the front of her blue button-down. I admired the color against her skin.

"Now?" I asked.

"Yeah, now," Claudia said earnestly. "I want to go somewhere where there's a lot of people. The movies or something."

Bad idea. Dark.

"Or maybe for a drive?" Tracy suggested.

Claudia stood up too and crossed her arms over her chest. "I can't believe you're being so calm about this," she said to Vicken.

Vicken stood up from the table. "What should I do, Blondie?" He threw his hands in the air and pretended to run around. "Scream?" He dropped his hands by his side, then stuck a cigarette in his mouth. "Death happens to all of us. Some just earlier than others." He walked out of the Union, leaving the smell of his cigarette wafting behind him.

"Lenah," said Justin, joining us. He immediately took my hand. I exhaled into the familiar cotton of his shirt and hugged him tightly. I lingered in his embrace, allowing his strength to overwhelm me.

"Want to come with us?" Claudia asked Justin. "For a drive. Get off campus."

Justin frowned. "I can't. Coach wants to have a meeting with the team."

I pulled away and he met my eyes. I could sense the question in his mind. Because Claudia and Tracy stood by us, he couldn't ask me what I knew he wanted to. Was Odette behind this?

A collection of cheerleaders passed by. They held their arms linked over each other's shoulders and held hands. One of them, in the middle, was wailing.

Claudia tugged on my shirtsleeve. "Let's get out of here. I can't handle this," she said.

"Be careful," said Justin, and kissed me quickly.

"I'll be all right," I said. "I've got the light of day."

⚜

I knew Rhode wouldn't like the idea of me leaving campus after Ms. Tate's murder, but going off campus to a public place seemed safe. Even if we were just going for a drive, we'd be in Claudia's car and I could suggest a public place if they wanted to stop somewhere.

"I just need my wallet," I said, and we walked back to Seeker.

As I walked up the stairs with the girls, it occurred to me they had never been in my room before. Not even during the previous year when Tony was still alive. Tracy stood directly behind me. She stood so close, I heard her breathing.

"I'll be right out," I said.

"We can't come inside?" Tracy asked. "You're Super Secret Girl or something, Lenah?"

Right. Should have thought about that.

"Of course you can come in," I said.

I stood at the door, unlocking it; the rosemary and lavender dangled in their usual spot.

"Cute," Claudia said, and lightly grazed the flowers with her fingertips. "Dried flowers. I always dry out my corsages or a flower whenever I get a bouquet."

I opened the door, and the girls stepped inside. They oohed and ahhed over the longsword, my furnishings, and all the space I had. It was Tracy who lifted a finger to touch the sword.

"I wouldn't do that if I were you," I said. "It's remarkably sharp."

"Why do you have a sword?" she asked.

"Passed down through my family," I said quickly. *We really do have to get out of here,* I thought.

"What is this? Ita-fert—"

"*Ita fert corde voluntas.* It's Latin," I said. "It means 'the heart wills it.'"

"The heart wills it," said Tracy after a moment. "I like that."

Together, we looked at the longsword. I had gotten so used to it. I supposed, standing there next to someone who had never seen it before, it was quite magnificent.

"What's all over your balcony?" Claudia asked, and I turned. She had her hands pressed against the glass of the balcony door. She lifted her chin to get a better view.

And there, still stubbornly sticking to the tiles, were my vampire remains. Most had washed away during summer rainstorms, but a few glimmers shone under the midday sun.

"Were you doing an art project?" Claudia asked.

"I'm not sure what they are." I decided that playing dumb was my best bet. "Let's go, shall we?"

Before I knew it, we were on our way. I opened the window of Claudia's BMW, feeling the late-summer air whip through the backseat and toss my hair about my face.

"Happy. Happy. Happy. Not thinking about Ms. Tate. I am haaaaapy," Claudia said, and turned up the music. An outburst of guitars, pianos, and multiple voices echoed near my ears. The singer crooned about love and bubble gum. This was definitely not Mozart. Tracy, I noticed, was exceptionally quiet, looking out the passenger window.

After a few moments, Claudia said, "What about the mall? We can walk around or whatever."

Yes. Smart. Bright. Loads of people.

As silly as it may have seemed in the moment, it was good to get off campus in September, while I still could go to the mall like a normal teenager. Before Nuit Rouge began.

Claudia ripped around a corner, and the engine revved as we climbed onto the highway. I had to hold on to the armrest or I would have slammed against the door.

"So," Claudia said. "Tell me about Vicken." I gripped the armrest as hard as I could as she peeled around another corner.

"Nice black eye," Tracy said sarcastically. It was the first time she had spoken the whole car ride.

"He kept wanting to touch it," Claudia said, but the tone in her voice was not disgust. It was, dare I say it, excitement?

"We're talking about Vicken?" I said, surprised. *Murderer. Excellent swordsman. You would have made a lovely meal for him.*

"He's from Scotland?" Claudia asked.

"Girvan, in Scotland, near the coast," I clarified.

"Isn't he your first cousin or something?"

"Right. He's my mother's brother's son," I lied.

"Just ask her already," Tracy interjected, and flipped her hair. "Is he seeing anyone?"

"I . . . don't think so," I said, slightly horrified at the thought of Claudia and Vicken dating. We pulled into the mall parking lot, Claudia whipping the car into a parking spot so fast, I was sure we were going to have an accident. But miraculously, we didn't smash into any other cars. In fact, the girls were getting out of the car before I even exhaled.

They seemed to be speaking another language. They were talking about trends I clearly knew nothing about.

Cardigans. Peplums.

Platform shoes, were they in?

What about a wooden heel?

Rhode had provided most of my clothing last year. I just wore it, accepted it. I hadn't paid attention to fashion since the Victorian era. I was a bit more knowledgeable now, but still kind of useless when it came to making the right fashion choices.

"Lenah!" Claudia said, and pulled me by the arm into a store. "You have to try this. That color would be gorgeous on you."

She pointed at a mannequin in the window. On it, a tangerine blouse flowed out over a pair of blue jeans. The material was gauzy and soft; the color brought a memory to my mind. A night in an opera house, a glorious orange gown. When I was Vampire Queen, the easiest way to draw victims in had been to taunt them with exquisite things. When they approached to compliment me on my clothing or my jewels—well . . .

Claudia snatched an orange blouse from the racks and thrust it at me. Soon after, each laden with clothes, we stepped into our own private dressing rooms. Claudia and Tracy ran through items, stepping out and modeling their ensembles. I had never shown anyone what I looked like in modern clothes. Asking for approval seemed silly, but apparently this was the thing to do.

"Lenah! I want to see that top!" Claudia called.

Feeling foolish, I stepped out wearing the blouse and turned to show the girls.

"Oh!" Claudia's jaw dropped. "You look amazing," she said. "You should get that!"

"Color looks good on you," Tracy agreed.

There, in the mall, I could almost forget Odette's note. Ms. Tate's death and Kate's too. I could be distracted with the possibility of wearing these clothes. I even considered going back to school and wearing them in front of Rhode.

Next, I slipped on a pink skintight dress, which was contemporary and revealing, with thin shoulder straps. I loved it. I hoped the girls did too. I wished the ladies of the 1900s, with their corsets and bustles, could see me now. I stepped out and looked down the dressing room aisle. The girls were admiring black dresses similar to the pink one I wore. Justin would like this dress because it was tight. He would notice I was wearing a color that was not black, and say, *You're beautiful.* He reminded me it was important that I was participating in this modern world, just as Suleen had told me to do.

Rhode hadn't seen me in contemporary clothes before. I wondered if he even noticed my body, now that it wasn't hugged tight by a corset or pushed out by a bustle.

A tall woman was admiring her reflection in the three-way mirror at the end of the hall. Long blond hair tumbled perfectly down her back. She smirked at herself and ran a hand down her abdomen to smooth the material of the dress.

Oh no.

The skin was perfect. Too perfect. That blond hair. Red fingernails. Sharpened to dangerous, horrific points.

Odette.

Immediately, I stepped back into my dressing room.

I held a hand over my mouth to stifle my scream. I trembled, unsure how to stop my body from shaking so badly. How was it possible? How could she stand the bright light of midday? I looked down and took an involuntary step back toward the mirror on the wall. One long leg slid beneath the separating panel. Catlike, she flattened herself and crawled from the next dressing room into mine and, in a shot, was standing in front of me. My back pressing against the mirror, I could hear myself breathing rapid, shallow breaths.

Her mouth curled into a red, lipstick-stained sneer.

"Come out, Lenah!" Claudia called from the aisle.

My friends . . .

"In a minute," I called back.

Odette took two steps toward me. I could see the marble-like sheen of her skin under the fluorescent lights. She looked like a moving statue. She cocked her head to the side.

"Surprised to see me, Lenah?" she said with a sneer. "Thought you'd be safe in the middle of the day? Thought you'd be with lots of people? Daylight doesn't frighten me. Not even a little." She slammed a hand against the wall just next to the mirror.

"What was that?" Tracy asked.

"Do you think this makes my butt look weird?" Claudia asked.

"No way," Tracy replied.

I continued to keep my back against the wall. The only way to escape would be to get the dressing room door open and run. Odette could kill both Tracy and Claudia instantly.

"I'm not afraid of you," I lied.

Odette smiled, but the smile quickly turned. Her white teeth flashed under the light, her fangs sliding down, pointed and sharp.

The vampire hunger that made the fangs descend was overtaking her. She pretended to lunge at me and then laughed quietly, pulling back. Her laugh was stifled by the dressing room music and Tracy and Claudia cooing over a blouse.

"The great Lenah Beaudonte. How I have waited. How I hoped it would be me to bleed you first. Did you know I danced with Heath? That big Latin-speaking member of your coven? Yes . . . in the 1920s." She leaned forward so her mouth was next to my ear. "While you slept six feet under the ground."

I shivered.

Like an animal, she lunged at me again, this time slamming her palms on either side of my head. She took a deep breath, running her nose at the base of my throat. "You smell like your blood would light me up."

I took a short breath. Light her up?

"Don't play dumb. The ritual endows you with the weapon of sunlight. It's how you killed your coven."

"That's not true," I said. "That's not what happened."

"Shhh," Odette said, so I could see the pointy tip of her fangs again. "Your lies are not welcome here. But you were once the powerful vampire, weren't you?" She raised one pointed fingernail toward the sky. "Guess who is now?"

She left her razorlike nail pointed at the ceiling and looked at me from the corner of her eyes.

"Of course, I didn't go by Odette when I was human. Do you remember me? You killed my mother, my father, and my love."

Images of the mass of victims hovering behind the Aeris bombarded me. Her mother, father, and her love were in that mass. I wanted to tell her they were safe and would be forever—never again victims, never again subjected to fear and terror. They had white souls now.

She slammed her hands against the wall again just as Claudia laughed loudly on the other side of the door. I loved her laugh. I had to protect her.

I had to make a plan. I focused on the knifelike fingernail. If I screamed for help, I would risk Claudia and Tracy being hurt by Odette. If I kicked out the dressing room door, I could run, but she was faster.

"Lenah!" Claudia said. "Seriously, you're taking forever in there!"

Then, with a flick of Odette's wrist, there was a ripping sound inside my head. My flesh. She had cut me so the blood seeped down my shoulder. It was not a deep cut, but the skin split open cleanly. It burned and the blood trickled down my arm. She leaned forward to whisper in my ear, so close that I could feel her cold lips on my skin.

"The blond idiot. Then the teacher. You know what I want," she sneered again. Odette gripped me around the neck and lifted me from the floor, holding me against the mirror. I could barely breathe. I coughed and she loosened her grip enough so I could speak.

"I want that ritual," she said through clenched teeth. The flesh over my collarbone burned as it bled.

"It won't make you human," I croaked.

A nasty grimace grew across her face, making her look like a strange circus clown. Her nostrils flared and she whispered, "Is that what you think I want? Didn't you hear me? I'm your replacement." Her eyes hardened. Then I could see the truth deep within them.

It was a kind of familiarity that I could not describe; a view I knew well; an ocean view or a field I once knew. In them was a terrified young woman who had been ripped from her life too soon.

I sputtered out the words as I dared to meet her unnatural green eyes. "It's the torment, isn't it? The endless torment."

She flinched. "What?"

"If you pour your intentions into that spell you will bring ruin. Release black magic you never intended. I see your heart. I see your need for power. Power releases the pain, doesn't it?"

Claudia's voice echoed from over the door. "Let's see if they have it in your size, Lenah. What size are you?"

"Answer them," Odette ordered, and with one hand she held me to the mirror. With the other, she scooped a thin river of blood off my shoulder and licked it away.

"Small," I croaked, with a lurch of my stomach as I watched Odette swallow my blood.

"I think I saw them over there," Claudia said, and two pairs of feet traveled away, out of the dressing room. Odette threw me against the mirror again. My head smacked against the glass, and white spots of light exploded before my eyes.

"Give it to me now, or by the time your friends walk into this room, you will be dead."

I tried to swallow but hacked a cough. I was going to die. I had died before.

Between the pops of white light, an image came to me. Rhode and me on my parents' orchard. Not as we were but as we appeared now, in the modern world. Hand in hand, walking toward the house. The chimney was smoking. An apple in Rhode's other hand. Was this possible? Was this the future?

My breath rattled in my ears and I tried to breathe, but an eerie hush began to drown out the rest of the world.

"Okay!" I croaked. She released me immediately and I fell to the ground in a heap. My hands hit the carpeted floor of the dressing room, and sound whooshed into my ears. Just then, as though choreographed, I heard Tracy and Claudia come back into the dressing room area.

"Write it down," Odette commanded. I found a scrap of paper in my wallet and started writing. *You are giving her the ritual. You are giving it to her.* I kept repeating it to myself so she would read my intentions. *This is the ritual. I don't want to give it to you, but I am anyway.*

I tried to hide the lie deep beneath my heart. She had to be convinced.

"Lenah, here," Claudia said and a blue top came over the dressing room door. Odette caught it and held it against herself admiringly.

I finished, handing over the piece of paper.

This is real, real, real. Real. I wouldn't think about anything else.

Before she slid back to her dressing room under the separating wall, she threw me a knowing, haunting smile. "I can see why he likes you," she said with an animalistic cock of her head. "So fragile."

With that, Odette returned to her dressing room. I watched her feet move as she gathered her things. Listened to her light footsteps as she opened the door and walked away down the aisle. Exhausted, I slid my back down the mirror and sat on the floor.

"Did you die in there?" Claudia joked.

"No," I barely said. "Just getting back into my clothes."

My reflection was a sad sight. My hair stuck to my forehead from sweat, and the horizontal cut that ran over my collarbone was raw and red. It had stopped bleeding but the blood was sticky at the opening. However, it would be easy to cover with my shirt.

She was bloody brilliant, as Vicken would say. I had to admire her style. Truly, Odette would have been decent competition had I still been a vampire. I had to get up. Had to get dressed. The girls couldn't see me like this. My hands shook as I pressed against the carpet to stand up.

I didn't know how long I would have until she figured out that I'd given her a fake ritual. Days? Weeks?

I got dressed, smoothed my hair the best I could, and shakily stepped out of the dressing room. I avoided the three-way mirror, but there was no need to look—Odette was gone.

"I'm hungry," Claudia said.

"Let's eat here," Tracy replied. "I don't want to go back to the Union yet."

We paid for our items and I followed them out of the store silently. I tried not to move my right arm because the cut pulsated. The moment we were back in the brightly lit mall, my trembling subsided, but only slightly.

I went through the motions of ordering my lunch but I kept reliving that moment in the dressing room. Vampires such as Odette could be in the sunlight, which meant they were powerful. But how? How could she have gained power so quickly when it took me 180 years to withstand full-strength sunlight? How did she acquire the strength so fast? Odette said I had killed her family, but I had killed many people. Technically, I had even killed her, breaking the contract of her human life. The Aeris had reminded me of that.

We sat and ate our lunch but I kept looking at every face that passed by. Anyone with blond hair. This vampire would not be alone. She was powerful. She fancied herself my replacement.

"What happened to Rhode?" Claudia said. At Rhode's name, I slammed to attention, back into my seat. I refocused on my lunch and nibbled a piece of lettuce. "Whose fault was the car accident? His face looks awful."

"He must be the most secretive person alive," Tracy said. "I tried talking to him about it in Pre Cal, but he brushed me off."

"He wouldn't tell me either," I said, and hated how true this was. I was used to knowing everything about Rhode, but not now. "Rhode and I aren't as close as Vicken and me."

"Bet he told Vicken," Claudia said. "They're always sitting together at dinner."

"I'm surprised he survived it," Tracy said, still talking about Rhode's accident. She delicately ate a forkful of her Greek salad. "He's still got bruises."

"His eyes are amazing," Claudia said.

I stared at a girl with her blond hair in a ponytail but then relaxed. She was just a girl shopping.

Tracy nudged me.

"Sorry," I said, and took another bite of my sandwich. "Yes, they're quite blue." It felt ridiculous as I said it.

". . . you're being very quiet," Tracy said.

"Sorry," I replied. "I'm just a bit tired."

"So what's going on with you and Justin?" Tracy asked.

I opened my mouth to join the conversation and . . .

There she was.

Odette walked the long length of the mall running parallel to the food court. I froze in the middle of lifting my sandwich for a bite and stared, unable to help myself. Though she wore a man's baseball hat over her eyes, her long blond hair fell down her back. She was stunning. Her beauty would sway most humans, but I knew why she shielded her face from the fluorescent lights. It would highlight the unnatural hue of her skin and the dilated pupils.

She turned her head toward me.

Her eyes slid over the people in the food court directly, purposefully—to mine. Her jaw dropped; her eyes fell to my sandwich filled with lettuce, chicken, and tomato. And then, with a horrible curl of her mouth, Odette smirked. And . . .

Winked.

Chapter Twelve

Vicken!" I banged on his door three times. When I banged a fourth time, Vicken's hall advisor stuck his head out of his room; he was a tall assistant professor who taught photography.

"Some of us are preparing lessons, Lenah," he said, slamming his door.

The door in front of me creaked open, and Vicken appeared, scratching his head and yawning.

"It's six in the evening," I said. "You're sleeping?"

"I have a few hundred years of sleep to catch up on, if you don't mind."

I stepped inside, and Vicken grabbed a towel from his desk and stuffed it in the crack under his door. He opened a window, clicked on a fan, and lit a cigarette. I paced back and forth across his carpeted dorm room.

"Odette attacked me," I said.

Vicken's head snapped up so his hair fell into his eyes. "Where?"

"The mall. I was there with the girls shopping, and there she was, trying on a cocktail dress. Vicken . . ." I ran a hand through my hair and grabbed at the roots. "I gave her a fake ritual."

"You did what!?"

"I had to. She was going to kill me."

Vicken took a drag on the cigarette, considered me through

the smoke, and then stubbed the barely smoked cigarette out on the windowsill. He dropped it into an empty soda can.

"Let's go," he said.

Together we walked to the end of the hall. I expected to descend the stairs, perhaps to another dorm besides Quartz. I had not considered which room Rhode would be living in on campus. At the end of the hallway was room 429, a single like Vicken's—Rhode's room. There was something strangely comical about Rhode living in a dorm after serving as a knight under Edward III.

Vicken knocked and, as we waited, he looked down at me, meeting my eyes with an encouraging wink. We heard a few footsteps from behind the door, and Rhode opened up. His eyes traveled back and forth between us. The bruising made his right eye tighter and smaller than the other.

"What happened?" he asked.

"Not something we can really talk about with the general brouhaha, my friend," Vicken answered, motioning toward the other dorm rooms.

When we walked in, I guess I expected opulence. I expected Rhode's life at Wickham to mimic our life at Hathersage. But how could it? There would be no apothecary tables, no fine furniture. We were in hiding now. With the exception of a telescope pointing out the window and his clothes in the closet, Rhode's room was nothing more than a place to lay his head. When Vicken shut the door behind us, out of the corner of my eye, I saw rosemary and lavender tacked on the inside.

Of course. Those would remain.

Rhode sat down at his desk.

"Odette attacked me. I gave her a fake ritual. Really convoluted items. It'll take her days just to find them. Ignacious plant. Rattletail wood."

"Good choices. Innocuous ingredients. Even with the worst of intentions, they won't produce much of an effect."

Love surged through me at Rhode's support. It made my chest tingle. He lifted his eyes to mine, and crisp apples and the rich earth of my father's house were on the tip of my tongue. I stumbled back a couple of steps, trying to break the connection. If I looked away, perhaps it would stop the memory from engulfing me. I inhaled but there were more apples, a fireplace too. The wood crackling, smoking, and the scent of rain. I stepped back onto Vicken's feet.

"Hey! Watch it!" he cried.

A vampire's mouth. Lips parted, going for the kill. Where the two fangs would descend are two black, gaping holes. A vampire with no fangs? I want to run but I know I can't.

"Lenah?" Vicken's hand curled around my arm. "Are you all right?"

"She grabbed me by the throat!" I said, shaking my head. "And cut me." I moved the collar of my shirt to the side to show them the wound.

"You'll need to clean that," Rhode said. He gripped his hands on the chair even tighter.

"Well, I imagine when she finds out the ingredients are fake, her retaliation will be swift," I said. "But she did say one other thing. . . ." I hesitated as the memory of Odette sent a rush of shivers over me. "She said she could see why he likes me."

Rhode turned toward the desk and brought his injured hand to his chin. "He?" Rhode asked.

"A member of her coven?" Vicken offered, leaning against the wall, one booted foot against it.

"You've bought us time but no resolution," Rhode said.

I tried not to be stung, but his words hurt. "In case you missed it the first time I mentioned the incident, she tried to kill me," I replied as the gaping, fangless mouths from Rhode's memory sifted into my head again. Before he could respond, I added, "She wants power—it's the only relief from the madness. It's her only goal."

Rhode leaned his arm on the back of the chair; a bruised circle marked his wrist. It didn't look like a vampire bite—those would be punctures. When he realized my gaze had shifted from his eyes, he lowered his arm.

"She's not after humanity. She wants to perform the ritual in the hopes it will give her power. Power to reign over the elements. With elemental power, she can draw beasts to her, control weaker beings. She can . . ." I remembered my dream again. I saw the abandoned Wickham in my mind, the disheveled stone of the buildings, and the vacant beach. "She can do whatever she wants."

"There's nothing we can do until she shows herself again," he said. "And she will. In the meantime," Rhode said, looking at Vicken, "You and I could be a target. Anyone close to Lenah. I would keep your dagger on you."

Vicken raised his leg, placing his boot on top of the desk, and Rhode peered inside. I assumed he was looking at the dagger.

"You do the same," Rhode said to me.

"And why do you think a simple dagger will work?" I raised my chin. He was so in control, telling me what to do, telling me he loved me but then keeping his distance. It was enraging.

"We can't walk around carrying a sword all day, can we?" Rhode said. "And you don't have sunlight coming out of your hands anymore."

Anger stirred within me. Sunlight. So he did know something about last year.

"I'll carry a dagger too," I said, placing my hand on the doorknob. My heart started to pound. "And I'm going to take that bloody sword off its holder so I can behead the next vampire that sets foot near me."

"That's the spirit!" Vicken said, and his eyes shifted back and forth between Rhode and me. "Given the circumstances," he muttered under his breath. I glared at Rhode.

"Why are you so angry?" Rhode asked.

"Because you keep all your knowledge tucked away inside. Tell me, Rhode. Were you here last year, or weren't you? Did you stand in the shadows and watch me fight for my life? Did you watch my best friend, Tony, die at the hands of a coven I created when you left? You know all about leaving, don't you?"

His lips parted slightly.

I turned and walked away. I almost couldn't believe how good it felt to say those words out loud. He was businesslike and battered with all his secrets and his bruises. But I still wanted to know exactly who or what had beaten him to a bloody pulp.

"Lenah, wait," Rhode said. I turned to face him, crossing my arms over my chest.

"You act like it doesn't matter. Like it's just some inconvenience that I had to fight for my life in a dressing room. But don't worry, Rhode. I'll keep an eye out," I said, mocking his instructive tone. "I'll be a good girl and carry a dagger."

Rhode's expression hardened. "I don't understand you," he said with a shake of his head.

I wanted him to hold me, as he had for hundreds of years. In my mind, for one moment, we sat in an opera house, in the 1700s. His mouth grazed the nape of my neck; his hands traveled slowly up my stomach. But I couldn't say any of that out loud.

I blinked the memory away.

"I know what I have to do," I said, turning away and leaving his room. My fury continued to build as I raced down the stairs of Quartz dorm. I did not need a dagger. I would not be afraid in a dressing room again. No one would tell me how to live or what weapons to carry, least of all him.

You are soul mates. No one can change that.

I didn't want to be soul mates if it had to be like this. I needed to take control of something. Anything. Anything to keep Odette away from me. So, I was going to do a barrier spell and protect myself in my own way.

"Wait!" I heard from behind me. "Wait!"

I stopped at the entrance to my dorm and turned.

Vicken ran to catch up with me. "Don't," he said between breaths, "perform any magic." He rested his palms on his thighs.

"If you stopped smoking," I jabbed, "you might find it easier to catch your breath."

He stood up, seeing something in the reflection behind him. "Damn it!" he said, and walked toward the glass front windows. "It's fading."

"What's fading?"

He turned to me and said with complete disgust, "My bruise!" He whipped open the door and after showing our IDs we climbed up the stairs to my room. I shook my head.

"Since when are you Rhode's messenger boy? Why no spells?"

"If you do any spells," he said, turning his body to avoid a couple of students coming down the stairs. "I mean, spelling!" he yelled to cover. We climbed up some more stairs. "If you do any spells," he whispered, "it could release enough magic to draw in energy, even more vampires. They can sense it, remember?"

I remembered Suleen's words about performing magic, but if Rhode was right and we had some protection until the start of Nuit Rouge, then we might be safe on campus. I told Vicken as much.

"Either way," I said. "I am doing a little something special to-night. A barrier spell."

We walked into the apartment, and the first thing I did was enter the kitchen. My fingers lingered on the black tins of herbs and spices that Rhode had left me when I was first human and came to Wickham. It seemed impossible that he was the same person. But so far, he'd stayed away from me. He'd done as he was told.

Back in the living area, I knelt before my old traveling trunk, and there was a click from the latches as I lifted the lid. Inside, hidden, were some things I would need for the spell. My fingers fluttered over a small sheet of satin. I moved it out of the way along with old crystal spheres, daggers with engraved sheaths, and other trinkets from my life as a vampire. From the depths of the trunk, I pulled out one of the few books Rhode had left for me. The book was bound in 1808 and titled simply: *Incantato*.

I opened it, flipped through the thick pages until I found the correct one.

"Barrier spell," I said aloud, and walking through the kitchen, I placed the book down on the counter.

I snatched the sage and an old scallop shell big enough to hold the combination of herbs. After checking the book, I organized dried dandelion, thyme, sage, lavender, and an apple. I held the book in the crook of my arm and sprinkled the dried herbs around the perimeter of the room.

Vicken stood in the doorway of the kitchen with his arms crossed over his broad chest, watching me.

"Do you know," I asked, continuing to lace the room with herbs, "the origins of the Invitation Myth?"

"What? That vampires need to be invited into a house?" Vicken asked, and sat down on the couch. "It's bollocks."

The aroma of the herbs came to my nose in waves of sweet thyme and soft lavender. Remnants of herbs landed on the open pages of the book.

"Hand me your dagger," I said, and he did. I sliced the apple through the middle and left it faceup. When cut in half, the core is a pentagram, a five-pointed star. The pentagram is known in the supernatural world to bring power to those performing incantations. It could also represent all four elements—earth, water, fire, and air—the fifth point for all the elements combined, sometimes called spirit. The thought of the pentacle reminded me of the Aeris, of their power. I turned the pentagram out to face the room. "Vampires created the Invitation Myth," I continued, "to keep out the truly horrible beasts. The shape-shifters, the half men–half animals, the reprehensible of all kinds. Drink a little blood and suddenly you're the worst sort!" I met his eyes and gave him a knowing smirk. "But we knew there were worse creatures than vampire. Creatures that came into your room through an open window, robbing you of your breath. Creatures that broke bones . . . for pleasure."

I found a gray candle in the trunk and lit it. Gray is used on only very specific occasions—a color between evil and good. A middle color. Do not trifle with gray candles.

The candle flickered and with the book opened before me, I read the enchantment soberly. I poured all my intentions into that moment. I wanted to protect us.

"I am safe and protected here in this space." I repeated the incantation and placed the book down on the table. I took the gray candle into the palm of my hands and circled the room again. "I am safe and protected here, with the blood in my veins, with these herbs, let no vampire or supernatural beast walk through this door. I am safe and protected here."

I walked five times around the perimeter of the room. When I finished, I placed the candle down on the coffee table. I tried to ignore a throb from my collarbone.

"We need to let the candle burn," I said. "And you can't leave until it's out. We can't disturb the energy."

"We aren't vampires anymore. How do we know if we can even summon this kind of magic?"

I watched the candle smoke flicker into the air.

"I guess we'll have to wait and see," I said. "If this works . . . well—" I hesitated and Vicken waited for me to continue. "—well, if it works, we can try other things."

"Other things?"

I shot a glance at my book. How many times had I used it in Hathersage? Thousands? Granted, it was usually used to draw an enemy to me.

"You know what I mean. We could try stronger spells," I said.

"Why would we be trying stronger spells?" Vicken asked. I thought of Suleen's warning on the beach. The longer I was a mortal, the weaker my connection to the supernatural world became.

"We won't know if it works unless vampires try to come in here and murder you."

"Only one way to find out," I said, and reached for the television remote.

❦

Slow. *Skin against skin. The low glow of a lantern. Two bodies together. A thigh rests against mine—lips whisper in my ear.*

Vampires love with their whole souls. Not just with their bodies. They cannot feel as vampires. Their sense of touch wanes, leaving nothing behind but the human shell. Inside, the tortured soul is driven mad from numbness. When two vampires come together, two vampires who love, they can touch souls.

But not in this dream.

Rhode and I are on a bed made of straw. The windowpanes are old; the candle flame reflects in thick glass. The wood is so dark, it is almost black.

Rhode's hand is behind my head; his lips graze mine.

In this dream . . . I can feel him as a mortal would.

Our bodies make heat in this old room. A fire blazes and it makes my skin sweat. "Rhode," I whisper, and he pulls back from my ear. He looks in my eyes—the blue is so captivating, I forget for just a split moment how close we are. "I wish I could feel you," I say.

"Can't you?" he whispers, and brings his face to mine. "Never," he whispers. "Never again can I be parted from you."

The word "you" echoes. Just one small syllable.

You. You. You . . . and the image fades to darkness.

The straw bed and the warmth of Rhode's body against mine shift. Suddenly, the space opens up and I'm floating in midair—maybe I'm hovering, flying above the bed below me.

"You don't understand."

Rhode's voice. I float back toward the ground; the air supports my body as though I'm a bird. I hover even lower and I'm below a black ceiling. I am on my feet, standing in a room. This is not the bedroom—I am somewhere else. Rhode kneels on the floor; he is bowing his head.

"You don't see," Rhode says to someone in the room. "I can't do it. I can't. Your demands are too much."

I turn to look at the person he is speaking to, but it is all shadow beyond my eyes.

"It's too much," Rhode says again.

I am aware of my mortal body lying in a bed. The straw bed? No. It's softer. I am sleeping in my bed at Wickham Boarding School.

I want to wake up. Wake up, Lenah. *The white light of the Aeris that has been haunting me flashes before my eyes. There—there is that vampire mouth again, the one where there are no fangs. Gaping black holes are where his fangs should be.* Wake up, Lenah!

Wake up!

My eyes flew open.

I gasped and cool air rushed down my throat. Through the open door of my bedroom, the television showed the early-morning news. The gray candle had long burnt out. Vicken had fallen asleep but all I could see were his motorcycle boots dangling off the end of the couch. He snored in a rhythmic pattern.

I breathed out and sat up. A small line of sweat trickled down my forehead. I wiped it away and ran a hand over my hair, my pulse racing. The cut on my collarbone burned, so I hunched a bit and touched at the sensitive wound. *Rhode,* my heart said. Rhode.

But Rhode was across campus without me.

I got out of bed because I wanted to find Rhode; I wanted his eyes burning into mine. But what I wanted and what I needed had now become two drastically different things. I stopped, holding a blouse in my hand. Despite the heat and closeness I felt to Rhode in that dream, he would reject me if I surprised him at his room. What I needed was someone who would comfort me. Someone who would accept my touch when I gave it.

I needed Justin.

Chapter Thirteen

When I stepped out of the newly broken side door (thanks to Vicken earlier that week), dark blue and black clouds swarmed over the gray sky. It was just before sunrise—an hour at most. I knew I wasn't supposed to travel on campus alone. The cut on my collarbone pulsed as I stepped down the path, as a reminder that I shouldn't have been breaking the rules. I brought my fingers to it, and the crackled blood and scab were rough under my fingers.

I checked to see if anyone was on the pathway that ran from Seeker to the bay; then I checked behind me at the parking lot. Besides the security guard booth, only one van parked near Hopper. With another scan of the campus ahead of me, I darted down the pathway, making sure to keep to the sides of the buildings and the darkness that still lingered.

I knew Justin's single room had been moved for his senior year and was on the first floor of Quartz, facing the woods and the ocean beyond. The wind whispered through the trees, shaking their orange and gold leaves. A shiver rolled over me, and I looked down the path to the beach, momentarily expecting Suleen to stand there, waiting for me. But it was empty.

When did Suleen think it was important to show himself? Before or after I was almost murdered by a hungering vampire?

He said he would come when I most needed him. How about now?

A car pulled past the school on Main Street, making a whooshing sound. My hair lifted from my ears as a gust of wind breezed through the campus. No. It couldn't be. No one would be watching me now. Surely my fake ritual was keeping Odette and her coven busy.

Run, Lenah . . .

I didn't want to look behind me at the alleyway of Seeker. What if one of the members of her coven were in those shadows? Someone she sent to watch me. I told myself to walk faster. If someone were behind me, they would grab me by the shoulders. A little faster now. I took short breaths; the Union was just ahead.

Faster, Lenah. They could come at any moment.

I skirted by the greenhouse, the science building, and then looked back at the path. If a guard caught me, I would lose privileges, and I needed as much freedom as possible, given our circumstances with Odette.

I ran toward Quartz dorm, skirted around the back of the building, and pressed my back against the stone. In the woods, a yellow light fell in long vertical lines over the barks of the trees. The first-floor windows stretched along the building. They were long windows, like those in the gymnasium, and opened by turning a metal handle.

Justin's room. Justin's room, which one? Yes. There it was. Even though all the windows were the same, his curtains were pulled back. Beyond the windows were various lacrosse sticks, and a foot dangled off the end of the bed.

I knocked on the glass twice, standing to the side of the window so as not to scare him. There was movement inside and a small grunt. I knocked again.

"Jesus!" I heard a few footsteps. The window squeaked open.

I stepped in front of it. Justin's hair was messy from sleep. He wore no shirt, just sweatpants. Even at that time in the morning, he looked incredible.

Absolutely incredible.

"Um," I said, taking a step back onto the grass that separated the dorm from the woods. He leaned on the window frame.

"Lenah? What are you doing here?" His voice sounded gentle, happy.

I stood in the morning sunrise and pulled my thin T-shirt to the side, exposing the long cut that ran along my collarbone.

"Holy crap," he said. "Get in here."

I leaned into the room, grasping the ledge. When I pulled myself up, the wound throbbed and I nearly fell back onto the ground outside. Justin grabbed me and hauled me into the room.

"Sit, sit," he said, and led me to his bed. Flashes of our bodies tangled under the covers of his bed last year popped in my mind. He knelt before me and pulled the shirt down again to examine the cut.

"Ouch," he whispered. He met my eyes. "You should probably take off your shirt and let me clean it up," he said.

"My shirt?"

He stood up and my gaze rested on his defined stomach. I looked all the way up to his chest, over the necklace he wore, to his eyes. I saw then, in the morning light, the pendant. It was a silver disk that fell at the base of his throat. I knew that symbol.

"A knowledge rune," I said, and stood up. I touched the pendant with my fingertips.

"Yeah, I just got it the other day," he replied.

"Why?" I asked.

"I got it in town," he said. "Supposed to help make sense of everything. When that guy with the turban did the water barrier—I just . . . I don't know. I had to try to make sense of everything. Make sense of you."

"Me?"

"You, the ritual. Rhode. Why you're still alive." He got up and walked to the back of the room. "Anyway, I have a first aid kit in my lacrosse bag."

I was touched by the gesture and let the topic drop. Justin had purposefully sought out an object that would connect him to my dark, unearthly world. I was sure then that I had made the right choice in coming to him that morning. He was doing his best to understand me.

He rummaged in the corner of the room and I looked out to the woods through the window. Among the darkness of the trees, I could see myself as a vampire. Sauntering from the back of the woods toward the dormitory in a long red gown, my hair flowing over my shoulders. My fangs dripping with blood.

"Lenah," Justin said, kneeling before me again. When I looked back at the woods, the ghost from my past was gone and the woods empty. "Your shirt," Justin said.

"Oh!" I said, and lifted it from my body, exposing my bra. Justin leaned forward so he was kneeling before me, and dabbed something on a white cloth along the line of my collarbone. I winced at the stinging feeling. Justin blew on the skin and dabbed at the cut.

He lifted his face to mine. "Should I stop?" he asked.

"No. It just burns a bit," I whispered.

We hovered there for a moment; Justin lifted himself higher on his knees. His lips came closer and closer until they were on mine, and our lips traced each other's movements. My heartbeat sped up and I wanted him to keep kissing me. So I could pretend that I was never that beast in the woods. He started to crawl onto the bed and I lay down. Just as his body pressure was on top of mine, he pulled away suddenly. I brought my fingers to my lips in surprise and swallowed.

"Your cut," he said. "It looks bad. Let me try something else."

The passion humming between us evaporated.

He dug in the bag. I came down to the floor so we sat opposite each other. He opened a different bottle, and a most familiar smell overwhelmed me. I placed my hand on Justin's wrist and he lowered it for me to look at the bottle.

"My mom makes it," he said.

"This . . . ," I said, taking the bottle from him and sniffing it, "is lavender and aloe. A medieval combination."

"Well, it should work," he said, dabbing at my cut again. I could see the rustlike particles of my blood on the cloth. He dropped it into a bin. "We would get cuts all the time as kids. Mom made this up. I brought it with me to school for lacrosse injuries."

Next, Justin lifted two fingers covered in a gooey ointment and rubbed them along the cut.

"Antibacterial. This way you won't get an infection."

After a few more minutes, he had covered various parts of the wound in gauze held on with tape.

"I won't ask how you got this cut," he said, pulling me back up onto the bed and joining me there.

"You already know," I whispered. "You saw her murder Kate on the beach. I couldn't tell you in the Union, but she killed Ms. Tate too. Not long after she spoke with me outside Curie."

Tears rushed to my eyes and I blinked them away. My voice cracked as I said, "She's probably seen you with me, which makes you a target and I—"

"I'm not afraid of her," he declared, and looked at me, straight in the eye. "I'm not. I've seen what a vampire can do."

"I just had to see you. I knew you would understand," I said as I continued to fight the threat of tears. He pulled me to him and I rested my cheek against his chest.

A large crack of thunder boomed outside and we both jumped. He hurried to close the window.

"What does she want? Has she been watching you this whole time? I should stay close to you, in case she comes around again. . . ."

Justin kept talking, but I lay down on the bed and closed my eyes. I meant to tell him all about the strange feeling I had talking to Ms. Tate, but I must have been so tired. I remembered his warmth as he lay beside me. He held me close and when I just barely opened my eyes sometime later, my nose was nuzzled into his chest. His breathing was slow, steady. I listened to him breathe in and breathe out until I was moments from sleep again. Then I dreamt. . . .

A field of lavender, and the smell is so wonderful, calming and cool. I hold the black fabric of a gown in my hands. The image changes. This is not the lavender field. I am somewhere else. A masculine hand with a bruised thumb grips a ceramic sink. It grips it harder, the forearm shaking. What happened to the field?

The hands shake and reach up, and in the reflection of the familiar bathroom mirror, the hands cradle a face—Rhode's face.

"Do you love her?" Rhode asks the sink.

This is a Wickham bathroom; I recognize the blue-checkered tiled floor.

"You don't need her," Rhode says, looking up at his reflection and tearing his eyes away. In this connection I can feel his distaste as though I am experiencing it myself. I can feel the misery and hate ripping through the center of his stomach. It is not hate for me. It is hate . . . for himself.

Rhode lifts his right hand. He has taken off the bandage, and long scabs are visible across the knuckles.

"You don't need her," he says again, this time stressing the word "need."

"You can do what they ask," Rhode says, and surveys his reflection. With a downward cast of his eyes, he says softly, "No, you cannot. What they ask of you is too much."

Like a bolt, he punches the mirror, cracking it into a kaleidoscope of lines. Fresh blood speckles the reflection. His blue eyes dotted in crimson blots. Rhode repeats, "I can't, I can't," again and again and again.

I shot up in bed, my chest heaving. The spot next to me was empty. Across the room was a closet filled with lacrosse helmets, men's shirts, and a football. That's right. I was in Justin's bed. On his night table, a note read: *Practice, even in the rain!*

I threw off the covers, pulled on my T-shirt, and slipped on my shoes. When I reached down to put them on, the bandage from Justin's handiwork the night before pulled on my skin. I touched it out of instinct. I hesitated before the window and watched the rain pelt the grass and the woods beyond. These dreams of Rhode were becoming so realistic. This one even had the Wickham bathroom tiles! I unhooked the clasps for the windows, and just as my fingers curled over the slicked edge, the reality hit me as a punch to my gut. I took a step back because I knew. Maybe it was because we were, as the Aeris said, soul mates, but I knew.

My dream wasn't a dream at all. It was reality. It was a Wickham dorm bathroom and Rhode was standing before the sink. So it wasn't just memories but his present-day thoughts I was accessing too. I ran a hand through my hair and stared at raindrops smacking the windowsill. So we were soul mates who could no longer be together, yet I was privy to Rhode's thoughts? This was unnecessarily cruel. There was nothing I could do about it either. This was what the Aeris had decreed. No matter how connected we were, our lives had to remain separate. *Unnecessarily cruel* echoed in my mind again. I stepped onto the window ledge and out into the storm.

The rain picked up as the day went on. A few hours later, I sat alone at one of the long dining tables in the Union, where I was making yet another list.

Memories from the past.
Rhode's present-day thoughts.
Why am I receiving them, and more frequently
 with every day that passes?

Outside, the rain lashed against the glass roof and massive windows. In front of me, a piece of iced lemon cake sat untouched on a plate. I crossed out another theory about Rhode and my connection when there was a scratch of ceramic against linoleum, and a drenched umbrella leaned against the table. I placed the book down gently and raised an eyebrow as Vicken took a bite of my cake and pushed a newspaper cutting across the table. It was from the British newspaper *The Times*.

HATHERSAGE, DERBYSHIRE
MASSIVE FIRE DEVASTATES HISTORIC MANSION

There it was: a photo of my glorious home. The great lawn was crawling with dozens of men and women. A moving company was carrying out a large bureau I recognized from my bedroom. The first-floor windows were blackened, blown out. Shattered pieces of glass pointed up from the window frames. A couple of curtains hung out of the windows as though trying to escape.

Vicken took another bite of the cake.

"Where did you get this?" I asked, resting my fingertips on the thin paper.

"I told you I was going to do some nosing around. I've been receiving *The Times* for the last few weeks. And by the way, despite my moaning and groaning about this school, I've been in the library." He turned the paper back toward himself.

"On August thirty-first," he read, "a devastating fire engulfed the historic Hathersage mansion, which dates back to the early seventeenth century and is reputed by locals to be haunted. Thousands of items of extreme rarity have been recovered from the house. No bodies have been found, and it's believed the house was empty when the fire occurred. The fire consumed the entire first floor and destroyed a tapestry that once belonged to Elizabeth the First."

"Her mother, actually—Anne Boleyn. I had it restored and preserved several times," I said. The sinking feeling in my chest was something else. The paper said the house was empty. That house wasn't empty. It was filled with my history, my past, and it had almost burned to the ground.

Vicken kept reading. "Local historians have uncovered rare daggers, unusual herbs, and strange amulets. Some believe the items in the house are occult in nature. Many of the objects on the upper floors were spared, such as a four-poster bed from the 1800s, as well as anonymous portraiture also dating from the 1800s.

"Expert David Gilford of the Occult Group of London," Vicken continued, "was most impressed by the weapons room. There were ninja stars, countless daggers, and some of the most rare longswords he had ever seen. One had a handle made of human bone. Gilford also commented on some of the oddities found in the weapons room. He was overwhelmed by the apothecary equipment and strange devices that looked as if they were for torture."

"They were," I added.

Vicken continued, "The house appears to have been in the same family since Elizabethan times. Strenuous efforts are being made to contact the current owners, whose identities have not been revealed. The recovered items will be cataloged under the management of the British Museum, which is coordinating the salvage operation together with English Heritage."

Vicken lit up, his whole face brightened, and he smiled.

"Did you hear that? The British Museum!"

The date on the newspaper cutting was August 31.

Today was September 5.

August 31? Rhode had returned to Wickham on September 3, which meant he could have been at Hathersage when the fire occurred.

I swiped my books into a bag, stuffed the cutting into my pocket, and stood up.

"Where is he?" I commanded.

Vicken didn't respond.

"Where!" I screamed, and slapped the Formica table with my palm. Other students studying and eating their lunches looked over with wide eyes.

"He's in his dorm," Vicken said with a sigh.

I tossed my bag of books into Vicken's lap and glanced at the rain pelting the windows. With an angry curl of my lip, I asked, "Whose side are you on?" I swept out of the Union and into the rain.

··-◀·

Rhode wasn't in his room. After banging on his door, I stepped back outside Quartz, and within minutes, my T-shirt was soaked and my jeans were heavy on my thighs from the rain. I'd intended to walk to my dorm when Rhode, clad in all black, cut across the pathway some distance away from me. He kept his chin toward the ground and held a large duffel bag over his shoulder. This was odd. I stepped off the path, attempting to conceal myself behind a statue of the school founder, Thomas Wickham. Rhode disappeared behind the greenhouse. Where was he going? Hadn't we agreed that it wasn't safe to travel alone?

I ran down the path and stopped at a large oak tree next to the greenhouse. When I reached the end of the building, I saw that he had walked into the woods that circled the school. I caught sight of a fresh bandage wrapped around his fingers. The white gauze stood out brightly against his black shirt and jeans. Back in our history, he had taught me how to follow someone without being seen, predator and prey.

Perhaps he was sneaking out for a good reason. Perhaps he was going somewhere that would clue me in to where he had been the year before. He wasn't going to tell me, no matter how many times I asked—that was clear. Either way, he was sneaking out of school without Vicken and me for a very specific reason—and I wanted to know what it was.

I wiped the rain out of my eyes and hesitated at a nagging thought: *He knows he shouldn't be going anywhere by himself. But he's going anyway.* As the cut on my collarbone proved, Odette wasn't afraid of the daylight. Granted, the morning hours were more dangerous than the afternoon, but she had shown herself to be able to withstand the sun's rays.

I took a step, watching him weave in and out of the trees. I rested a hand against the warm glass of the greenhouse. Rhode walked toward the stone wall that circled the perimeter of the school. If he jumped over, I'd have no idea where he went unless I kept up and followed him over the wall.

Go, Lenah. Go!

So I did. I made sure to keep my distance as I followed. Once, he glanced back to the campus. I jumped behind the cover of a stand of three maple trees and pressed my back against the hard bark. I was being careless, following too close. Just a few seconds. I could wait few seconds. I bounced on my toes. What if he was over the wall already? I peeked around the trees just as Rhode disappeared on the far side of the wall, onto Main Street.

I climbed over and when my boots touched Main Street, I stayed in the shadow of the wall, as though somehow the shade would protect me from Rhode's gaze. Rhode kept walking, duffel bag swinging in his hand, past the Lovers Bay public library, past the Herb Shop, past the last store on Main Street before it turned into a suburban neighborhood.

At the entrance to Lovers Bay Cemetery, Rhode hesitated. I pulled back into the shadows, listening to the rain patter on the sidewalk. I waited until Rhode walked through the entrance. He was going into the cemetery. Why? Was this was another hint? Another clue to what had happened last year?

I followed, keeping pace just enough so I wouldn't lose him among the granite tombstones and trees of the cemetery. He navigated through the pathways so easily. He didn't stop and refer to a map. He didn't need one. He knew exactly where he was going.

Ahead of me, I found a place to pause and regroup. There was an enormous gray stone mausoleum in the center of the cemetery, which I leaned against. Nearby was Rhode's tombstone, the one I had put up the previous year in his honor, thinking him dead. But he passed right by it. I pressed my back even harder against the mausoleum's cold stone.

He turned at the row where Tony was buried.

I hadn't gone to Tony's burial. I couldn't bear to see his parents' sorrow, knowing my part in his death. But I had known the location of his grave. Of course I had known.

Curiosity churned in my stomach. "Oh, go home, Lenah," I whispered, but I could not make myself turn around. My boots squelched in the soggy ground as I padded quickly over the grass. I had to fall back to avoid him hearing me.

Rhode stood, his back to me, and looked down at what I assumed was Tony's tombstone. A couple of rows behind him, I got down onto my knees and crawled forward. The earth was wet and smelled of fresh-cut grass. I stayed close to the ground; I didn't see any other way. If I stood, he would catch sight of me in the corner of his eye.

I stretched my arms forward and crawled down the wet row, peeking up to see Rhode unzip the duffel bag. Out of it, he pulled his longsword. I drew shallow breaths. What he did next was very calculated. He dragged the tip of the sword through the earth in a circle around Tony's tombstone. As he did so, he cut into the earth so it made a deep groove in the muddy soil.

Rhode was almost done drawing a complete circle around Tony's grave. This was no spell, at least not one I knew. Rhode lifted the sword high in the air and plunged the sword into earth. Imbued with magic, imbued with his intention, for whatever reason, the sword easily slid into the soaked ground. In the dark of my mind, I imagined the metal slicing through the soil, the point breaking the jagged clumps of earth protecting my friend and pointing at his wooden casket.

Rhode fell to his knees and wrapped one hand around the hilt of the sword, then rested his other palm flat against the tombstone. He dipped his chin to his chest and closed his eyes in a silent meditation. Silent until he began to whisper quick words.

"Honi soit qui mal y pense," he said, over and over like a chant.

This was the official motto of the Order of the Garter. "Shamed be he who thinks evil of it," was the English translation. Rhode was performing a ceremony from back when he was a knight. I had never seen him do anything like this before. I stayed frozen to the ground, not daring to look away.

He sat back on his heels and brought both his hands to his face.

Why? Why Tony's grave?

This made no sense to me. I wanted to call out to him but I knew better—I shouldn't interrupt him during something so sacred.

Rhode then fell forward, extending an arm so his fingers curled over the top of the slicked headstone. The gauze wrapping his injured fingers was soaked through from the rain, and my eyes locked on a bright red blood spot that had seeped through. It was so bright in the gray rain. He had punched the mirror in my dream, just as I thought.

Wait. He was speaking again. What was it? I held my breath so I could make out the words. I drew a gasp, for all I could hear, all that traveled over the air to me, lying with my cheek on the soft grass was "Forgive me."

❦

I could not bear witness to this in secret. It was a betrayal. I stood up in the aisle behind Rhode. I needed to make a sound.

I stepped loudly into a puddle, knowing the slosh of the water would alert Rhode. He lifted the sword from the ground, swung it through the air, and pointed it directly at me. The ferocity in his eyes stunned me. I watched the recognition pass over his face as he dropped the sword by his side.

"I taught you well," he said.

"Lovely day for a visit to the cemetery," I said. "What are you doing here?"

"Paying respects," he said, and squatted down, placing the sword in a leather wrapping and then back into the duffel bag.

"To my friend?"

Rhode started walking out of the cemetery. I followed behind.

He walked quickly down the soaked paths, back into the less wooded, more open part of the cemetery. We passed the mausoleum.

"You said we shouldn't be alone but yet, here you are," I said, trying to provoke him into having a conversation with me.

He stopped and looked at me. He said simply and definitively, "I am not without a weapon."

"Do you want to explain this?" I asked, pulling the newspaper cutting from my pocket. I wiped the rain out of my eyes. "It's in the bloody newspaper. The Hathersage house burned. Now it's overrun with historians! It's gone!" Just saying it aloud sent a stab of pain through me.

He glanced at the newspaper but did not respond.

I threw the soggy shred onto the ground. "Enough games. Explain yourself. The date on that is August thirty-first."

"Why are you doing this?" Rhode asked. The rain continued to cloud the air between us—I could barely see him.

"Did you see it burn?"

Rhode placed the duffel bag onto the ground and let the rain drench us both. "Yes," he said finally. "I saw it burn."

Sorrow laced through my chest. "How could you? Just let it?"

Rhode kept his infuriating silence.

"Fine," I continued. "So you're not just lying to everyone else about a blasted car accident. You're lying to me. I asked you if you were in Hathersage. You never answered."

"Should I tell everyone that I was beaten within an inch of my life? That the only way out of that house was to set the place on fire?"

"You set it on fire?" I asked, horrified.

The rain pelted so hard, the cold drops were actually hurting my nose and cheeks.

After a few moments, he said, "Vampires came looking for us. I had to torch the place to kill them and burn any evidence of my survival. So I did."

I ran my hand through my soaked hair, my fingers catching in the wet tangles.

"Who attacked you? It was Odette, wasn't it?"

Rhode bent over, snatched up the bag, and started walking out of the cemetery again.

"When the vampires saw me and realized I was mortal, they

attacked. I ran for my life." Rhode, my fearless Rhode, shuddered in the horrible, drenching downpour. "I didn't think I would make it out."

"You could have died," I said.

"What's it to you? You thought I was dead for a whole year," he said.

"And you think I could survive it again? That I don't worry whether you are all right every day? Every minute?" It took me a couple tries but finally I got the words out. "Tell me. Did you watch me last year? Did you know what I was doing?"

Rhode dipped his chin to his chest. He seemed to think it over a moment, then said, "Yes, I saw you. After your friend Tony's death, I could not come to you. At the time, it seemed," he paused, choosing his words carefully, "fruitless."

Relief flooded through me. Finally, something.

"But you knew the coven were after me. Yet you did nothing?"

Rhode's eyes were focused on my neck; he didn't answer.

"Rhode?" I asked again.

He took a step to me and lifted his hand. Was he actually going to touch me? My stomach jumped. But no. He took the collar of my cold, wet T-shirt between his thumb and index finger and pulled my shirt down a bit, to expose my skin. The bandage had slipped in the rain, revealing the cut. He examined it for a few moments, then let go, all the while careful not to touch me.

"There was a moment, that day when we discovered that I had a sister, you swore we would always be together," I whispered.

I took a step toward him, intending to take his hand into mine.

Rhode jumped away from me and I saw fear, actual fear, pass over his eyes. I drew my hand back, hurt and embarrassed that he had rejected me yet again.

"I can't!" he cried, and I froze. "I will never leave you, Lenah." He met my eyes, but the look in them was pained, struggling. "But I cannot love you anymore. Not like this."

After a moment of silence, when the only sound was the rain pelting on the grass, Rhode said, "Our circumstance is absolute."

Our circumstance.

"Our house. Our portraits. Our library," I dared to reply. "Are all gone. It's like they're erasing our history." I brought my hand to my chest. The water drenched my shirt and slicked my fingers. "And all those beautiful books," I said.

"You're worried about the books we left behind?" he said, and his blue eyes cut through the misty gray air. "You should be worried about the skeletons we left buried in the walls or the goblets of blood we left sitting on tables, forgotten. They'll test the contents of old goblets. But we don't have to care anymore. It's over, Lenah. Aren't you relieved? Glad you can leave it all behind?"

I pulled back from him. All my belongings. All the old photographs and jewelry. The great halls where we took life so willingly were now empty and ruined.

What Fire had said to Rhode and me on the archery field replayed in my mind.

Vampires are dead. Supernatural, night wanderers. We cannot hold you responsible for the killings you performed in that world.

Rhode was right. I was glad the years of destruction and sadness were over.

And then . . . the rain came down even harder. It pummeled the grass and I had to wipe the water away from my eyes with both hands.

"Everything was destroyed. It's irrelevant now," he said, his words clipped. "We're human." He picked up the duffel bag and took a few steps toward the cemetery exit.

"Isn't this what you wanted?" I asked.

"For you," he said gently. But my wonderful Rhode was hiding something more. I could tell from the curve of his back and the gaze of his eyes to the ground.

"If the Aeris had not interfered, would you be happy with mortality? Wherever you were?" I asked, hoping this would lead to him opening up more about his whereabouts the year before.

Rhode turned back to me, a black-clad figure in that drenching rainstorm. "I'm not really mortal. I may be flesh and blood, but I'm something else. Stuck."

"What are you, then?"

"Something forgotten. Archaic. Put me in a glass case and shut the door."

"You don't really believe that, do you?" I asked.

"I believe I met a girl in the rain. Who had lost her mother's earrings. And I killed her. Now I stand here in a time I know nothing about. I watched the death of kings far greater than any man living now. And I am still here," Rhode said, his mouth slicked with rain and his blue eyes piercing me through the gray of the storm.

The image of a pair of ancient golden hoop earrings came to my mind.

Rhode held my gaze through the long lines of rain. I understood him—we understood each other completely.

"My mother's earrings," I said, "were in the house."

Rhode considered his answer, then said, "And so were the ghosts of all our pasts." The rain pelted the bag housing the longsword. Rhode looked at me. *"Était-ce tout vaut la peine?"* he asked in French. "Was it all worth it? For the sense of touch?"

He turned from me then and left the cemetery. He did not need to say that I should follow; we both knew that neither of us should be alone.

As I walked back onto campus, I stopped at Seeker. Rhode

didn't hesitate. He immediately hurried toward his dorm. As I watched him go, I finally understood why the knight of Edward III had visited the grave of my best friend, Tony Sasaki.

He felt responsible.

Chapter Fourteen

ater that afternoon, I walked out of Seeker dorm. The sun had broken through the clouds and I was barely able to focus my eyes when Vicken screeched, "I was just coming upstairs to get you!" He grabbed my hand. "Let's go."

"What are you doing?" I asked as his strong grip led me down the pathway. "What's wrong with you?"

"We need a lot of people. We'll go to the Union, that's it. A lot of people are there usually."

"Have you gone mad?"

"There!" Vicken pointed at the lacrosse field behind Hopper. "Throngs of people." We had managed to walk into a crowd of middle and upper school students watching a Wickham lacrosse scrimmage. Half the team wore white jerseys; the others, a dark blue. Vicken didn't care; he led me to the sides of the crowded bleachers and let go of my hand.

"You! You there," he cried.

He pointed at a ninth-grader who clutched a backpack to her chest. She quivered under his pointed index finger. "Look at me. Look in my eyes." He waited a moment, then spat out, "Damn it!"

I grabbed Vicken by the back of his T-shirt. "Stop it!"

The girl turned away. Her little feet seemed to explode with speed and she ran off toward Hopper. Every few feet, Vicken stopped people. "You! Hey, you! What are you thinking! Get back here! Don't you run from me!"

"What are you doing? You've gone mad," I whispered to Vicken.

"Have I? I've lost my sodding ESP. Spend over a hundred years with something and then, poof, it's gone."

"Gone?" I parroted dumbly. This was not in our favor.

"ESP. Gone!" He yelled and slapped his hands against his thighs.

"Shhh!" I said, and motioned to the crowded bleachers behind us. Claudia and Tracy were sitting way up high, watching the game. Claudia waved at me and I smiled back. I could feel Tracy's eyes on me even though they were hidden behind her sunglasses.

"Oh, you think anyone knows what I'm talking about?" He extended his arms. "ESP! ESP!" he screamed to the sky.

I slapped his arms down.

It was as though Vicken suddenly realized where he was. He turned to face the field, his back to the bleachers.

"What the hell is this?" he asked with disgust, and raised both arms from his side.

"It's a sporting event."

"I realize that. What the hell are they doing?" he asked.

"It's called lacrosse."

A pause, then, "Well, I'm not staying for this shite. Let's go."

As he turned to leave the field, cheers erupted around us and I could hear Tracy and Claudia's voice chanting, "Justin! Justin!"

On the field, Justin, in his full lacrosse gear, ripped off his helmet, threw it to the ground, and marched up close to another player. He put his finger to the other guy's face and was yelling something I couldn't make out.

I placed my hand on Vicken's arm. He stopped and we stood at the base of the bleachers, looking out at the scrimmage. Vicken stepped close to me and said in a low tone, "You're a human for about two minutes, and now you're a sports fan?"

"No . . . ," I said. I couldn't remove my eyes from Justin on the field. "Wait."

Vicken sighed.

"Cut it out, Enos! That's my last warning!" the referee hollered and Justin picked up his helmet as the players reassembled.

I sat down on the bleachers. Vicken groaned, sat beside me, and crossed one motorcycle-booted leg over the other. He leaned his elbows on the row behind him.

On the field, one of the players slapped his stick against Justin's, and the white ball flew in the air. Once Justin realized who had the ball, he smacked his stick against the other player's so hard that the player stumbled backwards. Justin whacked the player's stick again and again, until the referee blew the whistle.

"What?" Justin yelled at the referee. He lifted his shoulders and arms out to the side. "What's your problem?"

"I'm not telling you again, Enos. One more and you're out!" the referee shouted back.

The whistle blew, signaling the scrimmage was beginning again. The players assembled, and immediately Justin slapped his opponent's stick, sending the ball into the air and down into his own net.

Justin ran down the field so fast that no one could catch him. He slammed into other players so hard, it was as though he wanted to throw them to the ground. When one defenseman from the other side smacked the ball out of his net, Justin threw off his helmet and punched the player in the stomach.

"I've never seen him play like this," I said.

"Like what?" Vicken asked.

"Like he's out for revenge or something."

Cheers and raucous rounds of "Justin! Justin!" echoed about us again.

Another whistle.

The referee pointed to the bench. Justin bowed to the crowd, and when he walked off the field, he passed by the defenseman who had smacked the ball out of his net. Justin lunged at him, pretending he was going to punch him. When the other player recoiled, Justin threw back his head and laughed. He then plopped down on the bench and shook the sweat away from his face. As the crowd continued to call his name, Justin turned back to the bleachers and laid eyes on me.

Justin licked his lips, and the twinkle in his eye reminded me of the first time we met. It was right after Rhode had performed the ritual and I was human for the first time. I saw him on a beach, walking hand in hand with Tracy Sutton, long before he broke up with her and dated me.

He broke our gaze and turned back to the game.

He's the one who's gone mad," Vicken said when the scrimmage was over. We walked with the rest of the students down the bleachers back onto the field.

"Hi, Vicken," a group of girls said, almost in complete unison, as he walked by. He nodded his head, his eyebrows creased and hands in his pockets. He had no time for girls at the moment, apparently.

"I've lost my ESP, and even I can tell you something is wrong with that nutter."

Justin lingered on the field, surrounded by his teammates and also a few girls, including Andrea, the junior from the other night at the observatory. Most were wearing early fall attire entirely too warm for a day like today. As I approached, I looked at the shorts I wore. My pale legs seemed long and too white

compared with the unnaturally darkened tans of the girls surrounding Justin. I stopped, and anger burned my cheeks. I hated
this. This mortal embarrassment. If only . . . No. I stopped myself. I would not wish it. I would not let myself even consider
wanting my vampire powers back.

"What?" Vicken asked. "You don't want to go over and talk
to Monsieur Aggressive?"

Not when he was acting like that, I didn't. Last night, he had
been so tender. So open, as he used to be. Last night, as I lay next
to him, dreaming of Rhode, it could have been last year. Even
though it didn't feel like it. We were together like we had been
last year, lying next to each other, and Rhode, as always, was
unavailable to me.

Justin caught my eye over someone's shoulder and maneu-
vered around people to get to me. He stopped before he reached
me, his eyes shifting to Vicken.

Roy joined Justin at his side and squinted at Vicken. Soon
another couple of lacrosse players, pads under their jerseys, stood
on either side of Justin. Vicken placed a cigarette between his
lips. If Justin and his boys were coming over, it would probably
not be cordial.

"Did I mention he punched me in the eye?" Vicken said. He
overdramatized his blinking to highlight the slight yellow bruise
still lingering around his eye. Then he turned and headed out
onto the campus with the rest of the crowd, leaving a plume of
smoke behind.

Justin broke from the group, and I waited as he walked over
to me.

A flurry of goose bumps suddenly erupted over my arms.

I drew a small breath, swallowed, and looked at the ground.
Someone was watching me again. I knew it. The feeling was mes-
merizing. Where were they? I turned my head ever so slightly to
the right, following the feeling crawling all over me. Odette. Surely

it was Odette. I kept turning until I faced the quad before Quartz dorm.

Students walked together toward the Union or the library. They passed security guards and maintenance crews erecting violently yellow emergency telephones at virtually every intersection of the pathways on campus. My eyes were drawn to a shadow by Quartz building, and my breath caught in my chest.

Rhode stood there, watching me. I would love those blue eyes forever. How they had looked at me when I first awoke as a human, the year before. I wanted to walk to him, be with him. And I knew—as all vampires know—when you are the watched, you are the wanted.

He could not love me anymore; that's what he had said. Not like this. I didn't know what "this" meant. It could have been many things: We couldn't love under the Aeris's decree. We couldn't love as humans. All I knew was that I couldn't answer for him. It was done. Love for me would be Justin Enos and a lifetime of reminding myself that I was human. Not a girl of the medieval world. Of stained glass windows and candlelight.

"Lenah," Justin said. I jumped and turned. He stood alone before me, wiping the sweat from his forehead. The definition of his biceps kept my attention.

"Sorry," he said. "Didn't mean to scare you."

"You didn't," I lied.

"You're beautiful." Justin smiled at me again. "Have I mentioned that?"

"Oh." I didn't know what to say. "Well, no," I said, my cheeks suddenly hot. A thrill rushed to my stomach. I looked back to Quartz and the shadow made by the building. Rhode was gone. To my surprise, I was glad Justin and I were alone.

"That was an . . . interesting scrimmage," I said, looking into Justin's eyes, not entirely sure what to say next.

"You liked that?"

I flinched, not understanding what he meant. "Liked what?" I asked.

Justin held his shoulders back and casually licked the sweat from his lips. He smirked at me, raising an eyebrow. "Lenah, come on. You like me."

He took a step closer—so close that I could smell the sunblock and sweat on his skin. I did like him. It was no act. His mannerisms were so thoroughly twenty-first century. Even the casual flick of his head to rid himself of the sweat rolling down his skin was a gesture that would be alien to Rhode. Gentlemen of past eras would wipe their brows with a handkerchief. Justin's movements were quick, abbreviated. This world was one of instant messages, instant communication and interaction. People spoke to one another with a casual cadence and clipped, colloquial words. Even though I had been born in the medieval era, I had come back to life in the twenty-first century. This was my world now. Justin's world.

"You know how I feel about you," he said softly before I could think any more. The way he spoke sent a shiver down my spine. He glowed and always would to me. He emanated a life force that I had loved when I was first human, and even now I wanted a piece of it.

He shook the sweat away from his eyes and lifted his hand, running his fingers lightly across the cut on my collarbone. It made me tremble.

"Your bandage came off," he said.

"You may have to re-dress it," I said with another sudden heat to my cheeks.

"I will." He took a step closer, his expression suddenly serious. "Any more sightings of the blonde?"

I shook my head. "No."

"Enos!" someone called from behind us.

Justin backed away, dropping his fingers. My skin cooled

where the warmth of his touch had been. Suddenly he stopped walking backwards and gestured by lifting his helmet toward me. "Hey! I almost forgot," he said. "Happy birthday!"

My jaw dropped. It was September 6, wasn't it?

"Of course," I said. "It is my birthday, isn't it?"

"You forgot your own birthday?" Justin asked, incredulous.

Ah, well, my soul mate of six hundred years is living here at school, but I can't be with him, because a supernatural force ordered us to stay apart. You're beautiful in every way, shape, and form but I probably blew my chances with you. My best friend, Tony, was murdered by my other friend, Vicken, who isn't a murderous lunatic anymore. And I'm being pursued by a vengeful vampire who wants me dead too.

"A lot on my mind," I replied.

"Well, I'm having a party tonight," said Justin with a glance at the other guys. "Down at the town camping grounds. I tried to find you earlier to tell you."

The moment in the listening room replayed in my mind. His arms traveling over my back and shoulders as we danced.

"So does that smile say you'll come?" Justin asked.

Was I smiling? It seemed impossible after everything that had happened over the last two days.

"Look—meet us at seven. Site 404. Lovers Bay camping grounds. You can bring Vicken—you know, because we have to keep in twos. It's a couple of miles up Main Street," he said. "There'll be a lot of us," he added before I could say no. "We couldn't book it unless there were at least ten people going." Once he said that, a part of me—the foolish part—didn't want to say no, no matter how bad an idea I knew it was. Justin gathered up his sports bag, and when he threw it over his shoulder, the pendant around his neck caught the sunlight.

He turned away to join the rest of his team, walking toward the gymnasium. As I was about to turn away, he glanced back at me with a bright smile.

Rebecca Maizel

He always lured me in this way. He so easily commanded a room when he walked into it. Everyone wanted to see the lines appear around his mouth when he smiled. The casual mess of his sandy hair. I couldn't help but want to go. I couldn't help but want to be happy, even if just for an evening.

Chapter Fifteen

As far as Ms. Williams was concerned, as long as the campus was safe, it didn't matter what happened off campus. This particular point enraged Vicken endlessly, who thought off campus was definitely not safe. Either way, I wanted to go to the party, and as long as we all signed out together, we could go. Odette had shown no sign of coming back yet. Presumably, the fake ritual was still occupying her, and I doubted she would make an appearance in front of so many people.

I guessed if Rhode knew I'd decided to go off campus without his supervision, he would be furious.

That evening, I looked at my reflection in the mirror next to my bureau. My eyes seemed a darker blue than usual, as though I could not hide the anxiety brewing and churning inside me. I smoothed down some flyaway strands of hair and then looked over at the photo of Rhode and me on the bureau. It was back in its rightful place, after Tony stole it last year, trying to uncover the history of my vampire life.

In the mirror, I could see the scabbard that had held Rhode's sword for the last two hundred years.

The sword was gone, the scabbard empty, as I'd expected it to be.

On the floor, I checked the herbs from the barrier spell, as I had every day since I first performed the spell. If a barrier spell works, the herbs ignite, leaving nothing behind of the intruder but charred ash. As long as whoever came into the room was accepted, the herbs were not dangerous.

I turned back to my reflection and started to put on a pair of gold studs I had bought in the early 1900s. They had been in my jewelry box, almost forgotten, but now that my mother's earrings were lost, gone in the Hathersage fire, I decided to wear these. I pushed one into my ear.

An overwhelming stench of apples burst in the room.

I slammed my hands against the wall and dropped forward, my body engulfed in the pungent smell. I grabbed at my gut because it twisted and turned. Fake apples. How could someone manufacture such a beautiful smell and make it so ugly? So sickly sweet? Its force knocked me to the ground, where I fell to my knees, the gold studs skidding across the wooden floor, and just when my palms hit the ground . . .

"She must be isolated so no one can find her."

It is Suleen's voice I hear first. I am in Rhode's mind again.

Together, Suleen and Rhode stand by a tombstone in the cemetery directly next to my mansion in Hathersage. Four or five headstones stand together in a small plot, surrounded by a wrought-iron fence.

There is my tombstone. No epitaph, no name. Just an L carved into the stone.

Rhode buried me in 1910 and uncovered me one hundred years later to perform the humanizing ritual. Based on Rhode's appearance, he is the modern-day Rhode, the Rhode I saw when I first awoke at Wickham Boarding School. He uncovered me in secret, without the coven's knowledge, without Vicken's knowledge. I recognize Suleen's appearance from modern day as well. He wears white and his traditional turban.

"You are sure of this, Rhode?" he asks. Rhode nods but Suleen's expression is dark. Rhode turns, looking at himself in the reflection of a

house window. In this memory, Rhode's marble-like eyes are colder than those of his human self. It's hard to believe I am now accustomed to his mortal face.

"It'll be easier this way. I don't trust her coven. Have you noticed how strong they are? Vicken, Heath, Song, and Gavin. They're all hand-picked for their strength and cunning. We need to do it while they are not here."

"That's not what I mean. This ritual? Sacrificing yourself?" Suleen asks. The sun is almost fully descended; above, a full moon brightens the sky. "Your death offers me no comfort, Rhode."

"This ritual is the only way for Lenah to live. The Hollow Ones will protect her. They'll make sure nothing happens to Lenah after I am gone."

"The Hollow Ones will keep up their end of the bargain only if you die. There is no telling what will happen if you survive. They cannot be trusted, Rhode."

Rhode stares into the hills as the sunset washes them in gold. "What about her soul?" he asks Suleen.

"What about it?"

"How do we know?" Rhode's eyes flick to Suleen's and then back out to the field. "How do we know Lenah's soul isn't damaged. That as a human she won't fall back into her desire for power. Even I—" He stops and considers what he is about to say. "She killed a child, Suleen."

"Do you question your forgiveness? It is key to the sacrifice," Suleen explains.

"I question her human self. Can she love after being capable of such evil?"

"I cannot answer this for you," Suleen says. He looks to the sky. "If you want to unearth her, you must do it now."

"Tell me, Suleen. Can someone who has done such evil really come back? Her evil has surpassed that of any vampire I have ever seen."

"Now, Rhode! You must start before the sun fully descends."

"What if I can never forgive her?"

The truth finally comes out. He has not forgiven me for killing a child. For falling into madness as a vampire.

"Now!" Suleen yells.

Rhode lifts a shovel and stabs the earth.

⸻ ◀ ⸻

Stop him! Stop him!" I screamed. Someone was holding my shoulders and trying to shake me awake. The hardwood of the floor cooled my back and I blinked my eyes.

"Lenah! Hey, Lenah!" Vicken was calling my name. I looked up at the ceiling. Vicken leaned over me so his shaggy hair fell into his eyes. He raised an eyebrow. "You fell asleep on the floor. You have a couch, a lounge chair, and a bed. But, hey, don't let me criticize your napping locale."

I sat up, swallowing hard, and ran a hand through my hair. I sat there, staring at the base of the bureau. I gazed at its carved legs and intricate woodwork.

Vicken squatted down beside me. "Does this need immediate attention? Should I be calling someone to help you?"

"I . . ." I concentrated on the floor and the horizontal lines in the wood. "I don't know."

It's not that Rhode couldn't love me anymore, as he had said in the woods after visiting Tony's grave. It was that, at one point, he didn't want to. Because I didn't deserve it. Perhaps that's why he didn't come back last year. He didn't want to return to someone with a heart like mine.

"Who are the Hollow Ones?" I asked.

Vicken frowned. "Hollow Ones?" He shook his head. "Never heard of them."

"Help me stand," I said, and lifted a hand. Vicken's warm fingers grasped mine and pulled me up. I walked to the wall and leaned against it. Vicken stood looking at me, his arms crossed over his chest. Rhode's memory swirled in my mind.

"I'm seeing Rhode's thoughts," I said in a rush. Vicken's eyes narrowed. "I see his thoughts, sometimes his memories."

Vicken dug in his pocket for a pack of cigarettes. He lit one, then said, "What do you mean? Thoughts . . ."

I slid to the floor and linked my arms around my knees. "I see him in my mind, but it's as if I'm in his mind. I verified it. I dreamt that I saw him punch a mirror. And then when I saw him in person, there was a fresh gauze wrapped around his injured fingers."

"Why on earth would he punch a mirror?"

"He couldn't stand to look at himself. So he punched it."

Vicken shook his head again. "Odd."

I exhaled, looking out the balcony door at the darkened space. From above, the moon lit up the tiles, and my vampire remains still sparkled. It felt good to tell someone the truth.

"Why would I see his thoughts now? I'm completely mortal. I don't have my ESP or my vampire sight now. And it never happened at any other time in our history. When he left before . . . before I met—" I hesitated and chose my words carefully. "—when I met you."

Vicken thought it over then shot up. "Remember that story Rhode used to tell?" Vicken said. "The one about the vampire who loved the human girl. The one during the plague. The . . ."

"Anam Cara?" I said, remembering Rhode telling the story by firelight. I had forgotten the phrase until now.

"Yes. The vampire had a deeper connection to her than to any other. So much so that he could sense her thoughts, not just her intentions. He hid his vampirism from her, and when she got the plague . . ."

"He let her die," I said, remembering the story.

"Yes!" Vicken said, and walked to the trunk pushed against the wall below the iron candle holders. He sifted around inside it.

"Uncommon for vampires, who are inherently selfish," Vicken said, the smoke from his cigarette wafting and hanging over his head. He pulled out one of the few leather-bound books Rhode left me when I was first human. *A Book of Celtic Magic.* "It would have been easy. Cure her—make her a vampire forever. Instead, he let her go to her death as she should have. Not a pleasant death, but she got sick. And she died as humans do."

I liked that story and I remembered it well. It reminded me of how I felt for Rhode. Except, he didn't let me go. . . .

Vicken opened the *Book of Celtic Magic.*

"Here it is. *Anam Cara.* A soul friend. When one finds her Anam Cara, the connection is undeniable. Unyielding. It is a white string of light connecting two souls through space and time. Some believe the Anam Cara share a mind. A mind of a past so deep, so interconnected, that they can share thoughts."

He looked up at me and took a last drag from his cigarette, which was down to the nub.

"So, soul mates can share thoughts?" I said. And then it hit me again. I had forgotten temporarily, but there it was: Rhode's voice wondering whether he could forgive me for killing that child and for making the coven. Disappointment flooded through me again. I picked up my gold studs from the floor and stood up, facing my reflection, and I smoothed my hair again, which was mussed after my tumble to the floor. What was the use of sharing thoughts if Rhode couldn't love me anymore? If I had a damaged soul?

"So that's it?" complained Vicken. "You ignore my moment of brilliance and go back to getting ready for your party?" He placed the book back in the trunk, shut the lid, and sat down on top of it.

What if I can never forgive her?

I put on the earrings and surveyed my reflection again. My hair fell down my back over the thin gauze of the tangerine blouse I had bought at the mall. I wanted the studs to be my mother's earrings, the hoops that were lost in the fire. Sadly, that was not possible. I watched as my nostrils flared and I clenched my jaw again.

"Anam Cara," I said aloud, letting the expression roll around on my tongue.

"Well," Vicken said, pressing his hands on his thighs and standing up. "I guess you're still going to go to this party despite the news of the mind meld."

"You're damn right I'm going."

"All righty," said Vicken, and dropped a dagger into each boot. He slid another into a leather strap hidden up his long shirt-sleeve.

"Preparing, are we?" I asked.

"Your life has been threatened twice, and you're willing to risk it for a little campfire? I have an idea: I'll light a fire on the balcony and sing you 'Happy Birthday.'"

"I know it's strange," I said.

"No, it's bloody ridiculous," Vicken replied. "But I'm not letting you go alone. I'd chain you to the wall if it weren't against school policy."

I opened the door, Vicken walking directly behind me.

"You don't have to come to the party," I said, knowing that Vicken would, of course, come.

"You got that right. With those screaming loons? Knowing them, they'll get lost and we'll have to search the woods to find them—it'll be a mortal mess."

"So where are you going to be?" I asked.

"Watching the perimeter of the woods. Making sure no one with fangs crosses into the park."

"There'll be too many people surrounding me. Don't you think they'll be less likely to attack when they're outnumbered? I wouldn't have attacked in those circumstances."

"Maybe . . . ," Vicken said as we descended the stairs.

"Also, it's my birthday! You realize this means I'm actually aging."

"Really? How old are you?" Vicken asked as we walked down the stairwell. His smile was a sly one.

"Seventeen," I said.

"Really. You look so much older," Vicken said. I could have slapped him if it weren't so . . . well, Vicken to say something like that.

A few moments later, we were walking toward the camping grounds from my car, parked on Main Street. I listened to the chatter of people around us. We parted as a woman walking her dog stepped between us.

"Maybe Rhode is connected to your mind too," Vicken offered.

"There's no way to know. He refuses to touch me and is barely speaking to me," I said as the smell of coffee wafted over us from the Lovers Bay café. "You know, there are other things, stranger things that I've seen outside of his memories. I see his thoughts too."

I turned my head as we walked past the busy café. I wouldn't have minded an evening sipping a cup of coffee and chatting to Vicken. One evening to forget about Odette and Rhode and all that lay before me. We kept on walking up Main Street and I explained about Rhode's odd behavior when he punched the mirror. But when I opened my mouth to mention Tony, I glanced at Vicken keeping pace beside me and said something else instead.

"I'm telling you," I said, "he punched the mirror and said, 'I can't,' over and over."

"Rhode? Going insane? It doesn't make sense," Vicken said, keeping his gaze on the road, scanning back and forth.

"I think it's deep-rooted. That he doesn't think he deserves his humanity or something. I told you. He kept saying, 'I can't.'"

Vicken let this hang in the air between us, then said, "Can't what?"

"I don't know, I just want to make it better," I replied. And I knew a way to alleviate Rhode's pain. I had wanted to do it for days now: call on Suleen. Or perhaps we could call on the Aeris. Call on someone, anyone who could help him. Perhaps Rhode hurt because we couldn't be together. Or—and I didn't want to admit this, because I didn't want it to be true—perhaps Rhode did not believe he deserved to survive the ritual and be human. He had meant to die—we both did. It was our connection as soul mates that linked us to this world.

My head hurt.

"Don't worry about Rhode," Vicken said as we walked through the crisp air of the late summer night. We entered the camping ground. "Try to have fun with the . . . screaming loons, was it?" Vicken said, placing a cigarette between his lips.

"Precisely," I replied.

I heard the music first. Something with electric guitars and a light melody. I remembered the hundreds of times over hundreds of years when I had stepped over branches, parted leaves, and walked through woods. Never, not once, had electronic instruments echoed through the trees and undergrowth.

Ahead of me was the orange glow of the fire. When I came upon two or three cars parked facing the campsite, I knew this was it. Music played out of Justin's silver SUV. Claudia and Tracy sat by the fire with a few others, drinking out of big red cups. Tracy was talking very closely with a guy from the lacrosse team whom I didn't know. Justin looked up at me from unpacking some hamburger buns and a small charcoal grill.

Claudia jumped up when she saw me. "Happy birthday!" she cried, and wrapped her arms around me. She had to rise onto her tiptoes to hug me, but when she came back down, she reached into a pocket of her light jacket and pulled out a small card in a purple envelope.

"For you," she said.

"Claudia . . . ," I said. "You didn't . . ."

"Yes, I did." She nodded.

"Thank you," I said, genuinely touched. I held the small card in my hand.

"This party was my idea. Don't let Justin fool you. I suggested it." She glanced back at him and gave a playful smile.

I opened my present. I couldn't remember the last time I had been given an actual gift. One that didn't involve its immediate murder, anyway. I opened the flap, and inside the envelope was a small card, like a credit card, but on it were the words CAPE COD MALL.

"A gift card," Claudia said. "You seemed like you had a good time when we went to the mall. And you're wearing the shirt!"

A gift card? For me? I turned the card over and over, marveling at the small present in the flickering light from the campfire.

"Thank you," I said to Claudia, whose eyes were warm. Tracy looked up at me and gave me a half smile, as if she didn't really mean it. She was roasting a marshmallow on a long stick. It looked wonderful and gooey. Her hair glimmered in the flicker of the fire, and her angular features looked more pronounced to me than they had a few days before. Perhaps I was only just noticing it now, but she looked like she had lost a lot of weight in a short time.

I slid the gift card into my back pocket. As I watched the marshmallow melt away in the heat of the fire, another collection of Wickham students walked onto the campsite. They were the normal variety—athletes, academics, just kids looking for a party. But when I really looked, I pulled back and blinked a few times to make sure I was in my right mind. Had I just—? Had I really mistaken one of these high school students . . . for Rhode?

There he was, trailing behind everyone.

"Hey! Hey!" Someone at the front of the group called out and hoisted some paper bags in the air.

"My peach schnapps is here!" Claudia cried.

Rhode was wearing all black and I couldn't look away. How did he know where I was? For a moment, I felt like a disobedient child; then I lifted my chin in defiance.

Claudia spun around and gasped. "There's Rhode," she murmured to me. "Have fun . . . ," she said, and went to join Tracy.

Rhode walked in long strides and stopped directly in front of me. When he breathed out, he dug a hand into his pocket. With the image of vampire Rhode still in my mind, I noticed the small, human things—the pouted mouth, the need to inhale, and the band of sweat across his brow. He reached deeper into his pocket and pulled out a black bag; then he nodded his head toward the woods. "Could you come talk to me?"

I tried to be as casual as possible. "Sure."

He wasn't here because he'd changed his mind; I knew that much. He had made that plain when he told me he couldn't love me anymore. I followed him into the woods down a worn path, until the fire and campsite chatter were far enough away that no one would overhear us. He looked up through a break in the branches. There were long stringy clouds over the moon.

"Lace on the moon," he said before I could. And when the wind moved the clouds out of the way, he added, "You remember the first time we saw that?"

I nodded and smiled. "Of course. You showed me in 1604, during carnevale in Venice."

We both knew lace on the moon was a harbinger of change—something was coming.

Rhode took a step toward me, but this time I stepped back, unsure of his intentions. "Now you fear me?" he asked.

"I could never fear you," I whispered.

What if I can never forgive her? Rhode had said.

The hurt from his words churned in my stomach again. I wanted to ask if he had, in fact, forgiven me. If he had found a way to see past my horrible actions and manipulations as a vampire.

"If you don't fear me," he said, drawing my eyes to his, "then open your hand." And I did—I held up my palm as though waiting for his heart to be placed in it.

The contents of the black velvet bag spilled out.

Anam Cara.

I didn't look up at Rhode—not yet. My heart pounded deep inside my chest. My fingers curled around two small objects. Gold. They felt cool to the touch. I looked down. My mother's earrings. He had saved them from the fire.

"Lenah?" Justin's voice interrupted, echoing toward us. "Come back! Food!"

I looked back up at Rhode. "Happy birthday," he murmured. The quiet, forlorn look drew me in, but he couldn't look at me for more than a few seconds.

"Rhode . . . ," I said, and reached out toward him. He backed up a couple of steps.

I inhaled quickly as tears stung my eyes. I wanted to touch him so badly, it made my teeth ache. The pain of wanting him ran down through my arms, into my fingers—it radiated deep down into my soul.

"They were all I could bring back. I only had a few moments. I jumped out of your bedroom window. Punched out the glass."

I recalled my dream, remembering his fist propelling into the mirror, sending it into a thousand fragments of light.

"I used a chair first," he clarified.

His eyes searched my face. He furrowed his brow so a line settled deep between his eyes. Blue. The ocean. The sky. The love of my life.

"Happy seventeenth birthday," he said quickly, and turned on his heel.

He set off through the wood back in the direction of Main Street.

"Wait," I called quietly after him.

He turned, highlighted only by the faint moonlight filtering through the clouds; then he moved on farther into the woods. The pain stabbed in my chest deeper than I ever thought it could.

"Rhode, you'll get lost," I called after him, my voice cracking. "It's dangerous."

He looked up at the sky, at the stars and the lace on the moon. "Who taught you how to track the movement of the constellations to navigate your way?" he asked, but by now he was just a black silhouette. I wanted to walk by his side, go home with him, talk and touch him—skin on skin.

I wanted someone to hold me and tell me it would be all right. To tell me that the sun, moon, and stars were not governed by invisible forces. I wanted to believe that I was free and had a will of my own. But in the caverns of these thoughts I knew the truth—Rhode and I were not free.

And he could not love me anymore.

I watched him weave his way through the shadowy forest until he was indistinguishable from the trees. I knew Vicken would patrol all night. Rhode might too. And maybe it was selfish of me, but I stood in those woods with the ghosts of my past resting in two earrings lying in the palm of my hand.

With a heavy sigh, I walked back toward the party, listening to the leaves crunching under my feet. I saw that most of the senior class had come to the campground. There were a lot more red cups and many more people milling about.

I stood at the end of the path where Rhode had led me into

the woods. knowing he was gone—but also knowing that the spot where he placed the earrings in my hands would always be ours.

"Happy birthday to you . . . ," a group of people sang together.

A candle bobbed in the darkness toward me. Justin handed it to Claudia, who walked toward me with Tracy. They were carrying a deliciously decorated cupcake. Chocolate frosting twisted and turned in a decadent swirl, and in the center of it a small candle glowed.

Justin sang the loudest of them all, and I wished—oh how I wished that Tony were there.

The candle flickered and I met Justin's eyes above the little flame.

"Well," Justin said, leaning close to my ear, "make a wish."

"A wish?" I said, still looking into his eyes. "What do I wish?"

"Anything you want," he said, nuzzling close to my neck. My body reacted with goose bumps rippling over my skin. "Any wish for your birthday."

I held my breath and closed my eyes.

I wish first for our safety. All of us. Vicken, Rhode, Justin, and me. And for Wickham. But my heart wants the hurt to go away. I wish for someone to tell me I am all right. That who I am and what I did is forgiven.

I blew out the candle with the wish still swirling in my mind, Justin's happy expression shone back at me from behind the flickering candle. He really did throw this party just for me.

"Happy birthday," he said. He took my hand, running his fingers over my skin.

Someone placed a cup in my other hand. I took a sip and the slick tangy peach liquor slipped down my throat. Still holding my hand, Justin drew me around the side of his car, where he had set up a small tent. He took my drink and placed it on the ground, then brought his hands up and cupped my face. With thoughts of Rhode and the earrings still pulsating in my mind, I wasn't sure what to do. And if Vicken was walking the perimeter, he could see what I was doing.

"I know you love Rhode. You've loved him for six hundred years," Justin said. His body heat radiated over me. "I can't compete with that."

"What?" I barely whispered. His words were so true that they took my breath away.

In the dark, Justin's expression was ferocious. He leaned forward and whispered in my ear, in a low growl, "But he has no idea who you are as a human. Not like me."

"Justin . . . ," I said, surprise rolling over me, down my back to my toes.

"No," he said, and he cupped a hand behind my head. "I want to be the one to show you what it's like to survive a ritual, Lenah. What it means to live. He doesn't know you like I do." His sincerity pierced me. He meant it, and I could feel it in the lock of his gaze. "Let me in," Justin said, and the intensity was in the rush of his words and the tightness of his jaw. "Let me in."

Justin brought my face close to his and leaned in for a kiss. He groaned as though he were hungry. My shoulders relaxed. My chest released. Because I wanted touch, I wanted warmth, I wanted what I could not have when I was a vampire. He pulled away and we both took a breath. Wow—I did love his kiss. As he pulled away, I saw the silver rune at the base of his throat.

I had to try to make sense of everything. Make sense of you.

I relived that moment in Justin's bedroom when he had delicately cleaned my collarbone wound. I touched the pendant lightly with my fingertips.

He put an arm around me, pulling me close. His passion

emanated. "I need you," Justin said. His eyes were fierce and he didn't move. "So whatever you did with that ritual doesn't matter to me. I want—"

Claudia appeared around the side of the tent. She wasn't alone. Tracy stood behind her, looking unamused. As if she had been forced to walk over.

"Come on, Justin, you can't keep Lenah all to yourself tonight." She grabbed my hand and with a tug, I was back at the party around the campfire. Throughout the rest of the night, I danced, drank cups of peach schnapps, and melted into the warmth of Justin's embrace.

Justin kept my arm in his, parading us around the party as though we were royalty. I didn't fear the woods. I didn't fear the vampires. The company of other Wickham students helped to ensure my safety. They were grieving for Ms. Tate and Kate and Tony and trying to forget the violence. I was reveling in the humanness of it all. I let Justin's hold ground me. When we were touching, skin on skin, I knew which version of Lenah Beaudonte I was meant to be. I could smile. I could be human.

There were no strange smells of apples. I was not a crazed vampire who could not be forgiven. I had already been forgiven. I was just a seventeen-year-old girl celebrating her birthday. We leaned our backs against a large oak tree and watched as a small circle formed. Claudia danced in the middle of it, shaking her body and laughing with some of the other senior girls. Tracy stood on the outside, watching. She did not smile, at least not like everyone else. Her smile was just a lazy lift of the left side of her mouth.

As the night went on, Rhode's gesture in giving me the earrings was easier to forget. They sat deep in my pocket, where I could not touch them. I could wrap my fingers around Justin's skin instead.

Hour by hour.

Sip by sip.

It didn't really matter at all . . . did it? So easy to forget on a warm night with friends. With Justin and his soft touch. He whispered words in my ear.

"I missed you so much.

"Don't go back to campus."

Words like this led to . . .

Justin's arms around me.

A sleeping bag . . .

Inside a tent.

In the darkness of my closed eyes were blue hydrangeas, whose petals were the symbols of love and hope. Love and hope. Love and hope.

"I love you," the deep voice said. Like in the listening room, this voice had no British accent. Justin whispered my name again and again . . . until we slept.

Chapter Sixteen

My head was filled with sand. What an odd sensation. My eyes were closed though I was aware my head was on a pillow. I squinted an eye open—too bright. That hurt! Was this a demon light that caused so much pain? I'd heard that a demon hell was so bright, it left a normal creature blinded.

Birds didn't chirp in demon hells.

I would just sleep, I was warm. Was I in my bed? I inhaled deeply: the woody ash of a campfire. Oh, right. I was at Lovers Bay campsite. I dared to squint.

The sun filtered through a blue vinyl ceiling, making the sleeping bag I lay in very warm.

I was in Justin's tent.

He lay asleep on his back, and his face angled toward me. I looked at his beautiful pouted lips and thin nose. He had a slight stubble on his chin. He adjusted in his sleep, moving his arms above his head.

"Lenah . . . ," he groaned.

The night's events slammed back into place.

Oh, Lenah, you fool. Worse than a fool. Idiot girl. Foolish, idiot girl. I had to figure out how to get out of the tent without waking him up. Oh no—what if Rhode saw me with Justin? What if Rhode never left the woods? He was bound to have been watching me, with those vampires milling about.

Calm down, Lenah. Get up slowly. Where is your shirt?

The weight of my blood made my head throb as I tried to get up. *Slowly,* I thought as my backside edged over the cloth of the sleeping bag. I grabbed on to my clothes, which were lying next to the sleeping bag. A wave of nausea overwhelmed me. Not because I regretted spending the night in Justin's tent.

But because part of me didn't regret it.

I watched him sleep for a moment. The silver rune necklace lay around his neck, shining in the early morning light.

I don't know, he had said about the necklace. *I had to try to make sense of everything. Make sense of you.*

He had sought out that knowledge rune so he could understand me and supernatural power. But what happened last night was not supernatural. I needed him to touch me, to remind me what it felt like to be mortal. To know that even I could be forgiven. Forgiven by Justin, who had been so angry with me, yet had found a way to let me in.

I scooted out of the tent as quietly as I could and peeked ahead. A large bush hid me from the campsite. I changed quickly.

We were so far back in the woods but I could see Justin's SUV near the campfire. Small silent tents circled the campsite and remnants of marshmallow bags and party cups littered the site.

I had to get back to Wickham campus and it looked as if I would have to do it alone. Somehow, I would have to explain to the security guards why I didn't have a buddy to sign onto campus. I knew I shouldn't be walking alone, but I would have to risk it.

Fully dressed, with a tip-tap of my toes on the crunchy grass, I headed for the woods, hesitating when I heard rustling in the tent. Justin must have been waking up.

I set off toward the pathway that led out of the campsite, surveying my options. I did not dare walk past the tent, where Claudia and Tracy slept. I took a few steps toward the campsite exit but stopped.

A figure clad in black stepped out of the woods and onto the pathway in front of me. My heart stopped. I drew in a shallow breath. And another. The figure had dark hair and a tall frame, but he stood in the shadows of a large tree. The morning light only touched the treetops. He took another step, and my throat constricted at the sight. A vampire? I could run into the woods, perhaps lose him that way. I could make a ruckus in the campsite, wake everyone up.

Wait.

This vampire was smoking a cigarette.

Vicken.

⬩❦⬩

I stuck my hands deep into my pockets as I finally crossed out of the campgrounds and onto the end of Main Street.

"You are monstrously stupid. Do you know that?" Vicken said. "I don't need my ESP. I was told not to disturb you by that Claudia girl. I slept with my back against a bloody tree to get away from her."

"Vicken . . . ," I said, but my tone was an apology as we walked back to school; our strides matched.

In the warmth of the pocket of my jeans, my mother's earrings bit at my fingertips. My peach schnapps headache ebbed as I kept walking. The sunrise kissed the buildings on Main Street.

"I was supposed to protect you," Vicken said in a low voice.

"Spare me," I said as a tingle of guilt spread from the pit of my stomach to my face. We kept walking, faster and faster in the early morning light. Up Main Street, past the shops and market until we were at the campus gates.

"Names?" the security guard demanded.

Vicken and I showed our IDs, and the pedestrian gate opened.

"Vicken," I said as we walked back onto campus. "You have to promise me you won't say anything to Rhode."

"Promise you! He was walking the perimeter too!"

I didn't know what this meant, so I bit at the inside of my cheek as we walked.

Vicken's dark expression softened. "Why'd you do it?" he asked.

I didn't answer.

"Never mind, let's just get upstairs. I'm dying for a coffee," he said.

Step by step, we walked past the security guard of my building and up the staircase. We were almost at my floor when—

Apples again, coming up the stairwell in a nauseating stench. Apples rotting. Apples fermenting in a broken wooden barrel. I could see them in my mind. An image from my past: apples sitting out in the sun too long, brown and leatherlike.

"No!" I shouted, throwing a palm against the nautical-themed wallpaper of the hallway.

Rhode stands in the center of his room. He lifts the sword from the floor. I see his chest—he breathes rapidly. He then hits the sword on the telescope, sending black pieces of metal into the air. He slams his lamp; glass shards fly in tiny pieces through the air. His rage . . .

"No!" I yelled, and fell to my knees. A few doors below me opened, their latches making metallic clicks.

"Everything okay up there?" someone called.

"We're fine. Fine!" Vicken called back, and I opened my eyes, trying to focus on him. But his wild hair kept coming in and out of my vision of Rhode destroying his room.

I held back a scream of horror as Rhode's anger pulsed through me in a series of heartbeats. I tried to recall the images of Rhode, close my eyes and see him. His anger rushed through me as sparks exploded in my body.

He knew I had been with Justin in that tent.

"What did you see?" Vicken asked, and it was only then that I realized he was holding my hand. "That was another vision of Rhode, wasn't it?"

"He's angry," I said. "He definitely saw me last night."

Vicken pulled me up. I could smell pine on his clothes and tobacco on his skin. No apples . . . luckily.

Somehow, the last set of stairs seemed impossibly hard to climb. But I managed them. I stepped up toward my apartment, where I would shut the door, walk into my bedroom, and crawl under my covers.

Do you forgive me? I had asked Justin. He had said yes. Only now I realized I was asking the wrong person.

I hoped as Justin touched my salty tears that he didn't realize I was crying because I wished he had been Rhode. Shouldn't I have been happy to be touching someone who cared so much for me? Exhilarated, just like last year, when we were together and I was overjoyed and happy to feel loved?

"If you keep gasping without telling me what's going on, I'll lock you up until you do," said Vicken.

"It's just about last night," I replied, and reached out to grasp the doorknob. My fingers clasped around the metal.

Searing pain radiated up and down my body. My gut wrenched in a knot so tight in my stomach that I doubled over. My knees hit the cheap carpeting, and the hard fabric raked against my skin as I placed a palm on the floor, saliva whooshing into my mouth.

The barrier spell . . . it worked.

"You used to be able to drink pints and pints of blood. You were a powerful Vampire Queen. This is ridiculous," Vicken said. He lifted a hand to touch the doorknob.

"No! No!" I cried, and raised my hand. It felt like a dead weight and I pressed it back onto the floor. "The barrier spell has ignited," I said. This sickness was the mortal reaction to powerful magic.

It meant that a vampire had tried to break into my room. If it was Odette, she would be a pile of ash on the floor. The spell would instantly have killed whoever it was.

Vicken sat back on his heels and stared at the door, his eyes wide in shock. "Guess they found out the ritual's a fake," he said.

The magic of the barrier spell meant all the herbs I scattered had ignited, sending powerful energy about the room. I reached a palm up and hesitated in front of the door. I had to see if it was hot or cold. If it was hot, the spell was recent; cold, and it had occurred hours earlier.

Vicken and I, almost simultaneously, placed our palms against the door. His knuckles whitened and then the palm dropped, hitting his thigh.

"Hot," he said, and his tone was grave. "They must have just tried."

My fingertips zinged as I also dropped my hand from the door. The energy of the spell sent shocks of electricity up my arms, and Vicken clenched and unclenched his hands. I grabbed on to Vicken to help me stand, and we both stood up. I hesitated, holding the key before the door; then I slid the key in the lock, turned the doorknob, and the door unlatched.

"*Hunc locum bonis ominibus prosequi,*" I said. "Bless this space" in Latin. My hands still tingled as though they had fallen asleep. I kept squeezing them into fists.

"Let's go in," Vicken said. The door creaked open slowly. We stood there a moment—waiting. A weird white noise echoed, as though hundreds of people were screaming from the end of a long tunnel. These were the reverberations of the vampire's screams.

Tiny specks of gray ash now lined the perimeter of the living room where the herbs had been.

In the center of the room was a collection of sooty gray ash.

I walked toward it, but something caught my eye, outside on the balcony. Someone was moving. It took me a moment to recognize her, but it was Odette rolling onto her side so her blond curls fell over her face, and struggling to stand.

I jumped over the pile of ash to the balcony door, but Odette was already on her feet. Vicken pushed past me through the doorway and shoved Odette so she fell to the ground again. Her arm was covered in blood, her fingers raw and nails cracked. Perfect. Injured. Perhaps we could get her while her guard was down. Vicken reached into his boot for a dagger, but Odette rocked onto her back and kicked out, sending Vicken backwards.

Why, now of all times, had Rhode taken the sword!

Odette ran to the edge of my balcony.

"Go!" I yelled, and pushed Vicken toward her.

But she was much too fast. Like her strength, Odette's speed outmatched that of any normal vampire. I made it to the stone ledge of the balcony, threw out my hands, and tried to grasp onto a pant leg—but the fabric just grazed my fingers as she propelled herself into the air.

She landed on the roof of the building next to mine. I expected her to land catlike, on her feet, as I had seen her do every other time. But she stumbled, her arms pinwheeling to keep her balance, and she fell onto her knees.

Vicken lifted a leg to step on top of the balcony ledge. He was going to try to jump!

While he was a human, there was no way Vicken would make it without serious injury. I grasped onto his arm, heaving him back onto the balcony, and we fell together onto the tiles.

"No," I said breathlessly. Our eyes met. "I will not lose you again."

He held my gaze for a moment, and the fight in his eyes softened. He sighed and pulled me up. We stood together by the ledge.

"Let's go down," I said, pulling Vicken by his shirtsleeve. I intended to meet Odette at the bottom of the building next door. Two on one, we maybe had a chance. If she didn't outrun us first.

"Wait . . . ," said Vicken darkly.

Odette pressed up from the roof but her arms gave out and her elbows hit the ground.

"What the—?" Vicken said. "Look!"

She pressed again and this time shot up straight. She stepped to the ledge of the building and raised her arms above her head. I gripped Vicken's forearm in anticipation as Odette jumped off the edge of the building and ran off into the darkness.

"How the hell did she do that?" asked Vicken.

"And her arms," I whispered. "She healed instantly. Did you see them when she lifted them above her head? They weren't bloody anymore."

"I'm more concerned that she can get on campus," Vicken replied. "She did it before October first too. The protection of the ritual is over."

The ash of the vampire who did not make it out of my apartment sat in a small pile, directly in the center of the room.

But for Odette, her cracked and bloody wounds had healed in minutes. No vampire I had ever known could heal that quickly. But then again, everything I knew about vampires was being tested by Odette.

We walked back inside my apartment and Vicken bent over the ash of the dead vampire. He squatted down and pulled out a thick silver watch from the center of the ash. It dangled on the end of his finger.

"A man's watch," Vicken said. "Odette's ruthless," he continued. "She sacrificed a member of her coven. She knew you would do a barrier."

As I surveyed the charred herbs of the barrier spell around the perimeter of the room, I could sense that the energy in that room had changed. Any supernatural creature who entered would know that the barrier spell had protected me. That was why Odette had been injured. The first vampire had probably incinerated by walking into the space. Only Odette's fingers and forearm had made it into my apartment before she realized what was happening.

Either way, it was now my space, sacred and holy. Just as Rhode always said . . . energy leaves an indelible mark. With the smell of the campfire laced through my hair, and the pulsating images of Rhode smashing his room, I knew what I had to do. We needed help. We needed protection. I couldn't let Odette and her minions dominate us anymore.

I turned from the doorway. "I'm going to perform a summoning spell," I said to Vicken. "I'm not going to wait and let her control me."

"Oh really," he said, his tone etched with sarcasm.

"Despite what you may think, Rhode is losing his mind and I need your help. Especially now that Odette is on campus."

"Do you want me to bow, or will an 'all right' suffice?" He lifted an eyebrow and leaned a shoulder on the wall.

"We're calling Suleen and we're doing it at sunrise."

Vicken didn't respond, but just kept on looking at me with that same smug expression: one eyebrow raised and an unlit cigarette dangling from his mouth.

"You're not going to fight me on this?" I said, disbelieving.

"I'm not going to win, am I? You did the barrier spell. I didn't think that would work and it did."

"Let's try it at sunrise. When the moon and the sun share the same sky. It's the most spiritual time of the day."

"Should I call you ma'am?"

"Stop it," I said.

"How about Mistress? Or Goddess?"

"She's lost a member of her coven. There's only four now," I said. "And we know she heals quickly. At least we know those things."

"That's not all we know, love," Vicken added, and lit the cigarette. He inhaled deeply, then on his exhale said, "We've uncovered something else of the utmost importance this morning."

"What's that?" I asked.

"She fell when she hit that roof. She's weakened when she bleeds."

If Odette was weakened when she bled, then we would have to fight her and bleed her, eventually stabbing her in the heart. It would be the only way to kill her. In the meantime, we needed help.

Vicken and I wasted no time. The next morning, I rested my head against the passenger seat, my eyes closed, my hair whipping back and forth from the breeze. If it wasn't for the sound of the motor, I could have been in a fast-moving carriage—but we weren't. Vicken was driving my blue car, and with another rev and a sharp turn, I was thrown against the door. I clutched onto the armrest and opened my eyes. When we pulled onto Lovers Bay beach, the moon hung over the harbor, creating wavy lines of gray blue light. Soon the sun would rise. I could feel it in my heart, in my bones. Perhaps, like a sixth sense, I would always be able to perceive the sun and its power. Its danger.

We sat in the quiet and looked out at the water.

"She's getting her strength from somewhere," I said, staring out at the ocean. "A spell or something. It's the only way her skin can regenerate so fast."

"Let's not worry about that," Vicken said. "Just focus on the spell."

"We need all four elements represented in this spell." Even as I said it, the Aeris came to my mind. Especially Fire and her crackling hair.

I reached into the backseat for our supplies and the spell book, which were all in my special spell bag. We got out of the car and when I stepped onto the small beach, the sand sank beneath my boots. The stars twinkled above us in a hazy gray light. This was called the Line. Vampires considered this a holy time of morning. A time for spells, when the world is unsure of itself; no longer night, not quite morning . . .

I checked the area immediately in front of the parking lot.

"Let's go down there, out of sight," I said, wanting to be far away from any common human's eye. "We need that driftwood over there, we can stack it by the shore." I pointed to the base of three trees. A stack of old wood, weathered from the seasons, lay broken and in a pile.

"You sure are bossy for someone who's most likely going to kill us both, doing this spell," muttered Vicken.

As I walked to the shore to acquire what else we would need for the spell, Vicken moved some of the pieces of wood from the pile. I stood at the water's edge and watched the ripples lap onto the rocky sand and then out again. This spell would act as a beacon—a calling. A vampire as powerful as Suleen, if he did not want to be contacted, could avoid it. But if now wasn't a time of need, then I didn't know what was. I reached into the warmth of my spell bag and unearthed a small empty jar. I scooped some of the bay water into the jar and walked back to Vicken, standing above the driftwood pile.

Jasmine was crucial for the success of the summoning spell. From the bag, I took out a small box of amber resin, some jasmine, and the matches, then handed the bay water to Vicken. As his fingertips touched mine, I smiled slightly, looking at my old friend. Our love, the one between Vicken and me, whatever it had been 160 years ago, was over now, replaced by the love of friendship.

"Let's just do this before Odette decides to show up," Vicken said with a sigh. "I'm all itchy. I hate anticipation, it's thoroughly human."

"You should begin the spell. You were the last one connected to the supernatural world," I said to Vicken. I meant that he was the last to be turned human by the ritual.

I reached into the bag and pulled out the heavy leather-covered spell book. My boots sank deeper into the sand as I stepped forward and handed the book to Vicken. The gold print of its title, *Incantato*, glinted as the morning sunrise crested the beach horizon. He opened the book to the page marked with a small red ribbon, looked from the spell to me, and said, "Ready?"

Draw a door in the sand . . . , said a voice from my memory. I had almost forgotten. Once, long ago, Rhode told me he performed a summoning spell. I surveyed the size of the driftwood and the area round it. When I stepped back from the pile, I placed my finger in the cool sand and drew the distinct outline of a door around the firewood. I met Vicken's gaze for reassurance and said what Rhode had told me all those years ago.

"As long as there have been doors—there have been summoning spells. Entryways. Passages," I said, backing away from the door.

"So we summon Suleen and he helps us with these vampires?" Vicken said.

And Rhode.

"That's the plan," I said, and lit a match so it flared between my fingers.

I flicked the match and it flew in a wide arc through the air and onto the driftwood pile. Sparked by the flame and the supernatural ingredients, the wood hissed and smoke rose up to the sky. Then I opened the resin box and took a pinch of amber between my thumb and index finger and sprinkled it over the fire. Orange flames flickered and crackled.

"Begin," I commanded gently.

Vicken looked down at the book.

In Latin, he announced, "I call on you, Suleen. I summon you to appear before me in this sacred space."

I bent down, took the jar, and unscrewed the top. I sprinkled the salt water so the fire sizzled. The water slicked over my hands, dropping pearls of water onto the flames. There was an unnatural crackle and the flames burst up. I pulled back in surprise.

"Wow," I said. "That was powerful."

Were the flames meant to jump in the air like that?

I knelt down and took a handful of sand in my fist. Then, with my arm fully extended, I sprinkled it over the smoking driftwood.

Vicken didn't need to hand me the book. I remembered this spell.

"I give you the earth and the water. I call to you, Suleen."

"Lenah . . . ," Vicken started to say in a warning tone. He too had noticed the growing flames. I ignored him, keeping my energy and my intentions constant.

"I summon you, Suleen, to come to us in a time of need." I dropped the jasmine flowers into the orange flames. The outline of the door we drew in the sand glowed a bright blue like the morning sky. Was it working? I needed to help Rhode. Needed to stop him from smashing mirrors and performing ceremonial rituals of the Order of the Garter at my best friend's grave. I wanted to stop him feeling the pain of seeing me with Justin. I felt a surge of need—someone had to come and help us.

"I summon you!" I screamed. "I call on you, Suleen!"

A blast of orange flames!

The driftwood exploded with a surge of energy like an inferno. It threw me into the air and I flew back onto the sand. And then . . .

My arm.

Red-hot flames crawled up to my elbow.

"Damn it," Vicken cried, and scooped handfuls of sand onto the flames.

I rolled onto my back and sat up just as the fire extinguished.

Swaying back and forth, only then did I realize I was clutching my wrist and screaming—I hadn't heard my own terror.

I drew in a deep breath. Those flames had come from nowhere. They should not have grown to that height. Vicken grabbed the spell book and dragged me toward the car, refusing to slow down as my feet kept slipping on the slope of the sand. I glanced back at the door that I had drawn in the sand and the now barely smoking driftwood.

The door was gone.

"What happened?" I grimaced as my arm throbbed. "Has it failed?" I groaned in pain and clutched at my wrist again. Vicken opened the passenger door and I slid onto the seat.

We were out on the road but the bumps made my stomach churn.

"Where's the hospital?!" Vicken roared, panic rising in his voice.

"Infirmary. Go to the infirmary at Wickham. I need to be near my room. The barrier spell!" I yelled, not daring to touch my forearm. "If we called anyone with the spell, we need to be in a safe place."

My skin seared—I wanted to plunge it into ice. I leaned my forehead on the glass, hoping to cool the pain as we ripped around corners. Every time Vicken turned the car too fast, it made my arm throb.

"It's best you don't look at it, love," Vicken said. "It's not having its greatest moment."

We turned a corner quickly and my shoulder hit the glass, reverberating pain down my arm.

"This was your great idea!" Vicken yelled. "Summoning Suleen. Using elemental magic to call him too. Who told you not to meddle? Fire, the element herself, told you not to meddle. But no! Lenah Beaudonte won't listen to the bloody Aeris!"

"Can you keep your criticisms to yourself, please!" I said with a groan, grasping my arm even harder. I shouldn't have looked, but I did, and my stomach lurched. The skin bubbled—a red raw blistering mess. Just when I thought I couldn't take the movement of the car anymore, we pulled through the Wickham gates, waved through by the security guard, who recognized us. It was busy for a Saturday morning. Even with the weekday students gone, dozens of students were out on the grounds studying and relaxing. We screeched to a halt. Vicken ran to the side of the car, opened the door, and the pressure of his arm around my shoulder comforted me as he helped me to stand. Voices. Pain in my arm . . . so many voices.

"Lenah!"

"Are you okay?"

"Someone get Justin!"

In a messy shuffle, Vicken and I made it to the infirmary door. I was sure my legs would give out. I wanted to scream; I wanted to cry. I hated pain. This pain was so intense that I was sure my arm was going to be scarred for life.

Vicken threw the infirmary door open and we stumbled inside. I could barely stand anymore. A nurse popped up from behind her counter and shouted for the doctor. I leaned on Vicken, grasping my arm. I couldn't help it—tears bit at my eyes. The burning of my arm and the waves of pain overtook me. I finally understood the human relief at seeing a doctor, as a woman in a white coat ran into the foyer and toward me.

I fell into the doctor's arms, and vomited on the floor.

Chapter Seventeen

ow did you manage to do this?" a nurse asked an hour later. Thick white gauze wrapped around my arm from my wrist almost to my elbow.

"I was cooking on a campfire," I replied. A blatant but necessary lie.

Why had the spell failed? I wondered again.

"Well, you were lucky, young lady," said Nurse Warner. "An open flame can result in third-degree burns. These are bad second degree. From now on, eat at the Union."

"Look at it this way," Vicken said as he leaned against the wall across from my bed. He had not left my side. "Now you're in the club." He pointed to his eye, which had almost healed; the skin was now just a tinge of yellow. Rhode's battered face flickered through my head.

"Lenah?" Justin's voice echoed from around the corner. He burst into the room and came to the side of the bed. "What the hell happened to you?" Justin asked. "You left this morning before I could—" He stopped when the nurse interrupted.

"Only a few minutes, Justin . . . ," the nurse said with a lift of her eyebrows. "We can't have a zoo in here."

"Yes, ma'am," he replied. He took my good hand into his own, then kissed my fingers.

"This is making me sick," Vicken said, rolling his eyes.

Justin shot Vicken a murderous look just before the nurse walked out.

"I'll be right back with some pain meds, Lenah," she said.

Once she was gone, Justin asked, "Was it Odette?"

Vicken frowned but didn't say anything.

"Not Odette. Vicken and I attempted a summoning spell," I said.

"Summoning?"

"To call Suleen," I explained.

"Guess it didn't go too well, then?" he asked.

"Yeah, guess not, mate," Vicken said, pushing away from the wall. I slid off the bed and when my feet touched the ground, Vicken held the fingers of my burnt arm and Justin held on to my other arm. I sighed, just wanting to lie down.

The nurse walked in, examining the label on a brown medical bottle she held between her fingers. "Vicken, you should take Lenah back to her room," she said, and looked up. Her eyes traveled back and forth between Justin and Vicken. "Or Justin. You guys figure it out."

"Justin needs to hurry back to his lacrosse practice," Vicken said with a chuckle.

"Stop it," I hissed to Vicken.

Nurse Warner handed the pill bottle to Vicken. "The instructions are on the bottle, Lenah. I suggest you follow them."

"How about I bring you some dinner tonight?" Justin asked, letting go of me as Vicken led me to the door of the examination room.

"Great," I said. "That sounds perfect."

As Vicken, Justin, and I walked out of the examination room, I kept glancing at the door of the infirmary, waiting for Rhode to walk through.

No, Lenah. This is how it's supposed to be. Justin is here for you. Not Rhode.

"You must keep this wrapped for the next couple days and don't touch any blisters that may come up. Leave them alone. Come back on Friday and we'll unwrap it and see how the burn is doing," said Nurse Warner, following us through the door.

"I'll bring her," Justin said, glaring at Vicken.

They made me take a pain pill before leaving the infirmary and said it would make me sleepy. Justin kissed me again before Vicken led me down the pathway toward Seeker.

Sleep would be good, I thought as Vicken prattled on and on about how much he loathed Justin.

Sleep, I thought again.

Sleep would keep me from wondering why Suleen had not come to save us. Sleep might lead to dreams, which might explain why the spell had backfired. Why, after all this, Suleen had not come to save Rhode.

Now, remember, when you shower, you have to wrap that gauze, cover it with a plastic bag to keep it dry. Are you even listening to me?" Vicken asked.

I lay back on the couch, looking up at the ceiling fan. Round and round it went. The blades. What happened to them? The spinning made them smear across the ceiling.

"Oh. Who painted the ceiling?" I asked in a daze.

Vicken looked up at the ceiling and then down at me. He raised an eyebrow.

"Why didn't he come? Why didn't Suleen come to me?" I asked. "Is it because Rhode doesn't forgive me? Did I tell you that? He thinks after all my unspeakable evil acts, my soul is black."

"He said this to you?" Vicken asked.

"No, not exactly." My eyelids kept slipping over my eyes again and again. My, they were heavy.

"Okay . . . time for you to sleep," said Vicken. "I think those painkillers are finally taking effect."

"I love sleeping," I replied dozily. "Do you think we'll die? That Odette will kill us?"

"Oh, good," Vicken said with a sigh. He pulled a blanket over me, tucking it around my body, a familiar gesture now. "Let's discuss this when you're in your right mind."

"Right mind?"

"I have to run," he said. "But I'll come check on you later. Don't perform any more spells."

Spells, I thought as I watched the ceiling fan again. *Spells that don't work. Spells where I am hurt.* Slowly . . . I fell asleep.

———————

I stand in the center of the gymnasium, alone. It's decorated with shining white stars and snowflakes covered in glittering sparkles. This is familiar; the room is decorated just like at the winter ball last year. I look down and touch the silk of a long gown. I'm wearing the same gown from the dance! Above me, the ceiling lights flash blue and red over and over, reflected on the floor. The DJ plays a slow song but no one mans the booth. The music is loud here, vibrating on the empty hardwood floor.

Where is everyone? I take a step but I pull my foot back— What is that? I almost stepped on something. A necklace? I look down and pick up a leather strap. Hanging on it is Justin's rune pendant. I look around. He wouldn't have lost it so easily. Not after everything he told me. He has to have this back.

"Justin?" I call out to the empty room, yelling and straining my voice over the music. "Justin!" I yell again.

"I always loved that dress," a familiar voice says.

I spin to face the gymnasium doorway.

Tony walks up to me dressed in a tux, looking exactly as he had at the winter prom. Alive and well.

"The girls picked it out," I say, referring to my dress. Tony stands before me, his hands in his pockets. The gauge earrings and sunny smile are just as familiar as the last time I saw him.

"I lost Justin. I can't find him," I say, looking around the empty gymnasium.

"He'll turn up," Tony says calmly. "Do you want to dance with me?"

"Yes." I smile and wrap my arms around him.

We spin in that gymnasium, my best friend and I.

"I would give anything to see you again," I say, taking in the handsome features of his face.

"You will."

"When?"

He spins me again so my dress twirls out around me. But when I face Tony again, Odette is standing before me; we're dressed identically. I gasp, backing away from her. Her hair falls long and straight over her shoulders.

She wipes blood from her mouth and says, "He tasted the best."

The next morning, dressing, I noticed the scent of tobacco in the air. Vicken must have checked on me during the night.

He tasted the best.

Odette's words kept ringing in my ears as I walked out of Seeker and across campus. Yes, Odette could be out in the daylight. But so could I. I had people on this campus who loved me and people who, if I needed them to, would help me. And after that dream, I had to see Tony's portrait. I hadn't wanted to until now. It was time.

I walked across campus, inhaling the warm morning air; I tried to clear my head. Students called out to me.

"Hey, Lenah—how's your arm?"

"Lenah, what happened?"

I tried to shake the haunting memory of the dream away in the bright sunshine among the crowds of students on campus. Tingles swept up and down my arms, down my legs to my toes. I hated those white pills that made me feel as though I had taken double opiates and absinthe combined, something I remembered from my vampire days. I kept walking, though it was difficult not to grab at my burnt arm; my heart pumped blood into that arm, sending a throb to my fingers. I squinted into the sun and shielded my eyes with my damaged hand. The top layer of skin pulsed in time with my heartbeat. I continued past the Union and the crowded meadow in front of Quartz dorm. Last night, my best friend had been alive. How cruel to have him near me again, then taken away in the morning, but I would find comfort from him even in his death. I was going somewhere I could feel close to him and have him around me.

Now that Hopper had finally been reopened, students pressed out of the building holding art easels and thick black portfolios. I looked at their hands, at the paint caked on their fingers, and the charcoal under their nails. It reminded me of Tony and his paint-smeared face and bright smile. I was so absorbed in my thoughts, I almost slammed straight into Justin.

"Heads up," he said, and smiled that lazy, cocky smile. "I was just coming to your room to check on you. I knocked twice last night but you never answered."

"Oh," I said, stalling. "Those pills really knocked me out. I didn't hear you."

He took a step toward me. "I was worried about you yesterday. First with Odette cutting you, then Ms. Tate dying, now this summoning spell and you getting burned."

The intensity of his gaze made me pause. An uncomfortable beat passed between us. It reminded me of the night of my birthday.

"I think I've been cool with this whole thing," he continued. "I want to help you. Because after your birthday, I thought we were . . . I thought you were with me."

"We are," I said. "I mean, I am."

"Good," Justin said, and caressed my shoulder with his hand.

"Look, can we talk later? I'm just going to go upstairs, to the art tower. And if I don't go now, I'll never go. You know what I mean?" I said.

Justin's back stiffened. "You're going to see the portrait?" he asked. I nodded in reply.

His eyes widened. With his free hand, he reached up to the pendant around his neck and rubbed at it nervously.

"I can't go up there," he said, and dropped his hand from my shoulder. I could see the twitch of his mouth as he tried to formulate the words. He shook his head and frowned, then met my eyes. Without blinking, he said, "I'm not ready. I didn't think Tony and me were friends, but when he died. And I saw what I saw . . ." His voice trailed off. It was clear he was still wounded by witnessing the horror of Tony's death. Justin and I had gotten there too late.

"I understand," I said as students continued to file past us out the door. He took a few steps onto the quad but didn't remove his eyes from mine.

"Come to my room after," he said. As he walked away, he slung his school bag over his chest.

"Okay," I said with a small smile. "I will."

I glanced around the campus again, surveying the students out enjoying the beautiful day. But I wanted to be in the art tower, even if people were in there working. They didn't have to know what I was doing. There was a quiet thud from the glass door as it closed behind me. Step by step, as I climbed the circling stairs to the art tower, I breathed deeply, relieved. I actually felt better instead of worse. This was what I needed.

As I climbed, I passed a few students coming down the stairs toward the ground floor. They had to turn to the side to avoid hitting me with their portfolios. I climbed higher and higher and stopped at the familiar window I once looked through when I first came to Wickham. My fingers grazed over the familiar stones and I hesitated when I caught sight of Justin walking into Quartz.

As I reached the last step, I walked into the doorway—and there it was. There I was. Tony had wanted to paint that portrait the whole time I knew him. It was based on a photograph he had taken of me during a snorkeling trip. I looked at myself in paint: a back view from my waist up, my head turned to the side, in profile. My hair was pulled to the side to reveal the tattoo on the back of my shoulder—the motto of my coven: Evil Be He Who Thinketh Evil.

I didn't notice her at first, but standing below the painting was Claudia. She was leaning down, zipping up a portfolio, and when she stood up, she glanced at the portrait and then at me. "No one's been able to take it down. We just keep putting up our paintings around it."

"I didn't know you were an artist," I said.

She pulled her blond hair back into a ponytail. "Oh, I'm not," she said. "Drawing's my elective."

Together, she and I looked at my portrait, at my profile and the curve of my smile.

"I feel like I'm looking at myself in a different time. A different life."

"Lenah, you're seventeen. You don't have to be so dramatic," she said.

"You're right," I said, just as there was the thud of a heavy door slamming.

"Did the—?" Claudia started to ask, but there was no need. I knew immediately.

The art tower door was ancient and wooden. It was always open. Now someone had closed it. Claudia and I turned to look.

Odette.

A flood of horror flashed through me but then something else replaced it. My cheeks burned. Anger rushed through me, along with the familiar determination I had once felt as a Vampire Queen.

Odette's perfectly coifed hair fell down her blouse in delicate ringlets. Her dark green eyes locked on me as a wide smile stretched across her face. How dare she stand before me? Here? I could almost feel the Vampire Queen within me baring her fangs.

"Claudia, get behind me," I commanded, and Claudia hid behind my back. I could feel small breaths on my neck.

"You see, I do not fear humans anymore," Odette said. "I could outrun any of them now."

"You should fear me," I replied.

Her eyes floated up to my portrait. "It's lovely, isn't it?" She smiled. "Such a shame about the boy."

Claudia let out a tiny cry.

"Did you think I wouldn't know?" Odette's said. Her words were clipped and short. She meant the ritual.

"Actually, yes," I said. "I don't think you're very smart."

Odette looked like a statue. She stood, legs slightly apart. She was stunning in her jeans and red top.

"Lenah . . . ," Claudia whispered. "Who is this?"

"Shhh," I said, not removing my eyes from Odette's.

"You don't think I actually tried that ridiculous fake spell, do you?" Odette asked.

"Yes," I answered. "I think you did try it. I think you believed me to be so stupid as to give it to you."

Stay strong, Lenah.

Odette walked around the circumference of the room and stopped directly below my portrait. I grasped onto Claudia's wrist, keeping her behind me as I turned to watch Odette. Her thin fingers pressed against mine.

If I made Odette bleed, we would have time to try to pull the door open. I just had to weaken her and stall for time.

Keep talking.

"You tried that spell days after you received it, didn't you?" I smirked. "You sent your men on errands to find the ridiculously rare items I placed on that list. Black crystal from the African coast."

Odette stepped onto a small stool near the wall, then lifted a hand and made a claw. She rose on her tiptoes so her hand now hovered in front of my portrait.

Then there was a horrible ripping sound as she scratched her knifelike nails down the center of my portrait. It felt as though she were ripping me in half as I watched shreds of Tony's painting fall like feathers to the floor.

"What's happening?" shrieked Claudia.

I clenched my teeth.

Odette started to walk again and I held on to Claudia's wrist and moved us away from her. We walked in circles for a few moments.

We had no choice but to keep backing away. My fingertips grazed the wood of the door as we passed by. Claudia body vibrated against mine as she trembled. Then I saw it—there beneath the painting were cubbies and I could see a box of X-Acto knives. Perfect! Stabbing her in the heart with so small a blade probably wouldn't kill her, but maybe it would buy me some time. And if we could get the door open, we could get out of the art tower.

"Claudia," I said. "Try to open the door."

Odette stopped her slow pursuit and instead marched directly across the room. In a blink, she had wrapped her fingers around my neck and lifted me, so the back of my head hit the wall of wooden cubbies. Her nails dug into my neck, and a hot pain erupted where she had broken through the skin.

My hands clawed behind me for the cubbies, raking through

the air for an X-Acto knife. I couldn't grab one. I wanted to open my mouth, croak to Claudia to hand them to me, but she had backed to the door, mouth hanging open. I lifted my knees toward my chest and kicked my feet out, directly into Odette's stomach. She stumbled backwards and threw her arms out. She caught her balance quickly, but the look of surprise on her face was victory enough for the moment.

My knees hit the ground as I fell forward. I was no fool; I had had my coven member Song teach me defense tactics. Odette would retaliate, and fast. When I tried to lean my body weight on my arm to get up, I collapsed from the pain of the burn.

"Do you know what will happen when I have that ritual? I'll have the most powerful coven in the world," Odette said, and walked slowly across the room. She was not walking toward me.

Oh no . . .

Claudia was pulling at the door handle and screeching as she heaved and yanked. Her blond ponytail flew in the air as she tugged on the door, but it was fruitless.

"I wanted to get you without Vicken or Rhode. And I have, but I can't kill you! Doesn't irony enrage you?" Odette shrieked and slapped her hands against her sides. "Rhode is never alone without a weapon. Stupid mortal. Always traveling with other people or talking to teachers. But you. Arrogant Lenah. Choosing to be alone with a human girl."

Odette grabbed Claudia by yanking on her ponytail, just as she had done to Kate. She then positioned herself so she stood with her right arm clutched around Claudia's neck. It reminded me of what she had attempted to do to Vicken at the Herb Shop. She couldn't kidnap Claudia in the light of day, but she could kill her.

"No—" I reached toward them, but worried if I moved, I might make it worse.

"Lenah . . ." Claudia's chin trembled. I knew her tearstained face and confused eyes would haunt me forever. Odette pulled back harder on Claudia's ponytail, exposing her neck. "Please, don't," Claudia's voice warbled.

Please don't. I have a family. I love my life. I don't want to die. I could speak these phrases in dozens of languages. They had been said to me so many times.

Odette bit into Claudia's neck. I shoved my hand into the cubbies until my fingers curled around a bunch of X-Acto knives; then I threw myself toward Odette and plunged them into her thigh.

There was a sucking sound. Odette lifted her head. Claudia, barely conscious, hung limply in Odette's arms. Odette laughed manically as a trickle of blood dripped from Claudia's neck onto her blouse.

"You think those pathetic knives would hurt me?"

Odette moved her hands over Claudia's ears, met my eyes with a smirk, and snapped her neck, sending Claudia to the floor. Her body crumpled instantly. When her limbs hit the floor, they made a horrible crack.

She lay motionless. Dead.

The knives in my other hand dropped to the floor with a meaningless clattering sound, and my stomach dropped.

No. She wasn't dead. I wouldn't let her be. I crawled to Claudia and took her small hand into mine. It lay limp and unmoving, still warm, and her hair fanned out on the floor, featherlike and soft.

"Get up," Odette said, pulling me by my hair and yanking at the scalp. The knives remained in her leg. I stood up, my fingers falling away from Claudia's as Odette held on to a fistful of my hair and snarled in my ear, "Every day that passes, I'll get stronger and stronger." She brought her face to mine and I could smell rotting blood. "I can't wait for Nuit Rouge." She let go of my head, releasing the tension in my scalp, and walked to a bookcase across from Claudia. "And because I can't have you in jail . . . ," she said with a horrific sneer while she used both hands to send a bookcase crashing to the floor, crushing Claudia's lifeless body.

I shot up, jumping across the room, away from Claudia's body and into the opposite wall.

"You better run," she said.

With a knowing, horrific smile, she pulled the door open as though it weighed no more than a leaf; then she cackled once at me, drew out the knives from her leg, and threw them to the floor.

"Vampire Queen," she scoffed, and descended.

* * *

The sand of the Wickham Beach made my kneecaps cold. With a shudder, I released my fingers, and the clean X-Acto knives clinked as they fell out of a sweatshirt I had taken from the Hopper lobby. Now that Claudia was dead, I couldn't leave any evidence behind.

My fingers trembled as I rewrapped the knives inside the blue Wickham sweatshirt. I curled my hand around the fabric, keeping the sharp knives tucked away. How could I think they would be a weapon against Odette?

I stared at the hills of sand, knowing that once, not that long ago, I could see their infinitesimal specifics. But I didn't focus, not really. My back shuddered as I drew in breaths. I expected to cry; that would have been a normal human reaction. But as I sat there on that beach, I could not find the capacity. I just stared at the sand, my whole body shaking.

There was a jingle of keys behind me, then a shuffling of sand as someone walked toward me.

Let it be Odette.

Let her take me away. Let us be done with it.

Out of the corner of my right eye, I saw a pair of black combat boots stop next to me. On my left, another set of boots, worn down, the front lip of the toe separated from the leather. I looked up at Rhode.

These boots were another small clue that he had lived the year before. That he had been mortal and walked through the world. He fell to his knees but did not touch me.

"Claudia Hawthorne is dead," Rhode said.

"I ran down the stairs just minutes . . . No," I said breathlessly. I couldn't stop the air from coming in and out so quickly. I looked at the waves rolling ahead of me. "I ran away mere seconds before security ran upstairs."

"You're better off," Vicken said. "It would have been an ugly mess of questioning and the human legal system." He knelt down on the other side of me. "The police are already deeming it an accident."

I shook my head, disbelief rolling over me. It trickled over my shoulders, down my back, all the way to my feet. Vicken picked up the sweatshirt holding the X-Acto knives.

"She has unbelievable strength. I don't know how. Not like us," I said, looking into Rhode's eyes. His eyebrows furrowed; his eyes jumped back and forth between the gauze on my arm and the sand. "Our strength was never heightened because we were vampires. And she can be out in the light of day with droves of people. She doesn't fear crowds."

"Come on," Vicken said, pulling me up by my elbow. "We should talk about this. But not here, not outside in the open."

"I agree," Rhode said, and glanced behind him at the stretch of trees that lined the beach. Anyone could have been hiding in the shadows.

Chapter Eighteen

That night, the whole school was abuzz with the news of Claudia's death. I was not sure which rumor was more ridiculous: that she was killed by a gang that had come in to steal tech equipment; that the art tower was haunted and a poltergeist killed Claudia; or that someone had purposefully unbolted the bookcases from their metal fixings so they would fall on her. None of it made sense, though I suppose to a normal human, it wouldn't. Extra maintenance had been called in, and classes were canceled for the next two days.

After yet another emergency school meeting, Rhode, Vicken, Justin, and I stood in my apartment. Rhode and Vicken stood by the balcony door, arms folded across their chests; Justin sat near me on the couch.

"So someone's gonna tell me what really happened, right?" Justin said, and looked to me. He rested his elbows on his knees and leaned forward, folding his hands. "Because I saw Lenah right before Claudia—" He dropped his head for a second. "—right before I heard."

"One by one. That's how it's going to go. The moment our guard is down," I said, looking at Rhode and Vicken with guilt running over me. "I can't figure out where she's getting this power. Without bleeding her, we have no defense. Especially if she can suck blood so quickly. How can she suck blood so quickly?"

My skin was too tight. I wanted to spit. I had been so selfish, going to the art tower. No, I had been selfish and stupid. She far outpowered me even when I was at my pinnacle strength as a vampire. She came to the mall, yes, but she could have sneaked inside through a basement, or stayed under cover in a car. There were ways to avoid direct sunlight. And she had purposely sought me out alone. This time she had walked onto a crowded campus. With hundreds of people. She was becoming much more powerful.

"We need a strategy," Vicken said.

"We have each other," I replied.

"We've got shite," Vicken said flatly. "Tell him what we did, Lenah."

"Thank you, Vicken," I said, hoping he caught the sarcasm in my tone.

"Tell me what?" Rhode asked.

I stood up from the couch and crossed my arms over my chest. "I tried to call Suleen. For help. But it was unsuccessful," I admitted.

"What do you mean, you tried to call Suleen?" Rhode asked quietly, leaning forward.

Vicken cleared his throat. "See, we did this summoning spell."

"You what?" Rhode said, pushing off the wall and throwing his hands into the air. "Vicken—you didn't think it necessary to tell me this?"

"What, he's your spy?" I asked.

"It seemed like it might be useful!" Vicken replied, but he was talking to Rhode.

"Have you no sense at all? It's as if you two were never immortal. I'm surprised she didn't find you while you were performing the bloody spell and stab you both through the heart."

"Some things are worth trying," I said. I kept my arms crossed but leaned against the closed door to my bedroom.

"Like hurting your arm? That's when it happened, isn't it?" Rhode asked. I didn't reply. "You let her do this?" Rhode said, turning to Vicken.

"Like I could stop her, mate."

"Suleen can offer us protection," I explained.

"Don't mention these things in front of him!" Rhode said, motioning to Justin. "He doesn't understand."

Justin sneered. "I understand fine."

It appeared Rhode hadn't heard Justin, because he kept staring at me, then continued, "Don't you think I tried myself? I called Suleen after you told me you saw Odette at the Herb Shop. He did not respond. You made that choice on the archery—" He stopped himself and considered what he would say next. He drew a shallow breath. "No one is coming to help us."

I had always believed that, out of any of us, Rhode would be able to reach Suleen. After the memories I saw, I'd been sure he would come.

"What does Odette want?" Justin asked.

"To be Lenah," Vicken said.

"The ritual," Rhode said to Justin.

"Can't we just give it to her?" Justin asked. "And avoid more deaths?"

Vicken laughed cruelly, the sound cutting the air.

"What's the big deal?" Justin asked, looking back and forth from Vicken to me.

"What's the big deal?" Vicken asked.

Rhode sighed. "If supernatural creatures pour their intentions into a spell that powerful, it will backfire. The ritual could anoint Odette with unimaginable powers. Could release real evil and draw entities to Lovers Bay that don't drink blood—but drink souls," he explained.

My dream from earlier that month of an abandoned Wickham and a ruined Lovers Bay resurfaced in my mind.

There was a palpable silence, then Vicken said, "It's not like we can barrier-spell the entire campus."

Rhode sighed. "What shall we do?" he asked, but it was rhetorical. "Shall we wear garlic in our hair? Crosses around our necks?"

"We need Suleen," I said again. "Or we could call the Aeris. They're more powerful than any vampire."

"We can't call on them," Rhode growled. "You just failed calling Suleen. Now you wish to call entities even more powerful?"

"Why not? We have time. Nuit Rouge begins in a couple of weeks. The barrier between our world and the supernatural world is weakening already."

"Lenah, you barely got out of that art tower alive," Rhode replied.

"So what, then?" I said. "Stay locked in our rooms for the rest of eternity?"

"We need to prepare ourselves," Rhode said. "We know Odette's weakened when she bleeds. We just have to find the right moment to attack in the only way we have left."

The only way. Of course . . .

There was a pause and then I said what I knew was on Vicken's and Rhode's minds.

"Weapons," I said, and met Justin's eyes.

Rhode nodded once.

There it was—our last and only hope. For our human bodies were no match for Odette and her unnatural powers.

"This is how it should go," Rhode offered. "We're never alone." He looked at me. "We're never unarmed. It's very simple. We remain at the ready at all times. Carry a dagger everywhere, stay in full public view." His eyes scanned the room, finally resting on Justin. "This is what it's like to be the hunted."

Claudia Hawthorne's funeral was held on the night of the harvest moon, the start of the month of Nuit Rouge, October 1. The tide was higher than ever in recorded history, with waves picking up twelve and a half feet and then crashing onto Lovers Bay shore. It was a short service, during which I kept my eyes to the cemetery ground. When the students boarded the buses back to campus, Rhode left a jasmine flower on Claudia's coffin. If only they knew why. If only they realized why we felt so responsible.

When we returned to school, Tracy walked quickly. She darted across the quad toward her dorm.

I watched her go. With Claudia's and Kate's deaths, all that remained of the Three Piece was Tracy Sutton. I expected her to leave this cursed place, to run home to the comfort of her parents. About a dozen members of the sophomore and junior classes had now left school permanently.

As the days went on, some students continued to wear black, but slowly color came back into the mix, as well as enthusiasm for the upcoming Halloween dance. It seemed to be the only thing we had left to look forward to on campus. In between discussions of the various carnival booths and the costumes people were buying for the dance, the school announced they wanted to plant a tree near Hopper in Claudia's memory. Didn't these mortals know pine trees planted unnaturally would bring sadness to those who sat beneath? Did they know that oaks are the trees to bring peace? Yet they wanted to plant a pine, and I couldn't exactly make my objections openly.

I wondered if Claudia had already joined the white light of the Aeris. The thought of her there dead because of me, victim of a vampire made by me, made me drop my dagger into my boot every morning after brushing my teeth. Any time I thought to leave it at home, I remembered Claudia's fine blond hair fluttering around her lifeless body.

A few days after Claudia's funeral, Vicken and I made our way to the Union to have breakfast. We watched members of the senior class bring streamers and cardboard skeletons to decorate the gymnasium for the Halloween dance at the end of the month—October 31, the last and most powerful night of Nuit Rouge.

Across the green, behind Quartz, Tracy emerged from the small dorm for senior girls. I had to look twice to make sure it was actually her. She had dyed her hair a dark brown, and her cheekbones were so pronounced, she didn't look like the same person. She was gaunt and sallow, so unlike the vibrant, glowing girl from the year before. The one who matched her outfits and paraded around the campus. The girl who wore makeup to exercise and had matched her pajamas with those of her friends. Friends who were now both gone. A strength emanated from her now; the steely hardness of someone who has held the hand of Death. I did not wish that for her so soon in life. She had a backpack over her shoulder and was dressed as she had been for weeks, all in black. She was heading toward the section of the woods that remained unguarded.

"Where do you think she's going?" Vicken asked.

Tracy glanced back onto the campus to see if anyone was behind her and tugged the backpack more tightly over her shoulder.

"I'm following her," I said.

"No, Lenah." Vicken held me back by my arm. I wrenched it out of his grasp.

"You know what will happen the moment she's alone," I said.

Vicken considered me, then said, "Well you're not going alone."

"Let me get a head start," I said, and jogged across the grass to Tracy, who was just passing in front of the library.

"Tracy," I called. "Hey! Wait up."

She turned and I was expecting her to smile at me, but instead she pushed me away roughly. "No. Stay away from me."

I found myself blinking stupidly. The blue of her eyes really popped next to the contrast of her darkened hair.

"Me?" I asked. "You want me to stay away from you?"

Tracy adjusted the weight on her feet, and something jangled in her backpack. A clinking metal sound. "Where are you going, Tracy?" I asked.

"Nowhere." She scowled and crossed her arms over her chest. Another jangle.

"This is ridiculous," I replied. Behind Tracy, down the side wall of the library, Vicken inched toward us. He lit a cigarette and pretended, with a leg resting against the wall, that he was simply sneaking out for a smoke.

"I have to go now," Tracy said. She turned and took two steps toward the woods.

"No, Tracy. It's not safe," I said, and almost as it came out of my mouth, I knew I had said too much.

But she didn't listen to me. She ran for it.

After a few moments, Vicken joined me at my side.

"She's carrying weapons," I said.

"What kind?" Vicken asked, and we started to jog along behind Tracy. She was already on Main Street.

"I don't know."

"Did she say where she was going?" Vicken asked.

"No, but I have a good idea."

·· —◆·:

Vicken and I made sure, as always, to keep to the shadows. The late-afternoon sun shone through the bare branches, and my black boots crunched over the jewel-colored leaves that sprinkled over the ground.

"I only have one dagger," I whispered as we turned into the cemetery.

"I have two," Vicken replied.

"How long until Odette arrives, do you think?" I asked.

"Minutes," Vicken said gravely.

I kept having to remind myself it was Tracy as we followed behind. Her hair now fell in long waves of chocolate brown. She grasped the straps of her bag and turned, as I expected, down the row with Tony's gravestone.

"What the hell is she doing?" Vicken asked.

"Come on," I whispered, and we inched our way up the pathway to join her. I stopped, gasping a bit when we reached Tony's row. Tracy had dropped her backpack and was kneeling on the grass. She ran her fingers over the strange circle of upturned earth Rhode's sword had made around the grave.

I wrapped my hand around Vicken's arm. We stepped back into the shadows of a nearby oak and I did what I had been trained to do for hundreds of years. I watched. She knelt down, lowered to her hip, and leaned on one hand with her other arm outstretched in front of her on the grave. She leaned her weight on that one arm and peered down at the even soil.

Tracy's hand gripped the dirt tight, her head fell limp, and she broke into cries. Her supporting arm gave way and she fell onto the grave, hiding her face in the crook of her arm. I watched her back heave. Her sobs were uneven, the kind of crying a person does when she thinks she is alone.

Daylight clung to the sky, but this was Nuit Rouge, so the light provided no protection. The attack could happen at any moment. I bent forward, eyes out at the woods surrounding the cemetery. The birds chirped as they settled down for the evening. The wind was light, bringing with it the musky smell of soil. As a former hunter, I paused and took the time to listen. A hunter listens for unnatural movement in the air. Even air moves. It can leave an echo. For now, it seemed we were alone.

I walked down the row from the cemetery path, Vicken behind me. Tracy snapped her head up, her eyes streaked with tears. She reached into her backpack and pulled out a crucifix.

"Stay away from me!" she screamed.

Vicken jumped back and pulled out a dagger. His arm dropped when he realized she wasn't holding something dangerous.

"You're kidding me, right?" Vicken asked. "First of all, those don't work, and second, we're not vampires."

"You know who did this!" Tracy shrieked at me.

"Who?" Vicken asked. "Did what?"

"Who killed Claudia!" she yelled, but looked at me. "Justin told me you were in there with her. In the art tower."

"I didn't touch Claudia," I said.

"Or is it you?" she spat, now looking at Vicken. "We all know what you're capable of. The art tower is your favorite place."

Tracy stood atop Tony's rounded grave. All I could see, carved into the granite headstone, was the word ARTIST. Her body blocked the rest of the epitaph.

"Tracy, calm down. It wasn't us," I said.

"I was the one who went into your room with Tony last year. I saw the picture of you and Rhode on your bureau from like a hundred years ago. You come to this school and guess who dies? Tony. Then both my best friends. Am I next, Lenah? Am I?" She finally broke, her face collapsing, and she sobbed, dropping the crucifix onto the grass.

Vicken and I shared a look. I walked to Tracy and wrapped my arms around her. She wept into my shoulder, making it wet almost immediately.

There was a clapping sound.

Someone was clapping.

Someone was clapping?

"So, the mortal knows you're ex-vampires?" Odette said, appearing through the trees on the edge of the cemetery. "If only she knew how you used to murder children for pleasure."

This time I was ready.

"Get behind me, Tracy," I ordered, and a memory of the art tower flashed through my mind.

I reached down into my boot and whipped out the dagger. I held it outstretched in front of me.

The heart. The heart. Aim for the heart.

Odette sneered, fangs bared. Tracy's fingers gripped onto my shoulders. Odette walked toward us, and Vicken—my wonderful Vicken—ran at her, dagger raised in the air. Odette got to him first. She wrapped her fingers around his wrist and tossed him as though he weighed nothing. Vicken flew ten feet high through the air, and his body crumpled at the base of a tree.

He lay unmoving. My gut clenched but I had to stay focused. I had to do this.

I would not fail Tracy as I had failed Claudia. Not this time.

I stood my ground and extended my dagger in front of me.

"Have you learned nothing? Why would you leave campus without your precious Rhode?" Odette said, and clawed at me. Tracy and I jumped back; Odette barely missed my chest.

"Tracy, run," I commanded.

Odette moved so quickly, she was a blur of honey and black, but I knew that was what she would do. I grabbed Tracy by her shoulders, throwing her to the ground, and planted myself in front of Odette. She clawed at my chest—her nails ripped through my shirt down to my skin—and I screamed out, pain searing through my chest.

Odette laughed, then threw a malevolent glance down at Tracy. I knew what I must do to protect her; I went for it. While she laughed at my pain, I stabbed Odette in the forearm. The blade plunged into the hardened vampire skin. No measly X-Acto knife this time. This knife stopped her. Odette stared at the wound, as though she couldn't believe I had done it.

"That's a perfectly good fisherman oozing out of my arm," Odette spat.

Down at her feet, Tracy pulled a large silver blade from her bag. It flickered in the rays of the setting sun, but Odette didn't seem to notice. She sneered and stepped toward me, intending to retaliate. I raised my dagger, ready to plunge again.

Odette hadn't considered the human at her feet. Why would she? Hope slid through me as Tracy stabbed Odette hard right in the center of her leather shoe. Odette screamed, falling back onto the grass.

"Go!" I yelled, meeting Tracy's watery blue eyes.

This time, she followed orders.

She ran away through the maze of tombstones and trees. Suddenly I was flying through the air. Odette had swept her good foot under me, making me fall to the ground.

I flew back and, with a thud, hit the ground on my back, sending more pain through the cuts on my chest. Winded, I tried to draw in air but I couldn't. *Breathe, Lenah.* A kick slammed onto the right side of me. Another kick on the left. Odette's hideous dandelion-colored curls dangled before me, and her devilish smile faded as tears flooded my eyes, washing out my sight.

"Did your little friend think stabbing my foot was going to stop me? Haven't you seen how powerful I am?" I struggled to draw in breath. "I am only to get more powerful as the days go on. Oh, darling, are you having trouble breathing?"

She squatted above me and lifted an index finger, showing me her knifelike nails again just as she had in the dressing room. Slowly, I was able to draw a shallow breath, my frozen lungs finally thawing out. She pointed to my bandaged arm.

No . . . don't stab me.

"Of course I'm going to stab you," she said, reading my emotional plea with her ESP. "I thought I warned you, but I guess you don't listen. Being a queen and all, you think you still call the shots. But not anymore." She hovered her long red fingernails over the gauze of my burned forearm. "Give. Me. The ritual."

"Never," I said, gulping down air.

She sneered and then stabbed my injured forearm. Her fingernails sliced through the gauze onto my still-raw skin. A ripping sound, then hot pain seared my burnt arm. I screamed so loudly that it scratched my throat. The pain was so intense, acrid bile made its way to my mouth. Where was Vicken?

"Why, Queen of all vampires? Why do you insist on making this so difficult for yourself?"

Queen of all vampires.

As she looked down at me, with her porcelain skin and bloody mouth, time seemed to slow. Our eyes connected. My blue—her green. Together. Yes. Within her eyes, I could see myself as a vampire, throwing my head back, mouth agape, laughing into the night.

How familiar was the overwhelming desire to feel once again. All we wanted to do was feel. So numb. No feeling in my fingers or hands. Release the pain. Need the blood running down my mouth and the power to surge through my body. I could sense the duality within myself.

I was the Vampire Queen again.

Catch them by surprise. A public spectacle. On Halloween.

These were Odette's thoughts. I knew her plan because in that moment as her unnatural jade eyes stared into mine, I could see her plan. It was just as I would have formulated it.

She was going to try to kill me at the Halloween dance, when I would be too busy trying to protect the humans around me. I could see the decorations; I could see Vicken's and Rhode's bodies, bloody and dead on the gymnasium floor.

And with this remembrance of my vampire evil came some of the memories I had forgotten in my human state.

Odette's murder, when she was made a vampire.

"I remember the day you changed," I whispered shakily. "It was only hours before my hibernation. I told Vicken to make you a vampire. But he did not. And I desired the rush, the high of bringing another night wanderer into the world."

She pulled back and the straight line of her fingers curled over for the barest second. My arm throbbed again, sending tears of pain to my eyes. It was easier to say this when I couldn't see her clearly.

"I'm sorry," I said. "I'm sorry for what I did."

She curled her hands over my shoulders. She lifted me just slightly and then with a push threw me back to the ground.

"Don't distract me!" she yelled.

Pain throbbed at the front of my head.

"I attacked Rhode in Hathersage in order to get the ritual, but all he could do was set the bloody place on fire. You're both cowards. I am going to take you with me tonight. I'm going to take you with me and then—" She gave me an evil, bone-chilling smile, "—when Rhode comes for you, and you are dead, chained to the wall, he'll tell me all about this ritual."

"It's useless to you," I spat. "You're not powerful enough to bring forth the darkness you seek." I tried to stare into her eyes again, to call back our connection, but it didn't work.

"You don't know anything about my power," Odette said, raising her fingers, ready to strike again.

I grimaced in anticipation.

Suddenly she hunched over. There was an awful thud and the sound of ripping flesh. Vicken's dagger was pinned through her neck. She fell over, grasping at her neck, and rolled onto her back, grabbing for the hilt of the dagger.

Vicken appeared next to me with his wild hair and a bloody scrape on his cheek. He lifted his boot and stepped lightly on her stomach. She bared her fangs and hissed.

"Now, now, play nice," he said.

"She's very strong," I warned.

"That's why I stabbed her, love," Vicken said out of the corner of his mouth. "Now, tell us, where did you get your super strength?" he asked, still resting his boot on her stomach.

"I've performed spells you've never dreamed of," she sneered. "Each time growing faster, stronger, and more cunning."

But now I could see fear in her eyes. She was bleeding from the neck so it fell over her shoulder and onto the dirt. She tried to push herself up but collapsed with a thud back onto the ground, still under Vicken's boot.

"Lenah, I need another dagger," Vicken said, gesturing at Tracy's knife, which lay near Tony's grave.

Odette struggled against Vicken's boot, baring her fangs like an animal.

Yes, I had made her a vampire, though I did not make her a vampire in the attic as I had originally planned. I had moved the misery downstairs. She hid behind my ancient furniture. Her eyes then had been beautiful and green, desperate for salvation. The first night I had tried to kill her, she outsmarted me, ran from the attic, and found her family by the stables out in the back gardens.

"Lenah! The knife," Vicken cried.

Her father had begged. Naturally, I killed him first.

I stared at the ground. Ella had been her given name.

"I have a life to lead," she'd said, pleading with me.

"Do you?" I'd said with a merciless laugh.

From out of my reverie, I heard Vicken's voice. "The dagger! She's healing!"

"No, you pathetic child," I'd continued. "I have a life to lead and I can't take my hibernation unless I am full. You are young and healthy."

I hated the sound of my vampire self.

"Please . . . ," Odette's human voice echoed in my head.

Followed by the same, dead laugh. How I had laughed and laughed as she cried for mercy and begged me to spare her life.

"Lenah!" Vicken shouted again. I refocused on the ground and on Odette grasping her fingers around the knife protruding from her neck.

I couldn't move. A sickening feeling passed through me. Unmistakable and undeniable.

Odette pulled the bloody knife out of her neck. She jumped up and kicked out at Vicken, who fell. In the time it took for him to get back onto his feet, she had run into the woods.

"What the hell are you doing?" he yelled at me.

I shrugged helplessly. His protest was cut off when Tracy came out of nowhere, snatched the knife from Tony's grave, and ran toward the woods.

"Hey!" Vicken called after Tracy. "Crazy girl, get back here! Now!"

Tracy stopped at the edge of the wood, the knife still hanging by her side.

Odette had vanished.

Vicken walked down the long lane of gravestones and stopped next to Tracy.

He offered her his hand, and she motioned to hand him the knife. He shook his head. She lifted her eyes to meet his and then considered his palm again. It was enough to make my heart break. She dropped the knife to the grass and wrapped her fingers in his.

Chapter Nineteen

W here did you come from?" Vicken asked Tracy. "I thought you ran out of the cemetery."

"I hid by the mausoleum. When I saw her run away, I don't know, I got brave for a moment," Tracy admitted.

I held Tracy's sweatshirt to my injured arm as we walked back through the campus towers and past the security guard. The sweatshirt soaked up some of the blood that had seeped through the cut on my arm, but aside from the throbbing, the pain wasn't bad.

"I'm sorry," I said, "that I didn't . . ."

"It's all right," Vicken replied.

"It's not all right," I said. "I froze."

Tracy's expression was pensive. "It took me all summer to accept Tony's death." Vicken bowed his head a bit. She looked at him. "Did you kill him because you were a vampire?"

"We do many things as vampires that we would never dream of doing in human form," he replied gently.

"She killed Kate and Claudia, didn't she?" Her eyes shone in the ghostly blue of the early-evening light.

I nodded.

"I've spent all summer looking up how to kill vampires. I know why you have a sword on your wall. Why you keep herbs on your door. Lavender is supposed to protect your home. And rosemary." She ran a hand through her hair. "Rosemary is for remembrance." She pulled a chain out from beneath her shirt. It was a silver locket. When she opened it, there was a sprig of dried rosemary.

My breath was short. I couldn't help staring.

"Tony researched you too," she said. "It's why you wore those sparkly ashes around your neck last year. Like the ones I saw on your balcony. Then Justin confirmed it," she said. "That you were—" She paused and her eyes met mine. "—that you were a vampire."

I had never believed Tracy to be that astute. Perhaps I had always underestimated her.

"I loved Tony," I said. The center of my chest ached, taking the pain away from my arm. "He was my best friend."

"I'm not going to say anything," she said. "About either of you. It took me all summer just to accept that the rumors could be true. And then Justin confirmed it." She ran her hand through her hair again. "Well, he didn't so much confirm it as I forced him to tell me."

"How?" I asked. The prickly feeling of betrayal dissolved as she spoke.

"I threatened to smash the lights of his car. When that didn't work, I showed him all my research. Everything I found. I told him about the pictures. He finally told me the truth."

"You and Tony are more alike than I thought," I said. Her tenacity reminded me of how he too had unearthed my secret all on his own.

"I want to know. Someday. Not today, but I want to know what happened to Tony." She looked at Vicken as she said it. "That's all. Can you promise me?"

"Yes," he said. "I promise."

213

We started to walk across the campus into the busy student body, all walking in twos and threes to the Union or the library or their dorms.

"What do we do about the Halloween dance?" Tracy asked.

"You stay out of the way, love," Vicken said, lighting a cigarette.

"If you need me, I'll help you," Tracy said, and pulled her bag from the cemetery tighter over her shoulder. "Any way I can."

That night, I stood at my balcony door, looking out at the tiles. Only when I moved did I occasionally see the flicker of my vampire remains. I reached into my pocket and felt the gift card Claudia had bought me for my birthday.

"So it felt like your extrasensory perception was back," Rhode said.

"Yes," I replied. "It was very clear to me what Odette wanted. I could sense her deepest desires. I saw images from her plans for Halloween night."

"What could have caused it to come back?" Justin asked.

The only explanation I could fathom was that the bond created between Odette and me on that dark day a hundred years ago linked me eternally to her mind.

"I was her maker," I whispered. "It's the only explanation. I understood her motivations, as much as I didn't want to."

"Why didn't you kill her when you had the chance?" Rhode asked.

I locked my gaze on him and kept my jaw tight. My heart thudded. I hated thinking of myself in that moment, with the dagger by my side, Vicken at the ready. I didn't know how to answer this. I knew this woman. She was alone and afraid and I had sucked the very life from her. I had killed her. Worse, I had created the monster she became. Her death circled in my mind—the memory of how warm she'd been, how her body trembled from fear, and my joy at taking both her warmth and her life.

I met Rhode's eyes. "Because I already have killed her. I'm sorry, but it's the truth, and it paralyzed me."

Silence, then Vicken said, "On that note, it's time for dinner."

There was a clink from Vicken's boots as he stood up, and the shuffle of papers being moved. I turned my back on the living room and faced the balcony again. I knew what was coming in a few days' time and I would have only an old sword and a couple of daggers to take down Odette. I didn't know if I could make myself do it.

"You okay?" Justin asked me, placing a hand on my shoulder. His voice was close to my ear.

The door closed and I realized that Vicken and Rhode had left without saying good-bye. It meant that Justin and I were alone together for the first time since the night of my birthday.

I leaned my back against the glass balcony door and looked at the knowledge rune on Justin's neck. I focused on it. He had put it on backwards and it hung upside down. I didn't have the heart to tell him he had put it on wrong.

Justin kissed my forehead and when he pulled back, he smiled at me. His eyes lingered on mine. I thought of him that day, the day I'd turned Vicken human again with the ritual. How Justin had fallen to his knees when I walked out onto my balcony. I had been so ready to leave it all behind.

"That's the most difficult part," I murmured to myself. "The ingredients are important, of course, but the sacrifice, the intent, it's always the most important part of any ritual."

The intent . . .

Images from the summoning spell floated into my mind: the jump of the flames and the door glowing in the sand. Were my intentions pure? Had I been channeling my intentions into the spell so that it would bring me what I desired?

"Of course," I said aloud. "Of course." The spell backfired because my intentions hadn't been pure. In order for the spell to work, I needed to channel my intentions in one direction only, but mine were split. I wanted protection from Odette, but really I was calling Suleen to me for Rhode's benefit.

I knew what I had to do!

My spirits lifted considerably.

"I need your help," I said to Justin.

"Okay . . . ," he said.

The bright spark in his eyes glowed at me. It reminded me why I had slept in his tent the night of my birthday. Why I let his touch take me back to last year, when I'd thought that being a human was going to be simple. That I could be a seventeen-year-old girl in love, with no repercussions from her past.

But there will always be payment for your atrocities. That's why the intent behind all spells matters.

"Lenah?" Justin said.

"I'm going to perform it again," I said.

"What? The summoning spell?" Justin asked.

"Yes." The fire in my belly was back. Yes. Yes. I would perform it again, keeping my intentions pure, and call Suleen. This time he would come!

"Let's go."

After grabbing Rhode's spell book, *Incantato,* a jar for the water, and all the ingredients I would need, I raced down the stairs of Seeker, ignoring the burn on my arm, which was twingeing. I ran past students sitting in the hallway putting together Halloween costumes.

"Wait, hey!" Justin called.

"Keep up!" I said, and stepped outside the dorm. I found Vicken sitting on the bench in front of Seeker, a cigarette in his hand.

"Hold on," Vicken said when he realized I wasn't going to stop and chitchat. "Where are you going?"

"I'm going to perform the summoning spell again."

"Oh, right," he said, following me. "So, you've officially gone mad."

I kept going, not caring what he thought.

Justin joined us in the parking lot.

"What's he doing here? Where are we going?" Justin asked.

"We're going back to Lovers Bay beach," I said, throwing a glance at Vicken as I unlocked the car.

"You're bloody mad, you know that? I can't even smoke, I'm so angry," Vicken said.

I opened the door and tossed the bag filled with the spell ingredients and the book into the car.

"Then I consider this trip a success already," I said.

I was about to slide into the driver's seat when Vicken stopped me again by turning my shoulder.

"Lenah. You could die. You're barely healed now." He glanced at my bandaged arm. "Didn't we learn our lesson last time we left campus?"

"If Lenah wants to do it, she'll do it without you," Justin said from the passenger-side door.

"Pretty boy, you've got no idea what you're talking about. So get away from the car and shut it."

Justin came around the side of the car so fast that I stumbled to get between them.

"You could die too," Vicken said to Justin through clenched teeth.

"I'm doing this," I said, my hands pressed against Vicken's heaving chest. "And we agreed not to leave campus alone. I'm not alone." I motioned to Justin.

"Then I'm coming too. Three is stronger," Vicken sneered.

He met my eyes and took a step back. "Triangles are symbols of infinity. It could work . . . better."

"Good," I said, and Justin also backed away. "If you promise me you won't fight. I have to stay focused."

"I will," Justin replied. "If he promises not to get close to me. I'm not a fan of murderers."

I spun round, anger swirling in my chest. "Then you're not a fan of me."

Justin's expression was stunned. His jaw dropped. "I didn't—I mean."

"Just get in the car," I said. "Both of you."

As I drew the outline of a door, the sand was cool on my finger. The moon hung over the horizon. This time we were doing the spell at dusk.

"You're ready? You're sure?" Vicken asked.

Justin's eyes were wide as he stared down at the door. And strangely, he was almost smiling. When he caught my eye, he quickly dropped his expression, his mouth becoming a thin line.

"Sorry, just—you know—never seen a ritual before," he said.

I unscrewed the jar with the harbor water and sprinkled it over the flames.

"I summon you, Suleen, to this sacred place." My eyes lifted to the moon still hanging low in the sky. "I call you here to protect us from the impending danger." And I meant it. I wanted to protect our souls, our lives.

The amber came next, and when the slick resin hit the flames, the doorframe, just like last time, burned a bright gold. Vicken and Justin stared at the fiery outline.

"I summon you," I repeated. The fire crackled again, the flames lower than the last time. Good! Yes! This time it seemed it would work!

The wind whipped through my hair, and a great blast came up from the fire yet again.

I jumped back. I expected a ten-foot flame to jump into the sky. But no. The fire was completely out, leaving behind charred and blackened wood.

A miniscule blue ball of light sat in the center of the wood, exactly where the flame had been. The blue orb hovered directly over the embers of the fire, glowing and expanding into a vertical oblong shape as the seconds passed.

"What—?" Justin said.

"Shhh . . . ," I replied.

The blue orb grew to the size of the door I had drawn in the sand. It glowed for a few more moments, and I expected Suleen, the man I had grown to love, to step through. I expected to see his white clothing and familiar turban.

The door did not open. Like an old-fashioned film, it flickered on, playing a scene in a ballroom in a familiar mansion. The blue light from the orb grew brighter and larger.

"Oh no," Vicken said.

Heartbeat—a pulse.

The blue orb took over almost the whole sky. So big—a portal to another world? No . . .

A blast of blue light and then . . .

HATHERSAGE 1740

Vicken, Justin, and I were part of the scene before us, standing on the edge of the ballroom.

"We're in Hathersage," Vicken said in awe.

"Shhh," I said, waving a hand across myself as though to wipe away the power of his voice.

Justin said nothing. He watched the scene play out before him, with his jaw dropping in disbelief, fear, or both.

Glasses filled with blood clinked together. A small orchestra of vampires played in the corner of the room. Chatter from dozens of vampires echoed throughout my banquet hall.

"Lenah, what is this?" Vicken asked. "I don't recognize these people."

"This was before your time."

I knew what this was. This was the horrific night that secured my infamy throughout the world.

This was the night I killed a child.

We three mortals stood invisible to the partying vampires.

I gasped as I caught sight of my vampire self spinning around, a goblet in hand. My gown was black and corseted, covered with large jet black roses. The 1740s was a colorful era, but I had worn black . . . on purpose. My silk dress was stitched with roses of jet and black pearls.

"Did you know," my vampire self said, "that Nuit Rouge is the month in which you can access black magic?" The corset pressed into her ribs as she laughed, leaping over the body of a man in a white tunic and black breeches. A local farmer drained of all his blood. "Tonight is All Hallows' Eve!"

The vampires around her lifted their goblets in the air.

Bright torches threw the hall into an orange, dreamy light.

A vampiric Rhode stepped into the doorway of the banquet hall in his finest silk. He wore his traditional black, his hair slicked back so his turquoise eyes glowed out from the darkness of the hallway behind him. He slid his palm over his mouth and ran across the room to the body of the child whom he'd buried only hours before. Now she lay in the corner of the room, where I wanted her placed. Just for the evening.

"I unburied her! With my bare hands!" My vampire self called to him, laughing and taking a deep swig from a goblet of her blood. The dancing intensified in the middle of the room, all the vampires jumping to a lively drum.

"Isn't it lovely?" she called to Rhode, who was on his knees by the dead child. "She sort of looks like me, don't you think? She could be my little sister."

The flowers bounced with the vibration from the dozens of feet jumping on the floor, up and down and up and down. Roses, lavender, daisies, orchids, all in a fragrant abundance. Vampire Lenah picked up some daisies and roses and brought them to Rhode, who still remained on his knees, staring down at the child.

My vampire self covered the child's eyes with daisy heads. The petals reached her eyebrows.

"I'm going to give her a proper burial," said my vampire self happily. "I've invited all of our friends in Derbyshire," she continued, dancing a circle around Rhode, holding her gown so she could scoot around him and the dead girl. She scattered roses and daisies over the body. "And this young lady! Here's a daisy: I would give you some violets, but they withered all when my father died: they say he made a good end."

Rhode stood up. As I watched, I knew what was coming next.

"Oh, come now, don't you enjoy Master Shakespeare?" asked vampire Lenah.

He looked to the other bodies scattered about the floor. His eyes met vampire Lenah's. She held his gaze for a few moments.

"Why?" he asked.

"Why? Her blood is the purest!" My vampire self walked to the body of the young girl, still in her white dress, and merrily scattered even more flowers over her.

"No more!" Rhode yelled. He gripped my shoulders, sending me back against the wall with a thud. "Lenah, what have you become!"

Lenah laughed at his earnest gaze. "Oh, come on, I'll have someone bury her again when the party is over."

He growled and it was almost a scream. His eyebrows furrowed together in a pinch. This was the pain of a vampire who wanted to cry. Rhode gripped vampire Lenah again and shook her so hard that her shoulders vibrated and her teeth chattered. I hated watching myself like this.

"Why can't you just let me love you?" Rhode said, his teeth clenched together.

"Because I am unraveling," my vampire self said. "And power is the only release from pain. Not love."

He let go and swept from her then, walking down the darkened hallway. I watched my vampire self run after him into the distance. I followed, Justin and Vicken in my wake.

"What are you doing?" she cried. "Rhode!"

But he did not answer. He kept walking until he reached the hall in the front of the house. By the door was a small black leather bag; he grabbed the small handle and whipped open the door. The sunset, a burning orange, scorched my eyes. Vampire Lenah instinctively threw her hands across her face, but this was 1740, and after 322 years, she did not need to fear the sun.

"Rhode!" she called.

"You are reckless," Rhode hissed, whipping around. "Power will not save you. It will only further the deterioration of your mind." He walked out the door and away from the house and toward the endless sweeping hills. Lenah took a few steps after him.

"I know what I am doing," she said, bringing her feet together and raising her chin defiantly.

Vicken, Justin, and I watched from the doorway. Rhode stopped and turned to face vampire Lenah again.

"Do you?" Rhode moved closer so he was an inch away from her face. His fangs showed as he whispered, "Do you? You murdered a child. A child, Lenah."

"You always said that infant blood was the sweetest. The most pure."

Rhode looked horror stricken. He backed away from Lenah. "I said it as a fact, not as an invitation to sample it. You have changed. You are no longer the girl I loved in your father's orchard in the white nightgown."

His eyes had a misty look, and even within a memory, I could tell he was formulating his thoughts. "I told you to concentrate on me tonight. That if you focused on the love you feel for me—you can break free. But you can't do that, I see that now," he said. I watched myself try to speak, but Rhode continued before Lenah could find the words. "You've seen it yourself. Vampires your age begin to lose their minds. Most choose fire or a stake through the heart to bring them to their deaths, to avoid a slow descent into insanity. The prospect of forever is too much. And for you, the life you lost has made you insane. Living on this earth for all of eternity has brought your mind to a place where I can no longer reach you."

"I'm not insane, Rhode. I'm a vampire."

"You make me regret what I did in that orchard," he said sadly, starting his long descent into the countryside.

"You regret me?"

"Find yourself, Lenah. When you do, I will return."

My human self remembered this moment so clearly. Back then, I could have watched him leave. I could have followed his frame until he was out of my sight, but this time, the pain was too much. I wanted out of that blue light, out of that memory. Instead, I watched my vampire self turn and walk back into the brightly lit hall. Music echoed from the ballroom, but it was another world to me. My vampire self placed a hand on the stone wall. I remembered that the stones held no temperature nor could I feel the thick ridges beneath my fingers.

Nothing . . . nothing . . . nothing.

"I want out!" I yelled, falling down to my knees. The house was gone. My life was Wickham now. "Out!" I screamed.

A blast of blue light and the cold sand of Lovers Bay beach hit my knees. I fell to the ground, holding my face in my hands. A kind of cry came up like a wave. A huge surge of sadness. I had to draw in a breath; I could smell the salt of the sea and amber resin on my hands. I wept a horrible wailing kind of weeping. The tears slicked my hands and as I drew in ragged breaths of salty air, I let the horror of that memory wash over me in waves of embarrassment and shame.

Justin and Vicken were silent.

I had not brought Suleen to me. I had summoned the truth, a reminder of my true self. I was a killer.

And I deserved no help.

Chapter Twenty

I ran as fast as I could, sprinting down the long street away from the beach.

Come and get me, Odette. My chest ached from how hard my lungs had to work as I ran, but I kept running. The sound of feet slamming the pavement again and again and again echoed behind me.

"Lenah!" Justin's voice. "Lenah, it's not safe!"

I didn't reply. The biting wind nipped at my cheeks. A car engine revved and then screamed to a stop ahead of me. The headlights of my blue car swung around, and the car cut me off from running any farther. I backed away and brought the heels of my hands to my eyes.

I heard the slam of a door. Vicken's boots walking to me on the cement. Justin's feet hitting the pavement as he caught up behind me, then stopped.

"Don't touch me!" I screamed. The words burned my throat.

I looked to my palms.

"How much blood did we shed, Vicken?" I asked. My back shuddered as tears pushed their way through me and down my cheeks. "Answer me."

I shoved him on the chest so he fell back a few steps.

"I can't do this. I can't kill her. I've tried and I can't."

225

Vicken came to me and silently wrapped his arms around me. I cried into his chest until his shirt was wet through.

"You can do this. We'll help you," Vicken said.

His eyes stabbed to Justin, and they shared a gaze, one that said, yes, we were in this together.

Somehow I walked back to the car, somehow I climbed in, and I knew that somehow, I would have to find the killer within myself once more, and finish Odette.

⁘

I was silent in the passenger seat, my hand resting on the car window as we made our way back to Wickham. The sky still held a blue twinge, like the blue of the orb that had showed us my past. My horrible past. As Vicken drove, I could only wonder what he was thinking. I had explained it to him so many times, but now finally, he had seen a glimpse of my life before 1850, before he joined my madness.

Justin sat in the back, throwing questions at Vicken. "What the hell was that?"

"I don't know," he grumbled.

"But why did we see it?"

"I don't know," Vicken said again.

"But we—"

"Look, mate. Just shut it, all right?"

When we pulled onto Wickham campus, everyone was in full preparation mode for the Halloween carnival and dance. I got out of the car and inhaled cider and cinnamon coming from the Union. I started down the main path. *How strange,* I thought as I walked out of the parking lot and onto the grass. Vicken's and Justin's footsteps echoed behind me. But they were like drumbeats to me. *How strange,* I thought again as orange pumpkins and black streamers blurred into October colors. Like a Monet painting. It was all just a smattering of color I couldn't understand.

Students wove black lines of ribbon around lampposts. A crew of men and women were standing far out on the lacrosse field, putting up tents and booths. They didn't seem like students. Or maybe I didn't. Maybe I didn't know what I was anymore.

"Wait," Justin called softly. I kept walking.

"Let her go," I heard Vicken say.

I walked past Seeker, past the Curie building, where once, I couldn't dissect a frog, because I couldn't destroy another creature.

I continued past Hopper building. A hallowed place where I could not even glance at the great stone tower, because my two friends had died within those walls.

"Lenah!" Tracy called to me as I walked by Quartz dorm. She sat out front on a blanket alone, reading a book. I could not explain what had happened, so I ignored her. I turned to the greenhouse and opened the door. The misty, humid air engulfed me, and I hurried down the aisle, snatching roses, sage, and lavender from various pots. I held them in my fists and clenched hard. The petals crumpled under the pressure of my fingers. I sank to the floor.

That child . . .

There was a creak from the door behind me. Sneakers squeaked on the wet cement. The sudden gust of fresh air brought with it the humid smell of the greenhouse mixed with the smoke of a summoning spell gone wrong. Justin sank to his knees next to me. His warm hand slid over my palm and curled over the petals in my hands and between my fingers.

"I'm sorry you had to see that," I whispered. It was all I could say.

"You were," Justin started to say. "You were really powerful."

I lifted my eyes to him slowly. He leaned toward me and kept my gaze.

"Is that what you saw?" I asked. "Power?"

He opened his mouth to speak. All he was able to get out was no; then he immediately dropped his hand from mine. "I don't mean it like that. Just that . . . you didn't fear anything back then. You were—"

"Pure madness. Nothing more. Nothing less."

"True, it was. But . . ."

When I met his eyes, even their green color looked different. They did not remind me of the trees swaying on his parents' street. I did not see the evergreen leaves of the woods that surrounded Wickham Boarding School. Despite his best efforts, he would never understand me. He could not possibly know what it meant to be alive after being dead for so long. To have kissed Death and lived to tell the tale.

Justin grasped my hand. The warmth of his grip grounded me in the greenhouse. I pushed away the image of the little girl. Instead, I focused on the sounds of the plant misters and the reflections of the orange and black streamers outside. In this space, with the flowers and herbs, I was quiet, my mind able to soften the atrocity of what I had done. Justin rubbed his hand over mine. Last year, with all its beauty and happiness and its horrors, had made me a different person. I wasn't supposed to survive that ritual, but I did. And so did Rhode. It was never going to be like it was between Justin and me. Too much had changed. I had changed.

I would never love Justin.

I could go through every motion, wear the clothes, wear the perfume, and say all there was to say. But I was never meant to live in this modern world. I was never meant to be here.

I would live my life for Rhode even if it meant I had to live without him. He was the only person. My soul mate. My love.

Even if he could never forgive me.

Even if it was over.

Chapter Twenty-one

Once, long ago, I ran through an apple orchard dusted with snow. The wind bit at the tip of my nose. Arms out, I ran and ran, wind flying through my fingers and through my hair.

"Lenah! Lenah!" my mother called from the door of our house. She smiled at me as I turned and ran into the depths of the orchard. It was the fifteenth century, which meant we would burn the fires at all hours. Without it, we would die in the cold.

I stopped at the end of a long lane of a row of apple trees. The chill licked at my nose and I could feel it in the air not as a vampire would, but as a child of the medieval world. Spring was upon us; the snow was wet, almost like rain. I stood at the edge of my father's land and looked out at the great world beyond it. The woods were my favorite place at that time of year, the beautiful trees laced with silver and diamonds of ice. I drew in breaths of cool, fresh air. I stared into those woods, absolutely unafraid of the world beyond.

So Rhode will get the costumes?" Justin asked. "We can hide the weapons that way."

I stood in the study atrium on the night before Halloween with my back to the window. Justin, Rhode, and Vicken sat at a table looking over a drawing Rhode had made of the gymnasium.

"We know our positions?" Rhode asked, looking up from his drawing on the coffee table. "Lenah?"

I had looked at that sketch ten times now. I knew exactly what I would have to do; I just hoped I could do it.

"Let's go over it one more time," Rhode said.

I sighed and recited our plan for what seemed like the millionth time.

"We'll isolate the members of her coven so I can get a clean shot. One stab," I said, finally meeting his eyes. "One stab to the heart."

That night, I dreamt of vampires with no fangs. They were faceless demons: no eyes, no nose, just a mouth with gaping holes in the roofs of their mouths. Blood rolled from their smirking lips and onto their chins.

It was hard to shake the image when I awoke on Halloween morning. What helped was that the campus had gone through a complete metamorphosis. Banners read HAPPY HALLOWEEN; pumpkins lined the pathways and decorated entrances to many buildings. Classes were canceled. After Rhode returned from buying costumes, we decided that it would be best if we stayed in the midst of other students all day. I had knocked on Justin's door twice but he had not answered. He was, I guessed, already out and about with friends. I wondered why he wouldn't want to check in with me after everything that had happened the day before.

I stood staring at a carnival booth overlooking dozens of bowls of goldfish.

"Oh, just play the game," Vicken said. "One game in honor of Nuit Rouge. And this one won't involve you murdering someone for sport." He rolled his eyes at me. "You're not abandoning the school if you win a fish."

If I tossed a small ball into a bowl, I would take the tank home and keep that fish for a pet. I scoffed. Me? Keep something . . . alive?

Just as Vicken leaned his back against the booth of the Goldfish Toss, there was a *boom-boom, boom-boom* of bass drums.

"Oh no, here they come . . . again," he groaned. For the fourth time that afternoon, the school band banged on their drums and marched across the football field toward the carnival, looking like one giant mass of white wool. They wore funny hats with what looked like a bright gold quill pen on the top; one of the Wickham School colors. Many of the students around us abandoned their carnival games mid-toss or -throw and ran toward the football field. Vicken motioned with a disgusted wave of his arm.

"Look at them all! Abandoning their games. If I were in the middle of the ring toss, I would most certainly not quit!"

"You would take it so seriously," I said, eyeing the dozens of fishbowls, each with a graceful goldfish swishing its tail.

Vicken reached into his jacket pocket for a cigarette, then patted down each pocket of his pants in search of a lighter. There was a mechanical click, and then a plume of smoke as he took a drag of his cigarette.

"Look, all I'm saying is if you're going to do something, do it right."

"Vicken Clough! You put that out right now!"

Ms. Warner, the school nurse, blazed toward Vicken, her finger pointed directly at his chest. Vicken dropped the cigarette and stamped it out with his boot.

"My dear Ms. Warner! You're looking lovely today."

"How many times do I need to tell you, Vicken? Smoking is not allowed on campus. And you're not eighteen, so it's illegal. Hand it over."

"Hand what over?"

"The pack."

Vicken scoffed.

"Do not give me that look, Vicken. Hand them over."

I abandoned the fish to a more capable owner and placed the ball down.

"Not gonna throw?" the man operating the booth asked.

"Not today," I said.

As I walked away from Vicken and Ms. Warner, I thought about those goldfish. How they would live their whole lives in that tiny bubble. They would swim, swish, roll up and around in their little world.

Ahead of me, I saw that the crew team had changed the boat cabin into a haunted house. Wispy strands of fake cobwebs hung in lazy designs across the windows. Someone had hung up a black curtain so I couldn't see inside. The door burst open, and a student dressed in a white sheet pushed out two younger Wickham under-classmen. The couple grinned at each other and ran back toward the football field.

"That was actually kind of scary!" the girl giggled.

The ghost looked at me from two cut-out eyeholes.

"Come in! If you dare . . ."

I glanced back to see if Vicken had emerged, but there was too much of a crowd. Students ran from booth to booth; the band collected far down at the end of the row on the field in a synchro-nized march. Suddenly Rhode turned a corner and I froze. He smiled at me just a little, so that one corner of his mouth raised.

We shared that small moment but it was over too soon.

"Come in! Come in!" Ms. Williams said, gesturing toward the haunted house. She was dressed as a cat, with black fuzzy ears, tail, and all.

"In a minute," I said to her. Rhode stopped next to me and I waited to try to talk to him. From around a corner, Vicken emerged with what seemed like every single candy and sweet at the carnival.

With a candy apple in his mouth, he said, "What?"

"I can see you're just frightened to death about tonight," Rhode said.

"If you don't mind, I'd like something sweet before I have to fight for my life."

"Lenah! Vicken," Tracy called to us. Her tone was off-kilter, a line creased between her eyebrows. She seemed even more porcelain skinned with her hair so brown.

"Are you all right?" Vicken asked as more students ran by us into the haunted house.

"It's Justin. He never checked in with the resident advisor last night. Hasn't checked in today either. The school has called the police."

Rhode, Vicken, and I exchanged glances. My heart gave a little twinge. I wouldn't panic. Not yet. It wasn't completely unlike Justin to saunter off with friends or his brother for an afternoon.

"When was the last time you saw him?" Tracy asked me.

"Yesterday afternoon," I said.

"Did anything happen? Anything where he could have been hurt?" she asked, and I could tell from her tone, she was talking about Odette.

"No, we were in the greenhouse. Safely on campus."

"What time?" Her eyes lit up. It seemed I had given her a new piece of information.

"Evening. Six? Seven?" I guessed.

"Okay, thanks," she said, backing away, a smile appearing on her face. "That's something. That's great." She turned and ran off down the lane of booths back out into the campus.

"Justin? Missing?" I said. I hadn't seen him at all that day. It also explained why he hadn't answered when I knocked on his door after breakfast.

"If Justin was truly missing, wouldn't they have called an assembly? Canceled the carnival?" Vicken asked. We both avoided the obvious. We both knew Odette could be to blame. "I'll have a second look around," he said. "Let you know what I find." He dumped the half-eaten candy apple and walked back out into the crowd.

"We should have a look too," Rhode said.

I didn't get it. Why would Justin have walked off? After everything that had happened? Did he have second thoughts about what he'd seen during the summoning spell?

Rhode and I walked past a shooting game and a ring toss. Interspersed between the student carnival tents were professional tents from a company that the school had hired. A large rented white tent read HOUSE OF MIRRORS in white light.

"Shall we check in here?" Rhode said.

Without replying, I walked inside.

I knew Justin wouldn't be in there, but I wanted to go in the tent anyway. I wanted to keep pushing away the thought that Justin could be in real trouble. Or worse, dead.

No, Lenah. Stop.

I turned around the first corner. Trick mirrors had been hung up against the wall. Some of the mirrors made me look long and stringy. Another brought my face together in a squish.

Rhode followed behind me, his strides matching mine.

"I thought you would want to search with Vicken," I said.

Rhode shook his head. "I just want this battle over."

We stopped and stood before the same mirror, which made our reflections bleed into each other. My arm was Rhode's arm. My chest, his chest.

"Your lies are overwhelming," I said, turning to Rhode. "Odette told me that it was she who attacked the Hathersage house."

He stood by the wall. "Yes, Odette arrived at the house first," Rhode admitted. "To begin with, I didn't know what she was looking for. She seemed generally cordial, but things quickly turned ugly. I tried to fight her, but as you saw, she is extremely skilled. Though she was not unnaturally fast at the time, so I was able to get away. That particular gift is a recent one," he said.

"Why wouldn't you just tell me?" I asked. "You don't have to hide everything from me."

He leaned toward me. "Because I thought I could protect you. That I could call Suleen or take care of it myself."

"And did you?" I asked.

"I could not do it alone," he said eventually. "Like always, I am better with you. Stronger."

And we were close again, standing apart from each other, separated by only inches. No longer battered and bruised, his skin was smooth again, like that of a young man with his whole life before him.

"Why do you fear my touch?" I whispered.

"I don't fear your touch," he said with a deep sigh. "It's never been about that."

I wasn't sure how to respond except to say, "You haven't let me near you for months."

"Lenah," he said gently. "I only fear what I am capable of with a beating heart. What the Aeris warned of. I can't promise to stay away from you."

"By touching me?"

Please, I begged, *don't let anyone disturb us now.* He raised his hand so I could see the inside of his palm. He looked at me, his eyes twinkling but his mouth a thin line, serious. He reached forward, palm out, and placed it on the center of my chest, right below my neck, right where Odette had stepped on me in the Herb Shop.

His skin, the smoothness of it—I had never wanted anything more in my life than in that second. Our world had been thronged by hunger for blood. We had been perpetrators of pain, and here we were, touching properly for the first time, as human beings. I reached up to touch his cheek and could feel my heart thumping against his skin. I wanted to breathe him, the way he smelled, to see every pore of his skin, to feel his heart beating.

I shuddered. Rhode continued staring down at the hand that pressed against my flesh.

"You," I whispered, "are worth every moment I have left on this earth. Even if I have to love you from afar for the rest of my days."

Rhode's bottom lip trembled and mine did too. I swallowed hard.

Tears spilled over his cheeks as he watched his hand rising and falling as I breathed. I couldn't look into his eyes while he cried tears for me.

Apples! No! Not now. Apples. Everywhere. The scent overwhelmed me. A white light blinded me.

Rhode stands in the center of a great library. I have never seen a library like this in my life. Huge wooden bookcases stretch to a ceiling decorated with an Italian-style fresco. But I cannot focus on the cherubs or the white billowing clouds of the painting.

Rhode has short hair. He stands with his hands behind his back and wears a black three-piece suit. It must be 1910 or close to it.

"She is in hibernation," Rhode explains to people I cannot see. "Below the ground in Hathersage."

"You wish to bring her here?" a deep voice asks from across the room.

"I wish to make a bargain," Rhode says.

"Lenah Beaudonte in Lovers Bay?" the voice says with a hoarse laughter. "The Vampire Queen herself."

"She will live as a mortal, sir," Rhode says.

"Fascinating! Let us discuss this bargain," the deep voice says again.

A white wash of light crosses over my sight, and the library disappears. Where did Rhode go? Rhode? Now I am back in that foyer I have been

seeing for months. Even though it is dark, he comes into focus . . .
slowly. A modern-day Rhode, a human Rhode, falls to his knees.

"*I can't do it!*" *Rhode yells.* "*I understand the consequences. I know*
the risk."

Images come in bullets.

A beach road lined by tall cliffs.

The ocean, stretching far into the distance.

A large house, a Gothic mansion, set far back, away from the ocean.

Number 42 chiseled in a stone plaque beside a massive front door.

I know instantly that this house is a terrible place. A place of dark power.
I have to find it.

Back in the House of Mirrors, Rhode touched me. I drew in
great heaving breaths and stumbled back into the mirror behind
me. It clanked on its hinges. I blinked hard, trying to recall the
images.

"What? What was that?" I asked. "That house."

Rhode wiped his eyes quickly and looked down at the floor.
My skin still throbbed where his hand had been.

"That house. What did you do?" I whispered.

"Did you have a vision?" Rhode asked, and stepped forward,
his arm outstretched.

Rhode had bargained with someone at that mansion. Someone powerful who knew me and exactly what I had done in my
past. And I was going to find them.

I stalked quickly out of the Hall of Mirrors, back out into the
sunlight.

"Lenah," Rhode said, coming after me. Students ran by us,
talking about their costumes for the dance that night.

"I have to go," I said matter-of-factly.

"Lenah!" Rhode ran after me but I was quick down the lane,
past many booths until I stopped short. Roy Enos and some lacrosse players held a very close and intimate court. Roy's expression was dark, his posture hunched and crumpled. *Nothing is wrong,*

I told myself. *Nothing is wrong with Justin. I am going to fix this.* I had to go to that house. Something within me told me it was of critical importance. That they could help us fight Odette.

"Lenah!" Rhode's voice echoed. "Lenah!" He was right behind me.

I spun. "No, Rhode. Whatever it is—I know that road. That house. And I am going."

"Don't," he said, and we stood at the edge of the field. "For once don't follow your own wishes."

"You can't stop me," I said. Rhode lifted a foot to step toward me when . . .

With a crash of cymbals, the band happily charged onto the field from the neighboring gymnasium for the fifth time that afternoon. The white wool and silly hats separated us. I watched Rhode try to duck through an open spot, but the band was relentless. I took that as my opportunity to turn and run.

Chapter Twenty-two

That house was the key. I knew it. Someone would help me. Help us. We could fight Odette and we could win. I found Vicken on the side of the boathouse as he watched Roy and his buddies in their huddle.

"I need you to come somewhere with me," I said. "While there's still daylight."

"No."

"I had another vision. I saw a place in Rhode's mind."

"What place? What are you doing, trusting his visions?"

"I can't explain it now. I need you to come with me. To a house."

"I seem to recall already saying no. No more spells, no more summonings." He tossed his cigarette into the grass and sighed, meeting my eyes again. "What's it worth going to this house? More burns? Your skin? Your soul?" Vicken asked.

"Fine," I said, and crossed over the grass toward the pathway, leaving the Halloween carnival behind me. I would just get in the car and go alone. I knew that road. It went past the town beach and led to Nickerson Summit, where I had bungee-jumped the year before.

I had to be quick, before Rhode could find me and stop me.

"Damn it! Lenah!" sighed Vicken. "You know I'm going to help you. But this house, this vision, it could be any house."

"No, it can't. It was a stone house and I've been on the road that leads there—I recognized it," I said as we approached the car.

"It's not good for us to go alone," Vicken said.

I opened the car door and slid inside. "Where we're going, we're not going to be alone. We're going to get help."

⸰⸱⸰

I knew we were close. The road grew steeper and steeper, rising higher and higher up into the air. Just as in Rhode's memory, the water to the east dropped below hundreds of feet of cliffs and sand dunes.

"We have to get back in time for the dance, Lenah," Vicken said. "She's going to start wreaking havoc."

"We will. We're going to get help."

"So you keep saying."

"There it is!" I cried. I slammed on the brakes, making the tires squeal. On a small stone plaque on a tree next to a long drive-way that led deep into the woods, away from the ocean, was the number *42*.

We turned off the road and followed the curves and bends of the driveway. We must have driven a mile, maybe more. When we finally came upon the house, we had to stop because a mechanically controlled gate protected the entrance to the grounds of an enormous gray stone dwelling. There were tall towers on the left and to the back of the house. Two windows stood alone on the front of the house; they were utterly black.

Vicken exhaled heavily, then said, "I don't know about you, but this house says to me: Come inside if you want to die."

I rolled down the window. On an intercom on the gatepost, a sign read, PRESS FOR ENTRY.

As my finger hovered over the button, a deep voice with an indistinguishable accent said through the receiver, "You are welcome here, Lenah Beaudonte."

"Well, that's comforting," Vicken said.

I gulped away fear. We had to keep going.

I backed into a space just next to the front door. The front of the car faced the woods, but in my side view mirror I could see the stone monstrosity. Just like my house in Hathersage, it was constructed from thick stone with barely any windows.

Vicken sat beside me. I loved his lionlike hair and pensive eyes. They looked at me from the passenger seat, waiting for me to say what we would be doing and why we had come.

"I'm glad you're here," I said.

"Wouldn't miss it for the world," he replied as he unbuckled his seat belt. He stopped me as I motioned to get out of the car. "We really may die in there," he said, his brown eyes serious.

I considered his wild hair again and the strong point of his chin. He was the soldier of my life.

"I won't hold it against you if you decide to stay in the car. This is for me," I said.

He got out of the car without another word.

Our feet crunched over the shells of the drive. Once I was out of the car, I realized just how well cared for these grounds were. Stone statues hid between flowers, and at the end of the long length of the house was the glass of a greenhouse. This was not just a house. This was a compound.

We walked to the front door and stood together before the thick black oak. Hand poised over the door knocker, I imagined that Vicken and I were going to a dinner party at someone's house. We were normal people, not former vampires. Just people. Just teenagers who wanted to live their lives. I was about to knock, when the door opened.

I recognized the man behind the door with a little skip of my heart. He was the man from my vision, but he did not wear a robe as he did in my dreams. He wore a cotton sweater and conservative brown slacks. He could have been a professor, from the looks of his spectacles and outfit. His eyes moved back and forth from Vicken to me.

"Oh, good," he said with a relieved sigh. "You're both unforsaken."

With a swipe of his hands, the entire outfit morphed into a mist of color as though it were made of nothing but dust. The man was suddenly clad in a pair of black dress pants and a set of black academic robes. This was the ensemble I had seen before.

"Unforsaken?" Vicken asked.

"You are both the damned. Once vampires. You are welcome here," he said, and opened the door to the foyer. As our feet stepped over the threshold, I sneaked a last glance behind me out the door. With a heavy thud, it closed—leaving us momentarily in complete darkness.

Vicken held his breath. He was primed to defend me.

"No need to consider tactics of speed and strength, Vicken Clough. They would be quite useless here," the vampire said. With a snap of his fingers, candles bloomed and their brightness grew. The candles stood in glass wall sconces and flickered from four corners of the room. Above us was a small chandelier. Five sconces, five candles— a pentacle star. This room held power.

"I am Rayken, Lenah Beaudonte," he said, and extended a hand. He was most definitely a vampire, for his hands were icy cold and the pupils of his brown eyes were wide and black. Rayken held my gaze, and a small smile played on the edges of his closed lips. "You are warm," he said, letting go of my hand. "Fascinating." He took a step back. "You may wait here and I'll alert my brothers of your arrival."

He walked down the long hallway and turned to the right. Vicken and I stood alone in the foyer. Vicken turned around and placed his hand on the door. There was no doorknob.

"We're locked in . . . ," Vicken whispered. "Whoa! The ceiling is onyx," he marveled, looking up.

The blackness of onyx will show the original soul. There, glowing above me, was the true reflection of my soul, and hanging right above my heart was a smoky orb. When I moved about the foyer, it followed. I looked down, trying to reach out in front of my chest to touch it, but I could not see it unless I looked up at the onyx ceiling.

"What is that?" Vicken asked, pointing at my reflection.

"I . . . ," I stuttered. "I think it's my soul. I've never seen myself in onyx before, so I can't be sure."

"We can't," Vicken replied. "As vampires."

I nodded, in awe of this strange orb. Vicken also had one, and it too was a silvery gray cloud hanging over his heart. We were both mortals now, so we could see ourselves in the onyx ceiling; vampires cannot see themselves, because there is no soul to reflect. Onyx, as a stone, harbors enormous power. Dark power. The darker the soul, the darker the onyx appears. It sucks up the negative energy.

"This way, please," a voice said from the darkness of the hallway. Vicken and I stole one more glance at ourselves in the onyx ceiling and continued down the hall behind Rayken. We twisted and turned down a labyrinth of passageways until we reached a wooden archway. Two doors were decorated with sculptures of hundreds of twisted and pained bodies with long serpentine tongues and bulging eyes. I looked away. The grotesqueness made me uncomfortable.

The vampire reached toward a doorknob shaped like a dagger. I had similar doorknobs in my own house in Hathersage, crafted by the Linaldi vampires in Italy. Master craftsmen—I remembered, as I had killed many of them in 1500.

"Good luck," the vampire said, and opened the door.

I glanced back at Vicken, who took my hand in his, and we

stepped inside a huge library. The library from Rhode's vision! As my eyes scanned the circumference of the room, I saw that every wall was covered from floor to ceiling with books. Above me, the familiar fresco re-created the brightest sky of the loveliest summer day.

A crackle of flames drew my eyes from the ceiling. An enormous fireplace was set at the back of the room, taking up half the length of one wall. The fire flickered, casting an orange light about the room. Before it sat three vampires in plush armchairs, each with a book in their hands.

In the middle was Rayken, who seconds before had been standing in the hallway.

I swallowed, trying to remain calm.

"Welcome, Lenah Beaudonte and Vicken Clough. It is with great pleasure that I see Rhode's ritual has worked—twice," said Rayken.

"You have impressive power. Your speed," I noted.

"I do not aim to impress, Ms. Beaudonte. My power is in my knowledge. Vampires cannot move any faster than the natural human being."

If only he met Odette, I thought. It was obvious Rayken had reached his seat long before Vicken and I had even stepped over the threshold. Either way, I didn't believe him. I had seen what Suleen and Odette were able to do.

"You know our names; I believe we should know all of yours. It is only fair," I said.

Rayken looked to the vampire on his left.

"Laertes," that vampire said.

"Like *Hamlet*," Vicken piped up from behind me, and he sounded pleased with himself. He cleared his throat. "If you read that kind of thing."

Laertes the vampire smiled, and it was warm enough to make him seem human.

"Fascinating," said the third vampire. He smiled as well, an openmouthed smile, and it was then I saw he had no fangs. Just two gaping holes where fangs would normally be. Just like in my nightmare.

"She sees we are different," Laertes said, and placed a hand on the knee of Rayken.

I saw they were different, but I also saw their power. I wanted them to help me fight Odette, but first I wanted answers.

"Ms. Beaudonte, you've already met Rayken. And to my right is Levi. We are—"

"The Hollow Ones," I said. The men from Rhode's vision.

The three bowed their heads in unison.

"The Hollow Ones?" repeated Vicken.

"I know very little of you," I admitted awkwardly. "But I have heard of you."

"Your friend Rhode has not told you of our expertise?" Levi asked. He had great folds of skin and deep wrinkles around his eyes, indicating that he was likely to have been made a vampire very late in life.

"He has come here, I know. I have seen it in my mind," I said, and dared to take a step toward them. "I had a vision in which you met with Rhode. He begged you to spare his life. He pleaded."

"Spare his life?" Rayken said. "Rhode Lewin never asked us to spare his life."

He didn't?

"Hmm. Hmm . . ." The Hollow Ones looked to one another, and their tone was one of concern.

"You say you saw it in your mind?" Laertes asked.

I nodded.

"Interesting. How was it you were privy to his thoughts?" Rayken asked, folding his hands in his lap.

"We are soul mates. Once the Aeris decreed we couldn't be

together, he refused to touch me. Yet I seemed to become connected to his thoughts. Sometimes his memories."

Laertes, Rayken, and Levi shared a glance and spoke in a strange, hushed language. I heard the phrase "Anam Cara." Then I heard the name Suleen.

"True soul mates, those whose essences of life are intertwined, will find a way to connect even when they cannot physically be together," Laertes explained.

These vampires knew me; they knew of my atrocities. I needed no summoning spell this time. I just needed their strength to help me deal with Odette—I didn't need to solve the mystery of Rhode just yet. I had to stay focused on the task at hand.

"I have come to ask of you a different favor than Rhode," I said.

"We do not partake in favors," Rayken replied.

"It's true," Laertes said with a sigh. "Knowledge, and knowledge only. Rhode sought our protection, which could only be achieved for a trade."

I knew this trade, whatever it was, would be dangerous. Perhaps kill me.

"What did Rhode bargain with?" I asked.

"Love," Laertes replied.

"What?" I whispered. This didn't make sense.

"That's what Rhode was here for. If he gave us his capacity to love, for us to study, we would protect you for the rest of your mortal life."

"How can you do that?" Vicken asked.

"We can do many things," Rayken explained.

"We cannot love, Ms. Beaudonte," Laertes said.

"Vampires can love," I countered.

"We removed that ability long ago; it would diminish our power to learn," Laertes said.

"So you would take away his love for me?" My voice wavered

as horror raced through me. "Did he do it?" My voice cracked. I thought back on all the visions. Today in the Hall of Mirrors, Rhode had touched me. He had wept.

I tried to draw in breath as this realization rolled over. I had been so foolish! I thought Rhode couldn't handle his mortality. But it was so much more than that. He had to consider giving up his love for me in exchange for keeping me safe? That was the source of his torment?

"He failed," Rayken said. "He could not."

"What is it you desire, Ms. Beaudonte?" Laertes asked.

"Rhode could not give up his love for me?" I asked. I wanted this confirmed before I asked for protection from Odette.

"No," Rayken said again. "He would not part with his ability to love you, despite your circumstances with the Aeris."

It had to be true. How else would they know about the Aeris?

Rhode could not give up his love. He had said it in his vision, *What you ask is too much.* And today in the Hall of Mirrors, he had finally given in to the torment. No matter what, we would never be able to stay away from each other. We would keep coming back to this moment again and again. I could call it any number of names—Anam Cara, soul mates, the love of my life—he was my Rhode.

Forever.

But it wasn't just about Rhode.

Images swam into my mind, and a different understanding of love overwhelmed me. It wasn't just my love for Rhode. . . . It was something else.

Tracy telling me she would help me—no matter what.

Tony's portrait in shreds.

Ms. Tate's closed eyes, almost sleeping. A note resting on her chest.

Claudia's tear-streaked face moments before her death.

Was this life? Was this what I'd begged for during the days

I spent in utter madness in Hathersage? My heart burned in my chest when I thought of myself scattering daisies like a madwoman over the floor of the mansion.

I looked up at the Hollow Ones. I knew what I wanted, and it wasn't protection anymore. What I had to do, I should have done months ago. It was the only way to finally let go of Odette and the life I had led in Hathersage. If I was truly no longer the monster I had been, the one capable of killing for no reason, then I had to let go of my human life at Wickham. I knew what I had to do and why all the events of this year had brought me to this moment with the Hollow Ones.

"I am willing to trade," I said. "I don't know what you could possibly want from me. But I am willing to give it."

"Lenah!" Vicken said, shocked.

I dipped my head; I had to get this out. "I came here to ask you to help me fight a vampire who is coming for me. But that's not what I want anymore. I want something far more important."

The desire within me shifted as I spoke.

"I want you to call the Aeris for me," I said. I wanted to go back to the medieval world, just as Fire had proposed all those months ago.

Laertes considered me. "You are very curious, Ms. Beaudonte. . . ."

"And foolish perhaps," I said. "I know I cannot give up my ability to love. Rhode and I are the same in that way."

Laertes waited a moment, then said, "Your blood will suffice as a trade."

"My blood?" I lifted my chin.

Vicken stepped to my side.

"No," he said, and his tone hardened.

"We will help you. Your ritual is very intriguing, as is the story of your ability to wield sunlight. We have never seen anyone's blood who has this capacity. Not even your Rhode."

Agreement echoed from the other two Hollow Ones.

"No," Vicken said again. "This is some silly ploy to murder you."

"Your bodyguard must remain silent or he will have to wait outside," Laertes said as he looked through a small box. There was a clinking of metal and glass.

"Lenah, no," Vicken said, putting his hands on my shoulders. "I beg you to see reason."

As I looked into Vicken's earnest gaze, I knew what I was doing was right. I looked at my old friend, knowing I never should have taken him from his father's house. Just as Rhode would never give up his love for me, I knew I could never live a life where all the people I loved could die at the hands of vampires. Or be hurt. All so I could be human. It was so clear to me now. For Rhode and me too. We would keep damaging each other, keep trying to find ways to be together without breaking the impossible decree.

That was no life.

I needed to go back to the medieval world to undo all this death, this pain.

Laertes took long strides toward me, his robe billowing behind him, sending waves of air that flickered the candle flames. The other two Hollow Ones remained seated, and Vicken backed away.

"I am going to drain you of nearly all your blood, Ms. Beaudonte. When you awake, you will be in a small room. Just there." Laertes pointed to an archway that materialized next to the fireplace. A large door made of dark brown wood. It was decorated with silver curling designs that looked like strange, alien flowers. "You will be in a bare room. Do not turn around. Do not come back inside until your meeting with the Aeris is over."

"You could kill me and I'll never get to have my meeting," I said, feeling my heart thump in my throat.

Laertes held a small knife in his hand—a tiny blade. Now that

I was close, I could see the gaping holes in his mouth where he had removed his fangs too.

"She must go alone," Laertes said, looking at Vicken over my shoulder. I turned to look at him, and our eyes lingered on each other's. Vicken's hands hung limp by his sides. He swallowed hard but said nothing. I did not know if I should leave Vicken like this. But I had to take the risk.

"I find it interesting, Ms. Beaudonte, that at precisely ten P.M. this evening, you will fight a coven of vampires. The newest Vampire Queen and her coven, in fact. Yet you choose no protection. Instead, you choose a meeting with the Aeris. Why?" Laertes cocked his head with an ever so slight smile.

"Because I think I can win that fight."

"Then if you die from this blood removal, it is no matter."

"Oh yes, it is," I said, and lifted my wrist to him. "I have to take her down with me."

Laertes replied only with a gummy, fangless smile.

Chapter Twenty-three

Vicken had to be held back by two men in black who came in through the hallway door. I did not watch as my blood flowed into the large glass vessel. I tried to ignore the pulsing of my heart through the cut on my wrist. Just when I felt woozy, just when my legs gave out, everything went black.

❦

I tried to blink once or twice but my eyelids were sticky. I wanted to lift my arms. *So do it. Lift your arms, Lenah.* I tried, but could not. I tried again, groaning while attempting to lift my hands, but they were so heavy. I tried to focus, but it was all blackness. Laertes leaned over me. His eyes traveled over my features.

Oh god. He was going to kill me. He did it. He tricked me.

"Can't," I whispered, but it was all I could say.

Laertes unearthed a small vial from his robes. A thin glass tube with a blue liquid inside. He lifted my hand from the floor, and it seemed to float there in the air in his hand. A dark line of blood ran from my wrist and down my forearm. Laertes dropped two small spots of blue liquid on it. It singed as though on fire but it did not hurt. The skin tightened as though being sewn back together.

Within a few seconds, the blood on my arm seemed to melt into my skin, becoming part of the flesh tone of my arm. Soon after, my hands and fingers began to tingle with pins and needles.

"Your blood will regenerate very quickly. Do not get up until you can move your toes. Good luck," he said, and with the sounds of a few footsteps, he was gone.

I lay paralyzed on the floor. It was cool against the back of my head, and the weight of my body seemed to sink into the icy surface beneath me.

Wait. . . .

I could sense its temperature. I tried to press down on the floor with my palms. I could. My fingertips gripped at the floor as I tried to push up, but I fell back to the ground with a smack of my head. I groaned and tried again. *Push up!* My stomach muscles shook. *Keep pressing, Lenah!* I sat up, exhaling and looked ahead of me. There was nothing but a stone wall. No windows. I stared at the ceiling, my feet still numb. The ceiling was black onyx and there were no candles, yet somehow I could still see. Behind me was a wooden door with a black handle. Along the bottom was a piping of golden light. The only way out. But I could not leave, Laertes had said. Not until I had finished speaking with the Aeris.

With my legs extended straight out in front of me, I surveyed the back of the room with a heavy twist of my neck.

The door started to glow as if a spotlight were being shone on it. With a slow twist of my hips, I faced the stone wall. I used my hands, which were stronger as the moments passed, to pull myself around to face the light. Like a fish tail, my legs tingled.

As on the archery field, a white light grew from a speck in the center of the room. It grew and grew until the whole room was bathed in a blinding light. Within that light were the shapes of hundreds of bodies. Even the small childlike shape.

The four figures of the Aeris materialized in front of the

sea of bodies, stepping forward in unison just as they had on the plateau. Fire stepped forward, ahead of the other three elements.

She looked down at my legs. The pins and needles had traveled down my thighs and calves. It wouldn't be long now.

"Forgive me," I said. "I would stand but I cannot."

Fire bent down so that her dress hung over her knees and flowed out over the floor. The other three Aeris joined her at my feet. Together, they stacked their hands one on top of the other and placed them on top of my ankles. The pressure of their hands was like soft petals on me; they were so light even though they leaned their body weight on top of me.

They sent something through me, a surge of light, a surge of love, or life—I didn't know. I heaved in a great gust of air. I caught it quickly and clenched my hands. I ran my palms over my thighs and could feel the smoothness of my skin beneath my clothes.

I came to my feet as the other Aeris retreated and stood behind Fire.

"Thank you," I said. I looked to each Aeris and said, "Thank you," once again.

Each Aeris bowed her head.

"You are very brave," Fire said.

I hesitated, then said, "I wish I could have worked it out sooner."

"Why have you called us?" she asked gently.

"I admit, part of me wishes to plead with you. To beg to break the decree that keeps Rhode and me apart. There's nothing I want more."

"But—?" she said, leading me. She wore her red gown, and her hair crackled, a curl of red flames that spit and sparked tangerine and gold light.

"I've burned myself, thrown myself in harm's way to fend off a vampire attack."

I lifted my wrist to show Fire the gauze still protecting my burn, but it had disappeared when they healed me. I dropped my arm.

"The Hollow Ones wanted to study my blood. They asked Rhode to give up love," I said, meeting the spooky red eyes of Fire.

She smiled at me in an understanding, almost proud sort of way.

"And after all that, do you know what I wish?" I asked.

"Tell me," Fire said, and her skin seemed to glow. I conjured the words from deep in my brain and deep within my human soul. I whispered my truest confession, that I had uttered only once before, to Tony before he died.

"I wish I had never walked out into the orchard that night. I wish I had died in the fifteenth century as I was meant to." As I spoke, my voice cracked and my eyes burned from tears.

Fire kept my gaze and nodded once, slowly. She then stepped aside and I looked to the white light behind her. A form came forward from the indistinct shapes. The form of a young man stood next to Fire and deepened in shape. Focusing again, forming, until I could make out who he was. Gauges in his ear, a warm smile, and he held his hands in his pockets.

Tony. Tony in color—unmistakable in color and life. Warmth exploded in the center of my chest, radiating down to my hands.

He met my eyes but did not speak.

"I miss you," I whispered in a rush. He backed away with a smile on his lips and disappeared into the light. The last clear, distinguishable features I saw were the apples of his cheeks as he smiled.

Fire bowed her head. "Sometimes, making the difficult decision is what sets us free," she said.

I tried to find Tony again but the shape of his shoulders and his artist's hands were a wash of light now.

I drew a deep breath.

"I want . . . ," I said, and looked into her eyes. I meant every word that came out of my mouth. "I want what you offered me on the archery field. To go back to the fifteenth century. But alone." I took a breath. "I know Rhode is a vampire in the fifteenth century and the only way for us to be together is by me joining him. That is too tempting. So I ask you that he will remain here in the present day."

"Remain?" Fire asked.

"He died for me, or at least he tried to. I want him to live. If he remembers his past, he'll go mad. So I also ask that he retain no memory. That he is with a family, free."

"And Vicken? If you go, if you return," Fire explained, "Vicken returns to the ninteenth century. He never becomes a vampire."

A memory engulfed me momentarily. Vicken in a blue soldier's uniform. He dances on a table, kicking out his legs, smiling. He is sweating. He is human . . . and he is happy.

"This is not a time in which he was meant to live."

Fire walked to me, out of the light and into the darkness of the room. She stood directly on the line separating us. The line that divided her world of white light and mine of darkness and light—the mortal world. She looked at me, cocked her head, and smiled another tight-lipped smile.

"All cycles must complete. The sun that begins the day must set. The spark that lights the world must go out. Finish what you started. Break the cycle of the ritual and it will be done."

"I defeat Odette and you'll send me back, as I wish?"

Fire nodded.

"And my victims, they'll be free? And those killed by the vampires I made?"

The white mass of souls behind the Aeris swayed and fluttered as though a light breeze had come through the room.

"They will all be free," Fire said.

"But they will not be white souls?" I asked.

"They must make their own way, as it should have been."

Like she had on the archery field, Fire started to fade; I could already make out the stone wall behind her.

"When it's over, you must go to the archery field. When the new sun rises, you will be sent back."

"And the battle?" I asked, because I knew she would understand. "If I die?"

Water, Earth, and Air faded with the light, yet Fire was as bright as ever. She stepped to me and lifted my hand in hers. Her skin felt like satin on mine. "I have faith you can do this, Lenah."

"I keep none for myself."

She moved even closer and in a grave whisper said, "Knowledge is your key."

"Knowledge? What does—?" I stopped because she glanced back at the fading mass of people behind her.

Then with purpose she said, "The dead do not show themselves to the living. Not unless they deserve it, unless they have a white soul."

"My soul was not white. I saw it in the onyx ceiling. It was gray."

She stepped away toward the wispy strands of white light. She too began to fade away. "You do now."

My mouth parted and for the first time in what seemed like an eternity, I smiled. "Wait!" I called, taking a step after her. Fire flickered before me as a candle about to burn out.

"Rhode. Will he be happy?"

Fire smiled and disappeared into nothingness.

⁓

I turned back to the door and twisted the knob. I expected to step back into the library. Instead, I stepped out onto the front stoop, back out into the late-afternoon sun, and onto the shelled driveway. I shielded my eyes from the light. Vicken shot up; he had been sitting on the bottom step, facing the long drive and smoking a cigarette.

He spun around and grabbed me into an embrace. I held on to his lean frame. He smelled of tobacco and lemongrass. I lingered there, taking him in.

"I actually feel sick," he said, and I listened to his deep voice vibrate within his chest. "Now I know why bloody idiot mortals say they're worried sick."

"I'm all right," I said, and pulled away.

"Ten P.M. is six hours from now, Lenah. We have to go," Vicken said. I dug in my pocket for the car keys and I handed them to Vicken. But he didn't run to the car. Instead he asked, "Well? Do we fight?"

"Fire said no matter what, we must succeed in beating Odette. It breaks the cycle of the ritual."

"Breaks the cycle?" Vicken asked.

"The ritual will be gone from the world if we defeat Odette," I explained.

"Excellent. Did Señor No Fangs or the Fiery Lady say what happens if we win?"

I couldn't tell him what would happen if we won. He would try to convince me to stay in this world, stay together, because that's all he had known for the last 160 years. But I needed to send him back to the world in which he belonged.

I shook my head and managed to smile as a strange sense of calm washed over me. We got into the car. As we drove, I leaned my head back into the seat, listening to the sound of the engine, the radio, and the gearshift. I watched the streetlamps go by. I watched everything and anything. Anything that would not exist in 1417.

⋅ ⋅●⋅

With a creak of the door, I walked into my apartment. I expected to be alone, but someone sat on my couch: tall body, hunched over, spiky black hair. Rhode held his head in his hands. When I was first made human again and Rhode walked out onto that porch to die, he was so sure, so absolutely sure of his death. He looked up at the click of the door.

"What have you done?" he demanded. I sat down next to him. He looked at me, eyes wide.

"For months, I thought you were trying to hurt yourself. That you thought you didn't deserve your humanity or something," I admitted.

"Why would you think that?" he asked.

"Since you came back from Hathersage. I connected with you. I could see your thoughts. Sometimes memories. And I misread your pain. That's what happened in the Hall of Mirrors."

"Connected?" Rhode asked, not understanding.

"What I thought was your unraveling was your struggle with the Hollow Ones. That you could not give up your love for me."

Rhode frowned and stood up from the couch. "I see. So you've uncovered my relationship with the Hollow Ones," he said, and walked to the bureau. He placed his hands on it and dipped his chin to his chest. I watched his strong back muscles contract through his thin T-shirt as he spoke. "When I awoke after the ritual, you lay on the couch, asleep. I just kept watching you. A human finally, finally, after you had wanted it so badly."

He turned to me and leaned his back against the bureau. I was too afraid to speak. As if interrupting his thoughts would stop him telling me what I had waited so long to hear.

"I could not help my reverence. I was proud," he said with a quick shake of his head. "Of what we had been able to accomplish with the ritual. It was unheard of. A simple combination of spells and herbs. But the intention—the crucial, most variable ingredient, was the most difficult to find. For we both had to find it within ourselves."

Rhode paced before me.

"So, I had two choices: Either I could wake you and we could begin our human life together or I could let you live a life unadorned by me. I had so many debts to pay. A large one to Suleen . . . I owed him." He met my eyes and although I didn't understand all of it, I felt we were there, on the verge of it, on the verge of truth.

"I owed you," he continued, "the chance to be human without me interfering. So I chose to pay off my debts. Believing you could acclimatize to your human life, and if you and I were going to come back together, surely I could explain it to you over time. So I went to the Hollow Ones. They vowed your protection for the entirety of your mortal life if I could . . ." He hesitated, and I listened raptly. "They sent me on an impossible task, Lenah. They expected me to find love. Actual love. If I could capture it, if I could find incantations or spells that might steal love away so that I might give it to the Hollow Ones, they would protect you. You would be free from the darkness that engulfed you for centuries."

Rhode picked up a photo of me from the bureau and I wondered momentarily if he would throw it across the room. "I failed," he said, and his voice was barely audible. "And then I found myself in the debt of the Hollow Ones. The protection for you lifted. Vicken arrived and I was too late to get you out of Lovers Bay."

It was silent and I looked down at my hands. I couldn't imagine Rhode failing at anything.

"Where did you go?" I asked hoarsely.

"Back out to search. To the farthest corners of the earth. I failed again." He came to his knees in front of me and placed his hands on my thighs. "Once you take love from someone through magic, they can never love again. They are not evil, they are not angry, they are hollow and empty, which is almost worse. I couldn't siphon life away from anyone else. I had done that for hundreds of years by taking their blood."

The thought of Rhode doing this sent goose bumps over me.

"I could not and do not understand that kind of evil. When I returned—" He gulped and took a moment to finish. "—when I came back to Lovers Bay to tell the Hollow Ones, I heard that you were a vampire again."

He gripped my knees and I wanted to hold him to me. I wanted to say it was all right.

"I saw your life as a golden orb hanging before me. Drawing me like the brightest of suns. I did not fear your light."

"You couldn't give up your love for me," I said.

"I could not," Rhode replied quietly. "Would not."

It was time for me to tell the truth in return.

"I bargained with the Hollow Ones, Rhode. I asked them to call the Aeris."

Rhode's eyes snapped up to me. He dropped his hands from my legs, and the mood in the room changed considerably.

"They never do anything willingly—what did—?"

"In exchange for my blood, the blood of a vampire who could wield sunlight and who had survived the ritual twice, they called the Aeris for me." I swallowed hard, trying to stay in control of my emotions.

Rhode stood up and kicked at the coffee table, sending books and pens flying into the air. I flinched and looked away from the falling debris.

"How could you? They can't be trusted, Lenah. You don't know what that transaction could mean for you years from now. They'll have that blood. Have that magic." He ran his hand through his hair. "You could have died."

"I did not die, Rhode." Exhaustion laced my tone.

I stared at the curve of his neck, the bit of flesh peeking out from beneath his black T-shirt. I wanted to touch his skin while I still could.

"And what did you ask the Aeris for? For protection tonight from these vampires? Lenah, there will always be more vampires. Did you ask to break the decree?"

"No!" I yelled, and Rhode sighed. His response was his silence. "You expect so little of me, always the selfish girl. Do you remember what the Aeris said? That we were soul mates and there was nothing they could do about that?"

Rhode nodded once.

"All this time I've been thinking about myself. About you, about me, about what we can't have. I was never worried about the people who really deserved justice."

"Lenah . . ."

"No," I said, and cut him off. "No more formalities. We have to beat Odette. Fire said it specifically. Once we do, once we kill Odette, the following morning, at sunrise, I will return to the fifteenth century, and Fire will undo all our atrocities. Erase our murders."

"What!"

"Why weren't we worried about the people in the white light behind the Aeris? About Tony or Kate, or Claudia? Even Justin? Who knows where he is now or if he's even still alive."

"The medieval world . . . ," Rhode started to say with a shake of his head.

"My life will be short. I'll marry young, die young. But I'll get to live, Rhode. And we'll save the lives of everyone we killed."

He seemed to consider something else, and then he spoke. "But I can't live not being able to love you," Rhode said, and when he said it, my heart ached. "I'll be a vampire in the fifteenth century, watching you. Waiting for you."

I swallowed. Gathering strength. I couldn't look at him when I said it. "I worked that bit out too. When I go back to the fifteenth century, you will remain here with no memory of your past. You will be seventeen-year-old Rhode, with a family. A young man with your whole life ahead of you."

"No, Lenah. This isn't fair. I've had no choice in this."

I lunged at him, pointing so he stumbled back into the bureau. "No!" I said with a shout. "No. I never had a choice. You walked into my orchard and made me a vampire. Everything that has transpired since that event will be undone by this choice."

I caught my breath in the silent moment that passed between us.

"Did you ever forgive me?" he asked quietly.

"Did you?" I asked. "I saw you. You told Suleen you were unsure if you could ever forgive me. That perhaps I was unlovable after—" I hesitated. "—after what I had done." My voice cracked; I was unable to help it.

Rhode and I were only a foot apart. I watched the realization of this pass over his face. "That was a memory I had a few months ago. I regretted what I said."

"So your memory was—?"

"A thought I was having in the moment. You were connected to my thoughts."

I allowed this to settle over me.

"You forgave me?" I said quietly.

I leaned to him and brought my lips within millimeters of his. He looked down at me, and we could have kissed so easily. His breath was so soft on my mouth.

"Didn't I always tell you, Lenah? You're my only hope."

Rhode bent forward just a hair; our lips grazed each other's. I was about to kiss Rhode as a mortal for the first time.

"I love you, Lenah," he whispered.

I was lost in the possibility of Rhode's lips caressing mine. My heart sang; every pore in my body craved his touch. I wanted to be one with his soul.

Bam!

Someone pounded on the door to my room.

We jumped apart.

"I'll get it," Rhode said, and when he backed away, the air between us felt strange and spoiled.

Vicken stood in the hallway, dressed all in black, his hair slicked back so his features were more prominent. He smiled with his lips closed as though he was hiding something. Then his smile widened and two very fine and very white pointed fangs gleamed.

"Wow," Rhode said, stepping back, and my spirits lifted when Rhode chuckled.

"You're dressed as a vampire?" I asked.

Rhode shook his head in disbelief and chuckled again.

"What?" Vicken said with a shrug, as though it were the most normal thing in the world.

"Lovely . . . ," Rhode said. He unzipped his duffel bag and pulled out his longsword. The silver blade caught the light and reflected tiny beams over the floor.

"Ith ironic," Vicken said with a lisp. The fake fangs made it difficult for him to close his mouth. Vicken shut the door behind him and took a couple of steps into the room. "Look at the two of you. Pathetic," he said. "Where are your cothtumes? You can't juth walk into a dance with a thord on your back."

Rhode motioned at the bag lying open on the floor. "I took care of that." He turned over the duffel bag, and five daggers spilled out. "Now, help."

Chapter Twenty-four

White ruffles hanging off cheap fabric: faces painted to look like demons or angels. These were only the snippets of costume that I could see around me on Wickham campus the night of the Halloween dance, the final night of Nuit Rouge.

The decorations were coupled with red and green flashing lights. Security vehicles lit up the pathways.

This was a new Wickham.

A frightened Wickham.

A Wickham tainted by vampire bloodlust.

I looked for Justin's tall frame but I did not see him.

Rhode, Vicken, and I stood in the alleyway next to Seeker and watched our classmates cross the green toward Hopper and go into the gymnasium. I tightened the strap on my back, a baldric, which was a leather strap that held the sword close to my body. It pulled down on my back whenever I moved.

"So tell me what Fire said?" Vicken asked for the tenth time.

"She said knowledge was the key."

Rhode kept his gaze out at the dark campus. "We can't worry about cryptic messages from the Aeris. We have to stay focused."

"Laertes said ten," I reminded Rhode.

"Well, that's easy, then," Vicken said. "We wait here until ten, then we strike."

"We can't leave those people in there," Rhode said. "We go to the dance. The first inclination that something's out of the ordinary, we fight. Remember, we need to get Odette away from her coven so Lenah can pierce her heart. It's crucial she succeeds."

"Yeah," Vicken said, trying to push his fake fangs tighter into his mouth. "But you're forgetting one important thing about this fight."

"Yes?" Rhode said.

"The hundreds of people in the room. We're going to have to reveal ourselves in front of them."

Rhode shot me a meaningful look. We both knew the changes coming at dawn. We had to succeed. Succeed, or we were both stuck here with the Aeris's decree and vampires looking for the ritual.

"Let's go," Rhode said, and we stepped out from the alley onto the pathway. I knew Vicken deserved to know about my choice to go back, but I didn't know how to explain to him the choice I had made.

"Did I mention this is a smashing look for you?" Vicken said, looking Rhode and me up and down.

"They were the only costumes that would make sense with Lenah's sword and my arrows," Rhode replied.

We were dressed as Vikings. I would have laughed or perhaps asked for photographs but the situation was not appropriate. The only costume balls we had ever attended were masks in the seventeenth and eighteenth centuries. This was different. My costume was a tank top, a pair of shorts, and boots with fake fur trim. Rhode's costume was a kilt and a black tank top. I tried not to notice the curve of his biceps or the cut of his muscular back.

Like my baldric, attached to Rhode's back was a quiver holding arrows. All I could see out of the top were the feathers. Rhode held on to his bow—a sleek, black, modern-looking weapon.

"You carry it," Rhode had said when he tightened the sword to my back at the apartment earlier that night.

"But it's your sword," I had said, feeling the weight of the metal as the straps tightened over my chest.

"I only borrowed it," he'd said, meaning about the afternoon he visited Tony's grave. "I left it in your possession for a reason." He'd met my eyes and raised the side of his mouth, giving me a sad, uneven smile. I had never asked him about the ceremony at Tony's grave.

As we walked, it was hard not to appreciate Wickham Boarding School's effort to decorate for Halloween. Finally we were able to see it complete. Black streamers wrapped the trees that lined the pathways; orange twinkling lights blinked like lightning bugs from all imaginable scaffolding. Wickham was trying to bring its students together. . . . Tony would have loved it.

Everyone was wrapped in their fall coats, so as they walked toward the gymnasium, I could see only glimpses of flashy costumes. I felt warm, but it could have been the adrenaline running through my body.

Vicken, Rhode, and I walked together, like a team, like soldiers, carrying our weapons. We turned onto the pathway that led to Hopper, and next to it was the hill that led up to the archery plateau. It reminded me of Suleen, who had not shown himself in months. Even when I really needed him, he had not come. The only remains of the carnival were the students' booths. It seemed that the professional company had taken the House of Mirrors with them.

I took some deep breaths of fresh air; the smells of Wickham campus cleared my head. Wet grass, clean air, and the ocean somewhere close by. I tried not to say good-bye as I breathed out, but I knew that in some way, I already was letting it go. Straight ahead of us was a large view of the campus, including a stretch of woods beyond Hopper.

There were screams of happiness when the door to Hopper opened just ahead of us. Booming music from the gymnasium sent ripples of sound out onto the pathway. I told myself to remember the way electricity lit up the darkness. That coffee could brew instantly into a cup. That music, the kind playing in the gymnasium, would have to hide deep within my heart, where I would always hear it.

"Lenah!" I turned and saw Tracy in a black overcoat and jeans. She jogged toward us, and when she caught up, I saw her eyes were red. She folded her arms across her chest.

"I tried to find you earlier," she said.

"What is it?" I asked.

"Justin," she replied, the panic in her voice apparent.

"Is there any news?" I asked. *Please let him be alive.*

"He's still missing. Officially, now," Tracy said.

"Are you all right?" I asked Tracy.

"I don't know," she croaked. "Just hoping he's okay." Her eyes told me that she hoped he would not be Odette's next victim. "They sent Roy home," she added. Tracy was almost shaking as she spoke. "The police have nothing. No note. No sign of distress," she said. "What about you guys?" she asked, and finally looked at us properly. I couldn't help but notice her eyes move from my sword to Rhode's bow and arrows. She finished by looking at Vicken.

"Are you—? Are you dressed as a vampire?" Tracy asked, taken aback. I gulped nervously. *Oh, Vicken, you nitwit.*

A creeping smile inched its way across Tracy's face. "You're kinda sick."

Vicken opened his mouth to reply, but Ms. Williams interrupted.

"Hey! Come on, you guys," she said, opening the door to the gymnasium. She wore her mouse outfit again and had drawn whiskers on her nose. Music echoed out over the campus once more. As we walked inside, Ms. Williams stopped and put a hand gently on my shoulder. She said quietly, "They're looking, honey."

I would have been more worried, but something deep within me told me what was going to happen. Perhaps it was a sixth sense, coming from the vampire inside me who once was so powerful, she commanded not hundreds but thousands of the undead. That powerful part of me said that Odette had Justin and he was going to be part of her power play. I couldn't say this aloud, because it meant Justin wasn't off somewhere being his typical mischievous self. That he hadn't gone back to being the boy who loved to race boats and was going to show up at the dance, brother Roy in tow, smiling and laughing. Somehow saying any of this made it all too real and too much.

Saying it to Tracy was too much.

"Lenah," Tracy said, stopping in the gymnasium doorway. "I love him. Not like before. He's my friend."

I placed a hand on her shoulder. "I know," I replied. "I'll do whatever I have to."

Odette was going to use him as bait. Bait to bring us to her and make us fight. I was prepared for that. Even if I knew I no longer loved Justin, I was prepared to save him.

As we walked, our boots joined the high heels and costumed shoes. Tracy looked back at me as she crossed into the gymnasium, and I could see the strength beneath her worry. Only a very special human could run through a cemetery prepared to fight a vicious vampire she had never seen before.

Rhode and I were silent as we followed behind the line of students.

Tracy turned to meet up with some of the other seniors who sat on the back ledge of the room.

I had plaited my hair so that it hung in a long braid down my back. I wanted it out of the way when I rammed the sword through Odette's heart.

"Okay," Rhode said. "We have twenty minutes."

"Should we circle the perimeter?" Vicken asked.

Rhode shook his head. "We should each go to a corner of the room and watch out for anyone or anything out of the ordinary."

I agreed. By standing in different corners of the room, we would be able to have equal perspectives if these vampires came into the gymnasium from any entrance. Next to where I stood were three tables of food, which made my stomach grumble.

If I was right and Odette had Justin as bait, there was no telling how she would use him in this scenario. Lead me out alone into the hallway? Make a spectacle? I adjusted the baldric on my back, drawing Rhode's sword closer to me.

Vicken and I stood against the back of the room in opposite corners, the bleachers stacked between us. His weapon was concealed in his boot, though I knew he had two more daggers hidden elsewhere on his body. We pretended to have a good time. When I first arrived at Wickham, I had hoped I would be able to be a normal girl, a girl who could forget the years she'd spent manipulating people and living off the joy of their pain. I had stood on the outside, and Justin had made me feel like I could be on the inside.

I would never be on the inside again.

I tried to pay attention the best I could. Everyone's costumes would have been entertaining had we actually been able to enjoy them: bunnies, superheroes, people dressed as cats and Knights of the Round Table. There was plenty of skin showing, so I didn't feel out of place in my skimpy Viking costume.

The gymnasium was overrun with people dancing chest to chest, so close that their hips touched. Small drops of sweat collected on foreheads and slid off cheeks. Rhode stood across from Vicken and me, watching the entrance. Every once in a while I would see him talk to a teacher. He was always quick to make an excuse and go back to the shadows to keep watch again.

I glanced at the large clock on the wall. If Laertes was right, then Odette was two minutes behind schedule. Rhode met my gaze and held it. I would always be lost in that blue. Like the many thousands of skies I had seen when I was a vampire.

With the scent of tobacco, Vicken stepped next to me. His head whipped to the right and his eyes stared unmoving across the room. He said simply, and gravely, "Well, this is an interesting twist."

I followed his gaze to the front of the room. What I saw I knew would shock me for the rest of my mortal days. I couldn't move. I knew I was supposed to protect everyone in that room, but my feet and hands seemed unattached to the rest of my body. My breath caught and I kept blinking faster and faster, trying to focus.

Then the screams began.

For Justin's costume was no costume. The youthful dew to his skin was gone, and the pores buffed away. The eyes that had softened for me, that had told me how much he loved me, were now glassy. Hardened. I could not mistake the madness.

Justin Enos was a vampire.

Chapter Twenty-five

Two security guards lay lifeless on the floor. Their necks fell at odd, disjointed angles. Dead. Immediate. Had they had time to call for backup? Had they reached for their modern-day technology to save them? And failed?

Justin stopped in the doorway, extended a hand into the hallway, and pulled Odette inside. He linked an arm around the lower part of her waist, dipped her so her back arched, and kissed her deeply. My lips parted in disbelief. Together, they stalked into the room, flanked by three other vampires. Justin wore the bright blue polo shirt that I had seen him wear hundreds of times.

With a simple bend of his knees, he jumped on top of a food table and kicked the chips and treats so they went flying into the air.

"Welcome!" Justin yelled, and pointed at the DJ, who lowered the music. "To the Halloween Ball. You know, I was looking forward to tonight." He squatted down and extended a hand so Odette could climb onto the table next to him.

Justin was a vampire. The horror rolled over me. She had won. Odette had won. She had stolen Justin away from humanity, taken all his beautiful warmth and life and made him into an icy, soulless vampire.

Odette and Justin stood on top of the table, reveling in the terror they'd created. Most people stood huddled together while others leaned against the wall, frozen. A junior I recognized from my science class last year slowly reached a hand out for a knife on the cake table. Before he could grab it, Odette walked along the table to him, snatched the knife out of the cake, leaned down, and stabbed it in the side of his neck. More screams echoed throughout the gym, and a herd of people ran for the exit.

Blood spurted out of the boy's neck in a wide arc and he grabbed at the knife, trying unsuccessfully to remove it. Odette stood back up as though she had simply brushed away a fly. I had to turn my eyes away. I did not want to watch his death; his cries made me sick to my stomach. But I had to look back; he had fallen lifeless to the floor.

"The next person who even thinks of fighting me dies." She turned to me with a sick smile. "Except for you, my dear."

I couldn't remove my eyes from Justin. How strange he looked as a vampire. How frighteningly regal and strong. How hard and statuesque. The morning I went to his window, he had been so soft. So gentle. So Justin. And now, he was nothing. Just a shell harboring anger and death.

I swallowed hard. I had to move—the rage inside me beat throughout my soul. I had to kill Odette. Then I could make things right. Justin wouldn't be a vampire. My friends would be alive and safe. Everything would be reversed come morning.

"We've come here tonight for a very special request," Odette announced.

Two vampires stood guard below Justin. My stomach lurched as I remembered the vampire I had killed with the barrier spell. Justin was the vampire that completed her coven.

Odette turned suddenly from Justin, jumped to the ground, and walked quickly toward the gymnasium entrance. The sea of students parted as she traveled toward them. Tracy stood firm against bleachers that were stacked by the wall. She sneered at Odette. She was planning something. She took a step forward, wielding something in her hand, but I couldn't see what.

Odette snatched at Tracy by grabbing and yanking on her ponytail. A flash of silver, and I realized Tracy had been holding a knife. It clattered to the floor. I had to get to her.

As I took a step, Justin jumped from the table in front of me, drawing my eyes away from Tracy.

"I'll take the two below Justin!" Vicken yelled, and he ran past me. I could not watch, because my gaze was locked on Justin's unnatural marble-like eyes. I looked for any sign of the human boy I had loved.

There was a crash near the door—I glanced at the shadows where Rhode had been, but he was gone. Odette had thrown a boy wearing a football player costume against the bleachers, while still keeping a hand locked around Tracy's wrist. He lay in a crumpled heap on the floor.

"The famous Rhode Lewin," I heard her say, and it ripped me in half. I wanted to run across the room, but Justin walked toward me in slow, long steps.

Instinct kept me backing away despite the fact that only twenty-four hours earlier, Justin had been holding my hand. I found my composure and comfort by pulling the baldric close to me. Ms. Williams and the other teachers were trying to usher students out of a window at the back of the room.

Come on, Fire. I thought to myself. *What is my knowledge? What's the key?*

Justin broke into a sneer, and I took this as my cue.

I slid the sword out of the baldric and held it before me.

"Lenah!" Rhode yelled from somewhere.

"I'm all right!" I yelled back.

"I always admired that sword," Justin said, stopping a few feet in front of me.

My body reacted but my mind still couldn't believe it. A vampire behind Justin corralled a group of students into a corner. They huddled together, black-streaked makeup running down their cheeks.

"You're going to give me the ritual," he said. He reached out and grabbed a girl from a group running toward the windows, then held her in front of him, smiling at me through his odd, cold eyes. His fangs slid down.

Maybe it was the connection between us, but I could feel Rhode's presence. I could feel his power, his concentration. I didn't need to look. All the times I had been unnaturally privy to his thoughts showed me now that he was lifting an elbow, ready to fire an arrow into Justin's heart. In my mind, I could see the sharp end of the arrow pointed directly at Justin.

I could see Rhode's face, spotted by specks of blood and sweat. *No,* I said in my mind. *Rhode, you cannot kill Justin.* I sidestepped so I stood directly before Justin, making it impossible for Rhode to kill him without first hitting me.

Rhode dropped the bow and arrow to his side.

"Give me the ritual, Lenah," Justin said, and he adjusted his grip on the student even tighter. "Or I kill her. No, wait. Better yet. I'll make her a vampire."

I held my sword out in front of me. It hit me only then that the student he had ensnared was Andrea, the girl he had romanced earlier that year. Tears ran down her face.

"Let her go," I said evenly.

I made myself forget the boy who made me feel so warm and human. I concentrated on the hardness of his eyes.

"Let. Her. Go," I said again.

I wasn't sure what to do. Around us there was the sound of glass breaking, and an alarm wailing somewhere in Hopper. What had happened to Tracy? Justin threw Andrea forward so she fell to her knees and scrambled away behind me.

"Justin. I know this isn't you. Sometimes the human within can remember."

"I remember your power, Lenah. From that day on the beach. I remember your power as a vampire. And I've always wanted it for myself."

He was going to lunge forward, I knew that. His green eyes—now so alien-like, so strange—burrowed into mine.

I was smaller than Justin, but I only had to choose one body part, one small body part, to disarm him. I could do any number of things to break his concentration, and then I would have to stab him directly in the heart or behead him.

The thought of that was impossible. He swiped forward, an unseen dagger in his hand ready to stab me, but I jumped aside.

"Go! Go!" Vicken yelled, and the sound of his voice comforted me. He was still alive. But where was Odette? Where was Rhode?

Justin and I did not falter from our stare. I was ready and as I raised my sword, I jumped forward, lunging my body weight on my left leg. I thrust the sword through the air but missed, and the sword arced through the air, the tip driving into the floor. A hard vibration rattled up the sword to my hand. I wanted to scream from the pressure on my fingers.

"I could have just brought a gun," Justin said as he neatly sidestepped my lunge. I kept my feet firmly planted on the ground without moving from my fighting stance, and pulled the sword from the floor.

"You wouldn't miss the opportunity," I said. "You love being the center of attention."

"Didn't you once tell me I would have been a great vampire?"

I gasped. I did say that, didn't I? What was worse . . . I had been right.

"You may be flesh and blood now, but you're still a murderer," Justin said. "You were responsible for Tony's death."

276

"You loved Tony," I said, and I hated it, but my voice broke. I looked at the gymnasium floor and the streamers trampled by our feet; then I lifted the sword above my head again. As Justin jumped forward to plunge his dagger into me, I stepped left, dodging him, but he rounded on me quickly.

"The whole vampire world knows about your ritual," Justin said, staring at me. "Give it to me. I can offer you protection."

"I'll die first."

"I should have let Odette catch you long before that day in the art tower. I thought you might have figured it out by then."

"What are you talking about?" I asked, unsure what he meant.

We circled each other, round and round, my sword held high, his dagger at the ready. For someone who had no experience of knife work, he was certainly agile. But then . . . his words crept into my mind.

"You, the ritual. Rhode. Why you're alive . . . so whatever you did with that ritual doesn't matter to me. I want . . ."

He had been talking about the ritual all this time. From that night onward.

I clamped my jaw together, biting my words away, but I couldn't help it. I'd had no idea Justin was in league with these vampires.

"How long?" I asked. "How long have you been under her control?"

"I knew your true colors, Lenah, the night of your birthday. You think I didn't set this up? I worked it all out. Planned it so you would trust me."

He was with me that night for the ritual?

Behind Justin, one of the other vampires jumped at Vicken. Vicken's back arched as the vampire hit him and he slammed into the ground, but then he flipped over quickly, dagger still in his hand. I had to stay focused.

Justin broke the rotation and took a step toward me. I was close to him, closer than I needed to be to drive the sword into him. I concentrated on the space just between his arm and chest. I was going to pierce him—to disarm. Yes . . . right there, right between the arm and the chest. My right hand gripped the handle tighter.

I leapt at Justin but he was too quick and kicked me in the stomach, sending me to the ground. Rhode's sword clattered against the floor. My stomach cramped. I clutched at it in time to see Justin preparing to thrust forward to stab me. I flipped over and grabbed for the sword again; then I kicked up, knocking Justin's dagger out of his hand. He snarled, lifted his foot, and stomped down on my stomach before I could roll out of the way. My hand let go of the sword. and the breath came out of me in a whoosh. I coughed a dry, hacking cough. My throat was already so sore.

Breathe, Lenah. But I couldn't. My chest tightened. I was on the floor of the gymnasium, but then, her words . . . Odette's words from so long ago in the dressing room came to me.

I can see why he likes you. She had meant Justin! The rune around his neck swung back and forth over my eyes as he towered over me. Knowledge, Fire had said. Knowledge is the key.

I needed to understand what she meant.

I also needed the sword. I tried to breathe in again. *Breathe, Lenah!* I yelled inside my head.

"Mortal," he grumbled, and lifted his foot again. "Give me the ritual!"

An enormous crash brought both Justin's and my attention back into the room. An arrow protruded from the chest of one of the vampires in Odette's coven. He collapsed into a set of chairs and the drink table, bringing all of them to the floor in a heap.

Time seemed to slow even further. By the base of the bleachers, I saw Odette. Her neck craned over Tracy as she fed off her. Tracy's eyes were closed and her mouth lay open and slack, just like Claudia before her death. Rhode appeared out of the chaos, kicking Odette away, so the blond beast fell back from Tracy. She grimaced, and before she could assemble herself to lunge at him, before she could reach for the knife I was sure she had, she glanced across the room at Justin. Her anger changed to wide eyes and a menacing sneer.

Pain was spreading through from my spine to my arms. Justin towered over me, bringing my eyes back from Odette and Rhode. He brought his beautiful face closer to mine—even more beautiful now that the pores had sealed. In his right hand was my sword; he lifted his arm just high enough to point the blade at my chest. But before he could do anything else, I rolled away, raising my foot, and kicked him square in the chest with what I hoped was enough power. My foot stung from the force of the impact. He stumbled but I was quick, and as I jumped up, I lifted my leg again, kicking him once more in the chest. His arms flew out as he hit the ground, and he dropped the sword. I snatched it up and held it, pointing down at the ground, my fingers resting on its hilt.

I let the weapon hang between us. I saw myself hundreds of years ago, snapping my finger and commanding hundreds of vampires to murder one helpless Dutch woman. I saw myself drinking goblets filled with blood. Death parties, Nuit Rouge.

"Do it, Lenah!" Vicken screamed behind me as he ran out of the gym, chasing one of the vampires who had fled the building.

A sneer crept across Justin's mouth, and he laughed. "I will get the ritual from you one way or another, Lenah," he said.

I threw the sword to the ground to confuse him, and just as I'd hoped, Justin's eyes followed the slide of the weapon as it hit the ground.

There, lying against the bareness of his chest, was the rune. The knowledge rune.

Of course.

I had no idea how long that rune had been controlling him.

Endowed runes, items infused with magic, could control the mind of someone weak, someone grief stricken, someone with a broken heart.

"Justin, your necklace!" Odette cried, moving fast. "Protect the rune." Then the blond vampire stood before me, using her body as a shield between Justin and me. I needed a clear shot to get the rune from his neck.

Now I knew it wasn't just bleeding Odette that would weaken her—it was taking the rune.

The rune was the connection between Odette and Justin. She may have summoned super powerful strength through spells and incantations, but the rune was the key. How blind I had been! That knowledge rune channeled that strength, bound it to her, along with her supernatural speed. She had fueled herself by feeding off Justin's mind.

Intention was what mattered. Intention in the soul, in the mind. Mind over matter, call it what you will. The mind was always more powerful than the body.

The symbol on the rune, the knowledge symbol, worn inverted can be used in spells of trickery and manipulation.

Knowledge is the key. That's what Fire had said.

An arrow flew through the air and embedded itself in Justin's shoulder. He cried out and fell to the floor, thrashing and clutching at the arrow.

Suddenly, Odette grabbed a fistful of my shirt and tried to immobilize me by holding me close to her. She squeezed me tighter whenever I moved, and I coughed, struggling to breathe. Something in my chest felt like it would burst.

I had to get the rune. I had to weaken her. But she squeezed me again, sending a tightness up into my chest. Justin lay motionless for a split moment, his hand grasping the arrow. This was it, my only chance.

I stretched my body forward. Just a little farther. Then my hand . . . almost there. I reached, and my fingers curled around the leather strap, snatched it from Justin's neck, and immediately, Odette released me. I stumbled away, the rune dangling between my fingers, but I spun around quickly—I had to keep my eyes on her.

"I'll destroy it!" I threatened, holding the rune in the air.

Odette lifted a foot, threatened to jump, but then stopped. Her eyes darted from the rune to me. A heartbeat passed between us as she seemed to think through her choices.

Then she jumped through the air at me, stretching her knife-like nails toward my face. I ducked but saw the red talons out of the corner of my eye. *Now or never, Lenah.* She turned to face me again. This was it. I lifted my right hand and I did what I had been trained to do by Vicken 150 years earlier.

I stabbed my dagger into her dead vampire heart.

"No!" she yelled—but it was hollow, animal-like. She fell to the ground, her weight thrown onto one hand, and looked down at the knife as though she couldn't believe I'd done it. That I'd outsmarted her. Then she seemed to crumple in on herself, down on her knees. She looked up at me, her lips parted. Her fangs descended but they were not scary now; they were sad. She looked like a shattered version of the young woman she once was.

She collapsed back onto the ground, lifeless. A beautiful woman who died much too young. At the strike of dawn, she would turn to dust. And, I was quite sure, she would join the white light of the Aeris, and would eventually return to the natural course of her life.

And me, I would get my wish. At sunrise, this would all be over and we'd go back to a time before sudden unnatural death and empty sadness. I would return to the medieval world. Relief rolled over me only momentarily, because Justin reached for his neck. He shook his head as though trying to clear his sight and swayed back and forth before me. He had ripped the arrow out of his shoulder. I placed the rune on the floor and knelt before it.

Rhode joined me at my side just as the distinct sounds of sirens echoed in the distance.

"You must break it," Rhode said. "His mind is connected to it even in her death."

He handed me his dagger and we glanced up at Justin one more time. He continued to grab at his now bare neck. I used all the strength in my upper body to come down and stab the silver rune so hard that it burst with a bang and a cloud of white smoke. I looked from the rune to Justin, who now held a hand to his head. But his chest was exposed, facing right at me.

I could stab him through the heart and end him. End his human life, and end his vampire life. The rune lay broken on the floor.

"Stab him, Lenah!" Vicken called.

The sirens in the distance grew louder, closer. The gym was nearly empty and we had to go.

Justin shook his head as though to focus his eyes. In this world, his eyes would never need to focus again. He was now the undead.

Again, Vicken called to me to stab Justin. But I would not. I wouldn't stab the chest where I once laid my head, not even if everything was going to change come morning.

Because of the Justin that day in the rain when I first got to know him. Because of the Justin in the hall of his parents' house the night I had slept there. Because of his love for life, and how one time, not long ago, he had shown me the way to be human and I had loved him.

Justin blinked in shock at me a few times, and his marble green eyes had a strange gaze. His beautiful lashes batted at me; he shook his head again, as if he couldn't quite see straight.

Rhode stood up and together we looked at Justin, who was holding his dagger in his hand. He looked down at it as though he wasn't quite sure what he was doing with such a thing.

"Welcome back," Rhode said to him. The gym was empty now, except for us and Vicken, who had a line of blood running down his temple to his jaw.

"What did you do to me?" Justin asked.

"I freed you from Odette's mind control . . . through that rune," I explained.

"Rune?" Justin said.

"This rune," Rhode said. and picked the pieces up. He showed it to Justin, resting it in the palm of his hand.

"You are a vampire, Justin," I said, and his eyes jumped to mine.

He reached up to his mouth and felt for the fangs, which came down on command. He pulled his hand back as his fang pierced his index finger and a droplet of blood blossomed.

"Don't waste that," Rhode said. "You'll need all the blood you can get, vampire."

"I know what I am!" Justin yelled, and backed away from us toward the door. "I know. You don't need to tell me."

A common vampire reaction. Hubris. The blatant inability to be wrong. The young vampire does not miss its humanity right away. They have a zest for knowledge. For power. Often, they are excited about their new immortality.

But, really, Justin had not known. He had not known what happened to him. This was perhaps worse than all our stories. The rune had prevented Justin from realizing what had happened. It not only provided Odette with strength, but it also clouded Justin's mind. It took him over. It made him someone else.

Justin backed out through the door, placing a palm on his arm where Rhode had shot the arrow. He looked at it, checking for blood, but just as I had thought, he healed quickly. He kept his eyes on me and then they fell to the floor, to Odette. After seeing her crumpled body—he turned and he ran.

He would not get away. I ran too.

"Lenah!" Rhode called.

I ran out the door as fast as I could follow in his wake. But Justin was an athlete and was faster than me. He pressed into the crowds of people and ran past the trees, past the crowds. I got caught in the crowd of people.

"Lenah!"

"Are you okay?"

From where I stood, near the great oak tree in the center of the Wickham campus, I turned to look up the archery hill where so long ago, Suleen had separated Justin from me by the water shield. Now Justin stood at the base of that hill and turned to me. Our eyes met. Early in vampire life, one can recall happiness and concern. What met my eyes was regret. But it was fleeting. He ran to the woods next to the hill and into darkness.

Within moments, I was enveloped by hands and concerned faces still splattered with Halloween paint. A group of people circled me and led me away.

Chapter Twenty-six

News of Justin spread like thousands of feathers fluttering through the air.

"What happened to him?"

"Did he join a gang?"

"Who was he with?"

All kinds of questions carried over the quiet campus, massing together like a thousand whispers. How? What? Why? Who? The questions of victims. Questions that would never be answered.

Vicken, Rhode, and I sat at the base of a tree, waiting for what, I wasn't sure. Rhode reached for my hand. It surprised me for a moment, in that I wasn't used to him touching me. Vicken held a bloody T-shirt to his head. We didn't say much as we sat there.

"It's going to be okay," a firefighter said gently. "It'll be all right." She was consoling a group of crying girls who sat huddled near Hopper building. Other firefighters and police officers ran past us, in and out of the gymnasium. They went with axes and a hose, guns and body bags in their hands. I didn't want to think about it, didn't want to know. The great clock on Hopper building said the time was four thirty in the morning. Only two hours left until sunrise.

I overheard a snippet of a conversation between Ms. Williams and a police officer.

"You're sure he is in a gang?" the officer asked, and took some notes in a small book.

"Yes. He is most definitely in a gang. A violent gang," Ms. Williams said.

"We're going to need to get these kids inside. Start calling parents," another officer said, walking by me.

Vicken, Rhode, and I met eyes and maintained our silence. A paramedic with a medical bag approached us. He bent over and squinted, examining Vicken's head wound.

"Come with me," he said. "You've got to get that stitched up." He removed the T-shirt, and a little line of blood ran from Vicken's head down toward his top lip. When it curled over, for the first time, he didn't lick it away.

"Do you mind explaining to me the shape of this head wound, sir?" Vicken asked as he walked after the paramedic.

Rhode and I sat, backs against the tree, our daggers, bow and arrows, and sword hidden on the side of Hopper building. I leaned my head against the bark of the tree and looked at Rhode. He was out of his costume now, the only remnant of it, the black T-shirt. He was back in his jeans. So modern. And it hit me then . . . he too was aging. Though I would never see it.

He squeezed my hand and it sent my heart racing. How right, I thought as the chaos ensued around us, that now, after all this, he could make my heart pump so solidly.

It had waited for it for so long.

"What you did was very brave," he said. I exhaled, losing myself in the softness in his blue eyes.

"It didn't feel brave. It felt like—" I searched for the words. "—the end."

"How many were there?" The police officer's voice pulled my attention away. He was still interviewing Ms. Williams.

"I think four or five," she answered.

"Do you think, at sunrise," I whispered, "that Justin will still be a vampire? I mean, when I go back to the fifteenth century?" I asked Rhode.

"I think Fire will keep her promise," Rhode replied. He lazily rolled his head to look at me. "He'll be Justin, I suppose."

"Where do you think he went?" I asked.

"To find other vampires. It won't take him very long." Rhode sighed, then said, "Perhaps your plan is, in fact, the best thing for everyone."

He didn't meet my eyes when he said this. Then he broke our grip to reach into his pocket, and he pulled out the broken rune, holding it flat in the palm of his hand. I did not take it. I didn't want to play the guessing game as to when Odette had gotten to Justin.

"Hey . . . ," Rhode said, his eyebrows narrowing. "Where is your onyx ring?"

I held my hands out before me and spread my fingers wide.

My onyx ring—it was gone.

"It must have fallen off during the fight," I said in disbelief. I glanced at Hopper building. "I'll go and look for it," I said, pushing against the ground to stand up.

"Ah, let it go. It's a cursed stone anyway. It makes people linger. Souls too. Connects people to their pasts in a world that may not want them anymore."

I nodded. Knowing that somewhere on the gym floor my ring was discarded under Halloween decorations and party punch, the ring that had linked me from life to life, human to vampire to human.

Rhode offered me the broken rune again. This time I took it and let the two pieces lie in the palm of my hand, cool against my skin. And it came to me then. How easily I had taken Justin's word for it. How easily I had listened to him when he said that he wore the rune because he worried for me, because he wanted to understand me. Every time he got me alone, he'd asked about the ritual. He was so eager to come to watch me do the summoning spell. So interested in power.

"You couldn't have known," Rhode said.

"When . . . When he and I . . ." I stopped, choosing my words. "That night. Of my birthday. He told me in the gym . . . he wasn't in his right mind."

"He was probably captured early. I don't think he did any of this of his own accord." Rhode sighed. "Either way, it's over now," he said quietly. He leaned forward and tucked a piece of my hair behind my ear. Justin had done that to me, but when Rhode did it, and his fingers grazed my skin, my pulse thudded.

"Remember the story you told me about Suleen? The Anam Cara?"

Rhode nodded and lovingly held my cheek with his hand.

"Do you think we're like that?" I asked. "Or is it only reserved for really powerful vampires like Suleen?"

"I think Suleen would say the love between us is even stronger than the love he felt for that woman."

He didn't remove his hand from my face, and its warmth reminded me of all the cold moments in my life. During those long years, his touch had brought comfort to me. Yes, I was human now and the touch was different: there were nerve endings and senses now connected to that hand.

But the love was the same.

"Lenah," a feeble voice called me.

I twisted to look for the source of the person calling my name. Everyone was still in their costumes, their eyes were lined in sparkly glitter, lips and noses were painted or furry. Beyond the groups of students huddling together on their way to Quartz dorm, two paramedics carried someone on a stretcher. As the stretcher passed by, Tracy turned her head slowly to me.

"Lenah!" she said my name again.

I jumped up from the grass but stopped and groaned as a shooting pain traveled down my arm. I reached up to hold on to my right shoulder; I hadn't needed such arm strength the last time I wielded a sword.

I walked past students talking about Justin and his changed appearance. There were dozens of theories: drugs, an adrenaline junkie, maybe he'd joined a gang. All words and phrases I had learned over this human year. They were just excuses people made to explain what they could not understand.

"Can you wait one moment?" I asked as I approached Tracy, and the paramedics stopped.

A tear rolled over her cheek. She wiped it away and looked at me. "I tried," she said. "I brought a small knife but she just kicked it away."

"I couldn't get to you," I replied, squatting down to her eye level.

"Is everyone I love going to die?" she asked, and her voice was so shaky. "I don't want to go home, Lenah, but they're closing school."

"Not forever," I said.

"Is he going to come back and kill us all?"

"He's a vampire," I said softly so only Tracy could hear. "But I don't think you have to worry about him anymore."

She wiped her eyes. "What you did. Tonight. It was amazing," she said.

"It's because of me you had to see that at all."

Under the moonlight, I could see her pain so clearly.

I reached out and took her hand. I was so used to embracing Justin or Vicken, who were young men with strong shoulders and wide backs. But Tracy was just a young woman—like I should have been. Her hands were frail to me, as if I were holding the hand of a small child.

"I can't believe they're canceling school," she said, and let go of my hand to wipe tears from her cheeks again. The men who carried the stretcher continued walking toward a collection of ambulances in the center of the green. In front of those ambulances were six bodies. Four vampires, including Odette, and two students. Just when I turned away, someone behind me said, "The news crews are coming."

"See you soon, Lenah," Tracy said, and she was carried away into the fray of emergency workers and flashing lights.

"Sure," I said, though I knew I would not, in fact, see her soon.

When I turned back to face the chaos on campus, the police were corralling students by their class groups. Everyone was on their cell phones. Ms. Williams pointed some students toward the dorms.

I met Rhode's eyes as he and Vicken stood by the oak tree. Vicken had a white bandage wrapped around his head and they talked with quiet confidence. It was hours since Justin had run off to the woods, and only now, with midnight long past, did the police officers and firefighters usher the students back to their dorms. Statements had been made, notes taken—it was time to go inside and try to rest for whatever was left of the night.

I exhaled as a cool wind swept through the campus, making the leaves shiver. I knew that a shiver was a sign. A familiar knowing feeling swept over me.

I looked past the students, up the archery hill, where at the top—finally, finally—stood Suleen.

I walked toward Vicken and Rhode. On my way, Ms. Williams stepped before me. Her mouse nose had worn off. All that was left of her costume were some smears of whiskers over her cheeks.

"I've been waiting to get you alone," she said.

Her eyes, a blue gray color, penetrated mine in that late night. "What did you do?" she asked. "How did you know? You, Vicken, and Rhode?"

"Ms. Williams, I have to go."

"Those men. And Justin . . . ," she started to say.

I touched her on the shoulder, as she would have done for me, like a parent to a child. Because, really, I was so much older than she would ever be.

"It's over now," I said, repeating Rhode's words to me, and walked toward the tree.

As I walked, I tried to ignore her calls.

"Lenah, wait. I don't understand. I don't under . . ."

When I reached the tree, I saw that Vicken's bandage stretched from his eyebrows to his hairline.

"Are you all right?" I asked.

"Nothing but a bee sting, love," he said, and we shared an exhausted smile. At the top of the hill behind him was the white garb of Suleen. He reminded me of the gray orb that hung over my heart in the reflection of the onyx ceiling at the Hollow Ones'.

I looked back to the crowds of people behind us. No one turned in our direction; no one demanded we go inside. I knew this was Suleen's doing. He made us invisible, to allow us a clear getaway.

It also gave me time for one last look. And I did look. My eyes swept over the campus, stopping, of course, on Seeker dorm in the distance. Its brick structure was framed by trees bursting with orange and yellow leaves. My heart ached.

"It's time to go," I said to Vicken, and started walking up the hill.

"Go?" Vicken asked. "Go where?"

"Come on," I said gently, and took his hand into mine.

He looked down at it and then up at me. "What's going on?" he asked.

Rhode squeezed my other hand hard as we ascended the hill. Three generations of murderers walked to their rectification. This reckoning was by my own doing this time. When we crested the top of the hill, Suleen stood ethereal and silent.

I wanted to be angry with him. Wanted to know why he didn't come when I'd called him with the summoning spells.

The truth was that I already knew the answer. He didn't come, because I didn't deserve it. Because coming to save Rhode wouldn't have solved anything. I would have just found another way to try to break the decree, to do magic that I was specifically asked not to do.

As we walked toward Suleen, I drew a breath. Fall was finally upon Wickham campus. As we made it to the top of the hill, huffing and puffing, we could see our breath in the air.

"Suleen," Vicken said in wonder. He had never seen the vampire before—not in the flesh. "You came," Vicken said. "We didn't even have to burn any appendages."

Suleen smiled kindly but then turned his gaze to me. "I am proud of you," he said. Rhode stood by my side, and Suleen looked to him next. "And even prouder of what you could not give up."

Rhode nodded once.

"Now for a proper introduction," Suleen said, and turned away from Rhode and me. "Vicken Clough of the Fifty-seventh Regiment," Suleen said, and Vicken puffed out his chest. Suleen reached out and held Vicken's forearm. Vicken held his in return. A common way for vampires to greet one another, it was a shake that protected the wrist. Vicken's eyes lit up, more than I had ever seen as a mortal. This must have been a very important moment for him.

"He doesn't know," I said to Suleen.

Suleen stepped back and it was only then that I realized the sky was no longer black but gray, soon to be lavender, and then the burning orange of the day. The sun—the harbinger of change. The reminder, though this time my chariot.

"Tell me what? What's happening?" Vicken asked.

I threw a glance at Suleen. "How long do I have?"

"Just a few minutes," he said softly.

I turned to Vicken and put my hands on his cheeks. I found his gaze and held it. It seemed hard for him to keep my gaze; his nostrils flared a little. He would cry, though I was not sure if he would know it yet. Or if he was fighting it. I watched his eyes slowly remembering the human reaction when the body cries. I met his brown eyes and said, "Do you know why I saved you in the gymnasium last year?"

He shook his head.

"Because when I met you, you danced and sang on tables. You loved the world, and I had made you a spectator in it."

"Lenah?" he said gently.

"You'll be a spectator no more."

"I don't understand you, love," he said.

"I'm going back to the fifteenth century," I said.

"No!" he cried, and I dropped my hands from his face.

"And you, to your father's house. At dawn, you will return to the night I stole your soul and made you a demon. You will be the navigator I met, with maps tacked to your walls and socks hanging over a washtub."

The sky was purple now and the sun was coming soon to crest over the hill. The first golden glimmers kissed the hilltop.

"Lenah, no!" Vicken cried again, but I turned away anyway. "What does that mean?" he called behind me. "Suleen, what does that mean?"

I turned back to Rhode, whose eyes were cast to the ground. His arms hung by his side; he could have been a modern-day statue, he was so still.

I walked to him, stood just as we had for months now, inches apart. "I'm going kiss you now," I whispered.

Rhode lifted his eyes to mine. "I was hoping you would say

that," he whispered back, and we both cracked a smile. "Lenah," he said, and I could feel his body heat humming off him. "What will I do without you?"

I shivered as one word traveled through me. "Live."

Our lips met . . . the beautiful pressure of his mouth against mine. The heat of his mouth and his taste. I followed the movement of his lips and the soft pressure of his tongue. His hand rushed up my back, sending goose bumps over my arms.

It was better than I ever expected. My Rhode kissed gently. He cradled the back of my head and pushed deeper into my mouth. *Don't pull away.*

The apple scent, which had haunted me all year, overwhelmed me again, but this time it was coupled with the familiar white light of the Aeris. The images that came to me now showed thousands of memories from my past with Rhode. A slide show of our years together.

Gold earrings in the rain. Dancing at balls. Laughing under the stars. Rhode and me on a straw bed. Rhode laughing at something I said by a fireside.

It wasn't all pain and death, was it? It was love.

He pulled away, and the air between us was warm even though the chill of the air bit at my ears. His eyes traveled back and forth between mine.

"Off to have an adventure?" he whispered with the slight lift of his mouth into an uneven smile. He had said that familiar phrase to me hundreds—no, thousands of times. It lifted my heart.

"Anam Cara," I whispered. He gave me a small smile, and that was enough for me. I didn't have to explain what I meant. For it was a new world now, one where our histories no longer mattered and we were set free.

"Lenah . . . ," Suleen said, and I could see the gold coming up over the horizon. Perhaps it was because the Aeris had told me, or that I knew the sun was Fire herself, but I knew. I was supposed to walk toward that sunrise. I knew it would take me home.

The blue of Rhode's eyes was so fierce, as always. He loved me. I could return to the fifteenth century knowing that, for once, I had truly loved and been loved. Rhode cupped my face in his hands and gently kissed both my cheeks, my forehead, and then brushed his lips over mine.

I backed away from him, chills rushing over my whole body. When I looked to Vicken, tears—large, gorgeous tears—ran over his face. He wiped them away and stared at his fingertips, momentarily shocked by the power of a cry for which one has waited over a hundred years.

Suleen held his hand out, and as I had seen him do the year before, he drew it toward him and held it over his heart. The golden glow of the sun warmed me; my whole back was engulfed in its heat. I was going. The trees behind Rhode, Vicken, and Suleen were blurred into orange and red smears against the sky.

Last, I looked to Rhode. I wanted him to be the last thing I saw in this world. His lips were just barely parted. We could have said any number of things then. But I was going quickly. I could barely see Vicken anymore; he was a white wash of light. I thought I could smell apples.

There was nothing left to say between Rhode and me. Words would never be enough. So I brought my hand over my breast, where my beating heart lay. He had been willing to die for it— for my ability to breathe and live. I left it there and didn't break eye contact from the blue that I loved more than love could possibly explain.

I love you. I love you. I love you.

The light was all around me now, overtaking me.

This would be a different world. One without Lenah Beaudonte.

And just like that, with the light before me in a wash of gold and silver . . .

. . . I was gone.

Do all our mistakes remain lodged in our hearts? Can we ever really let go? That which is written in stone may be undone. For stone cannot hold sway.

Even stone can be broken.

Chapter Twenty-seven

1417

Apples. Great crimson orbs glisten in the morning sun.

"Lenah!"

Someone is calling my name. Round apples dangle from a branch outside the window. I know this view. I know this raw smell—the straw of the bed. I am on my family's orchard. The sun filters through the window, washing the wooden floor with yellow light. Roosters crow outside the window—they wake with the dawn. I remember this.

"Lenah!"

My father! Joy blooms in my chest. "Sleepy girl! Are you ill!" My father's voice echoes and I have not heard it in so long. I shoot up. Momentarily, I raise a hand to touch the thick glass of a medieval window. The light is more natural than in the modern world—it is real, not made by lamps. It filters through the old glass, thick and imperfect.

I don't care that my sleeping gown is long, covering my feet, I raise it up as I run down the stairs, jumping two at a time. There is my father, with his heavy beard and working clothes. My mother is before the fire with a tub of water and dirty clothing. I can recognize some of my gowns. I remember!

I throw myself around my father's scruffy neck. There is a hint of lavender to his skin; he has just bathed.

He pulls back from me. "Have you stolen the monks' tomatoes again?" he asks.

I kiss his cheeks. "No," I say with a smile. "Give me two secs," I add, and motion to the stairs.

"What did you say?" my father asks.

Oh. I turn. "Secs" is a modern word—a measure of time. My family cannot measure time this way. He follows his routine by the movement of the sun. Instead I say, "I shall follow."

"Quickly now," he calls.

I peek out the window, with the sounds of my mother's washing behind me. I forgot over my long history how quiet the medieval world was. The harvest has long passed; most of the trees are bare. I look about—I recognize this exact scene. The Medici family has taken most of our crop, and the rest has gone to the monks, whose property we live on. To make cider to drink and for food.

Today is a day of cleaning. After the harvest—we must clean the rows to prepare for the oncoming winter.

I think I know what this day is but I don't want to believe it— not yet. I will be able to tell this evening—when I watch the sky.

I spend the afternoon in the orchard with my father. I have missed him for so long that I find myself standing behind a bare tree, watching him rake through the ground, humming. For the barest moment, I long for the easy push of a button. I had seen workers at Wickham use motorized leaf blowers. I think how much easier this would be for my father's weathered hands. I wish we could play some music as well, and of course, I think of Wickham and the long fields. The lacrosse practices I watched, where they blasted music to help the time pass.

Lacrosse.

I blink away the sun in my eyes and pick at the dirt below this bare tree. I hope Justin, wherever he is now that I am gone, is happy. And human.

I wipe the sweat from my brow, watch the sun move across the sky. This world has no cars, no medicine, no Rocky Road ice cream. I smile at the memory of Tony's hands running a paintbrush through cerulean-colored paint. I will suffer with the loss of not only my friends and Rhode, but also my newfound love for the modern world.

I want to tell my father everything. But I cannot. There is just no way that he could possibly ever understand. I squat at the base of a tree, running my fingers through the rich earth. This routine has come back to me quickly. I remember so well how to prune the branches, how to cut them so the apples will return fragrant and strong.

"Lenah!" my father calls, and he points at the house just as darkened, bulbous clouds hang over our orchard.

I call back and hold the hem of my dress up to walk easier. Dirt covers my hands as I follow my father and make my way home.

·· ◄·

We are due for church, my mother tells me over dinner. I look forward to this. To seeing Father Simon and hearing him speak of God and religion. Once, so long ago, those services taught me how to live my life—to serve God, to live a life for the afterlife. These were medieval thoughts. I never imagined I would have my own views on religion, on God, on the ether, and life before and after death.

My mother smiles at me over our meal. "You seem happy," she says.

"The food is good," I reply.

It's only a simple stew, and she says as much. I remind myself that food here is food you cook yourself. You either catch or kill or buy it from someone who does. Food here is made by hand, not created in a factory.

Rhode once told me long ago that love was an emotion that existed beyond the confines of the human condition. It could rise to the highest peaks, he said. Even out there in the heavens, love flew, soared, and spread between the stars. I believe this is true as I sit here across from my parents.

"You are so quiet," Mother says as a crack of thunder vibrates our small house.

"Rain again," my father says with a sigh.

"Harvest is over. Rejoice," Mother says, and kisses him on the head.

The oncoming rain is a downpour I know.

As it finally hits, I know this pelting on the roof as well as I know my soul.

This is the night I died. This night is the night Rhode made me a vampire.

Hours pass and soon the night's fire is almost burnt out. My mother's earrings are safe—I did not ask for them today. I did not lose them in an orchard lane.

The Aeris have sent me back to this day to remind me of my choices. I walk to the stairs, to the window that hangs over the eighth stair. It has always been a childish inclination to count, yet I do it anyway.

I place a hand on the cold glass. My fingers warm it; a halo of condensation billows out from my body heat. So many things I know from my modern life. How science changes, how music changes, that people get to live many, many years.

I spent five hundred years becoming a monster, feeding off people, making them my misery. But I also saw the way of the world. I focus on the end of the orchard lanes. Though I cannot see the end, once, in a different world, Rhode waited for me. There.

There is no Rhode at the end of the orchard lane; I know that. I saved him. He is safe.

I also know I will never meet Justin . . . or Tony.

Wickham will exist hundreds of years from now, when I am long gone, gone from the world.

I leave my hand on the glass. My jaw clenches. This hurts, this standing here knowing what I know, knowing how much lies before me with this whole world and all its beauty.

Even though he is not watching me, I do it for history. For the souls that were saved in one moment. I whisper the words:

"I will love you forever."

I bring my hand over my heart, and the tears well in my eyes. Shivers cover me head to toe; they roll and soon the tears do too and I say the words only vampires share: "Go forth in darkness and in light."

I gulp away the tears, turn from the window, and stand in the doorway of my parents' room. They sleep, back to back, close together. I wonder if I will live out the rest of my days here in this house. If I will get sick or if the immunity I picked up in the modern world will extend my life. Perhaps even, I could settle for a kind man from this world and marry. One thing I know is that this time, I shall meet my sister, Genevieve. I will witness her birth and see her grow.

I lean harder on the doorway, watching my parents for some time. I know the night, the ebbs and flows of the hours; I can feel it passing by. The turn of the dark sky from black to blue to a lavender tinged with pink. It is only when I am sure the sun is rising that I dare lie down in my bed.

No more bloodlust. No more needless death. Only one more thought passes through my mind as I finally drift off. . . .

Oh, oh, how I will miss him.

Epilogue

Dear——

I don't even know your name, dear. I cannot write it here on this paper, for it escapes me. Every day it sits on the tip of my tongue like a sweet candy. I can taste it for the barest of moments and then it is gone, gone before I can hold it to my tongue and swallow.

I burn for you.

There is a halo of condensation here on this window that looks out onto a campus barely clinging to summer. Fall will be upon us soon. Yesterday, I dreamt of you again. You wore your hair clipped above your ears and you wore a long gown. A gown not found in the modern world. It was corseted to your body, and you stood on a great hill that stretched out far into the distance.

You're beginning to haunt me in my day too. Randomly, as people speak to me, your face, with your dark blue eyes and knowing smile, will sift into my mind. Always, always, that knowledge plays on the edge of your lips.

What is your name? Why do you torment me?

Why do I want to tell you that there are students disappearing at this school? Three in total. The first is still missing—his name is Justin. The second, her funeral is today, and the third, she went missing yesterday morning.

They discovered the body of Jane Hamlin by the beach, two holes in her neck, drained of her blood. Why is it that your face came to my mind when I heard this information?

You, with your porcelain grace and your unnatural skin.

I would scream for you if you would hear me. I would burn this place to the ground if it meant you would see the smoke. I love you, I know this. Yet, I do not and cannot recall who you are.

I must go and close the pages of this journal. I sit here in a dress suit, ready to attend the funeral of Jane Hamlin. Someone has already knocked on my door. The whole of Wickham Boarding School is going. Odd. Just now, as I was about to place down my pen did a phrase come to me as though it were coming up to my mind from a very long slumber. I wonder if my parents taught it to me before their deaths, though I was too young to remember.

Evil be he who thinketh evil.

Do you know the meaning of this? Perhaps it is another clue. Another way to find out who you are.

Evil be he who thinketh evil.

Whoever is killing these students should heed this advice.

Until then,

Rhode